SCALES OF RETRIBUTION

June, 1510: the Burren, west coast of Ireland

Upon going unexpectedly into an early labour, Mara is alerted to the disappearance of Malachy, the local physician. Mystery follows birth, as shortly after the entrance of her son into the world the body of Malachy is discovered. But who stands to profit from this death and who therefore are Mara's lead suspects? For starters there is Malachy's new wife and her two sons, not to mention the very daughter who helped to deliver Mara's child. But soon we discover that the list of people bearing Malachy a grudge is even longer that Mara could have anticipated...

The Burren Mysteries by Cora Harrison

MY LADY JUDGE
A SECRET AND UNLAWFUL KILLING
THE STING OF JUSTICE
WRIT IN STONE *
EYE OF THE LAW *
SCALES OF RETRIBUTION *

* available from Severn House

SCALES OF
RETRIBUTION
Cora Harrison

Severn House Large Print
London & New York

This first large print edition published 2013
in Great Britain and the USA by
SEVERN HOUSE PUBLISHERS LTD of
9-15 High Street, Sutton, Surrey, SM1 1DF.
First world regular print edition published 2011 by
Severn House Publishers Ltd., London and New York.

British Library Cataloguing in Publication Data

Harrison, Cora.
  Scales of retribution. -- (A Burren mystery ; 6)
  1. Mara, Brehon of the Burren (Fictitious character)--
Fiction. 2. Women judges--Ireland--Burren--Fiction.
3. Physicians--Death--Fiction. 4. Burren (Ireland)--
History--16th century--Fiction. 5. Detective and mystery
stories. 6. Large type books.
  I. Title II. Series
  823.9'2-dc23

ISBN-13: 978-0-7278-9617-9

Severn House Publishers support The Forest Stewardship Council
[FSC], the leading international forest certification organisation. All
our titles that are printed on Greenpeace-approved FSC-certified paper
carry the FSC logo.

MIX
Paper from
responsible sources
FSC
www.fsc.org
FSC® C018575

Printed and bound in Great Britain by the
MPG Books Group, Bodmin, Cornwall.

For my brother, James, in fond recollection of all the fun we had as children, particularly in the caves, cliffs and icy seas of Ballycotton Bay.

ACKNOWLEDGEMENTS

Gratitude must go first of all to my family: Frank, my husband, always willing to listen to my latest bright idea; William, my son, who keeps my computers running smoothly, and is invariably full of creative solutions to knotty problems; Ruth, my daughter – always my first reader – who encourages and assists; my son-in-law, Pete, who designed and maintains my website and Shane, my grandson, just for being himself!

And then there is the team of professionals without whom there would be no book: Peter Buckman, my agent, who serves up a palatable mix of honesty, understanding and expert judgement, seasoned with a liberal sprinkling of humour and fun, and James Nightingale who edited this book so deftly and sympathetically – it was a pleasure to work with you, James.

Anyone who writes about Brehon law must acknowledge the huge input of dedicated people, like Daniel Binchy, Fergus Kelly, who translated these ancient laws from medieval Gaelic: I feel an immense debt to them.

7

Prologue

In June 1510, Henry VIII of England had completed his first year of kingship. He was at peace with France; the Pope himself had approved the league between the two countries; the country was prosperous and the people contented. The young king was approaching the first anniversary of his marriage which had taken place on the eleventh of June in 1509. His wife, Catherine of Aragon, though she had lost her first baby, was now pregnant again. Ireland, as always, was a problem, but he had plans for that troublesome country. He had appointed the Earl of Kildare as his deputy and had promised him arms and men to deal with those small Gaelic kingdoms which would not accept the rule and the laws of England.

The Earl of Kildare, Garret Mór Fitzgerald, was a good choice – in fact the only choice. Known as the Great Earl, he was the descendent of a family who had been given land in the east of Ireland by Henry II in the twelfth century. Over the three hundred intervening years they had become assimilated into their adopted country – married the daughters of Irish chieftains and took up some of its customs. Garret, however, was ambitious. When he became head of the Kildare family, most of Ireland had slipped back into Gaelic ways and Gaelic rule. Garret saw an opportunity to get even greater lands and riches by spreading the rule of English law throughout the whole of Ireland. By means of open warfare, strategic ties of marriage and friendship with many of the Irish clan leaders, he and his family were already ruling the south, north and east of the country. He appealed to the greed of the young king to grant him the means to totally subdue this country full of rich forests and fertile grassland.

The west of Ireland had stood out against the combined might of England and the Earl. It had remained strongly Gaelic, presenting an obstacle to Garret's overweening ambition. Without control of the west he could never be considered the prince – some said king – of Ireland. And so it was that in the first week of June in that year of 1510, Garret Mór set out to conquer the remaining chieftains who could not be bribed nor frightened into surrender. He mustered a great army, equipped with guns and cannon, and marched west against his poorly armed opponents with the certainty of victory in his mind.

In the far west of Ireland, King Turlough Donn O'Brien, king of Thomond, Corcomroe and Burren, was one of those unwilling to accept the rule of England. When the news came about the Earl's raid on his Limerick lands, he summoned all who owed him loyalty, such as Ulick Burke, the Clanrickard, from north of Galway city, the MacNamara from west of Limerick, and his own lords and vassals from the three kingdoms. He asked them to rise up in a great *slógad*, and to defeat this false Earl who had turned his back on the country which had enriched him and his ancestors.

And they swore the old traditional oath of the Gael to support him and to follow his leadership. They swore 'by the sun and the moon; by water and air; by day and night; by sea and land' that they would be his men and would fight by his side while breath remained in their bodies.

When the king and his great gathering departed, he left behind Mara, his wife and the Brehon (investigating magistrate) of the Burren. Mara was heavily pregnant and looking forward to the birth of her child in July. Until then she would work on, teaching her scholars the law of their forebears, resolving disputes between the people of the kingdom and praying for the safe return of her lord.

The land was peaceful – the second glorious summer of the reign of Henry VIII appeared to be as good as the first. The hay ripened early, the oats flourished, the exquisite spring flowers of the Burren – the dark blue gentians and the creamy white mountain avens – had finished their brief show of glory, and had given way to

11

the orchids, the roses and the silken harebells of early summer.

But one man, not an evil man in himself, nevertheless driven to evil by his greed and his passions, a man who betrayed his profession, was to destroy that peace and to bring suffering and death to the small kingdom beside the Atlantic Ocean. And when the secret and unlawful killing occurred, Mara had to gather her energies and ensure that the penalty was paid according to the law of the land.

One

Sechus Mór

(The Great Laws of Antiquity)

Nófis *therefore is the name of the book; that is the knowledge of nine persons, for nine persons were appointed to arrange this book of the ancient laws of Ireland, namely: Patrick, Benen and Cairech, three bishops; Laeghaire, Corc and Daire, three kings; and three learned men: Rossa mac Trechim, a doctor of laws, Dubhtach a doctor of laws and a poet and Fergus the Poet.*

And all the laws that were known in the country of Ireland, and were allowed by Patrick, were written down in this great book.

The limestone pavements and the swirling terraces of the surrounding mountains in the kingdom of the Burren shimmered silver in the heat of the mid-June sun. Pale pink roses glowed beside the flat platters of scented elderflowers in the hedgerows, the grykes were filled with frothy white and mauve orchids and deep blue vetch, the clints were carpeted with mats of

13

bright purple thyme and in the still-green oat fields, the poppies and hawkweeds flamed scarlet and gold.

It was judgement day in the kingdom of the Burren. Mara, the only woman Brehon in Ireland, waited by the ancient dolmen of Poulnabrone, one hand on the huge, sun-warmed capstone of the table-shaped tomb and the other holding a scroll. As judge and investigating magistrate, she held the scales of justice for all crimes and all legal disputes in this tiny kingdom on the shores of the Atlantic Ocean. In front of her were her scholars – six of them, ranging in age from nineteen-year-old Fachtnan to eleven-year-old Shane. Around her, some standing, some sitting on the flat stones of the clints, some leaning on boulders, were the people of the Burren. Most chatted together in low tones and from time to time cast a look towards the north. Soon the bells of the abbey would ring for vespers and when they finished then Mara would begin.

Nothing too complicated today, thought Mara, and she was glad of it. She was eight months pregnant; her back ached, her head ached and her stomach had now begun to ache; the sooner this baby is born, the better, she thought and waited eagerly for the first clang of the abbey bell. Ryan O'Connor and his wife were already there, she noticed, standing side by side. That was a good sign. It probably meant that the divorce would go through quickly and each

14

would be satisfied with whatever portion of the goods that would be allotted to them. She passed a few minutes regretting the differences that had arisen between them – there seemed to be no question of infidelity on either side, just, as they both firmly asserted, that they disagreed on money matters and how to run the farm – a fairly unusual reason for divorce. They were a good-looking pair of young people, the man tall and strong, the woman small, but well built and with the appearance of wiry strength. She was holding a baby of about six weeks old in her arms. What a shame to deprive a child of one parent over something so trivial, thought Mara, and resolved to try once more to see what she could do to prevent them from taking a step that they might regret.

'The bell, Brehon,' said twelve-year-old Hugh in a low voice. His young ears had caught the sound before she had, but now she could distinguish the sonorous boom. A few people crossed themselves and muttered a prayer, but all faces turned towards Mara and responded eagerly to her greeting once the last stroke had ceased to reverberate.

'There is just one case to be heard today,' said Mara, turning to one side so that her clear tones bounced off the cliff wall behind the clint-paved field and reached to the furthermost person in that field of judgement. 'This is the case of the divorce between Ryan O'Connor and Cliona O'Connor who wish to part and to go their

15

separate ways. No fault is cited, each has respected their marriage vows, so the law is only involved in order to divide the property in a fair and equitable way.'

To her amusement she noticed that two fifteen-year-olds, Moylan and Aidan, her most idle scholars, were watching her with rapt attention. Of course, the examinations were next week and, as Mara always paid a lot of attention to practical experiences, they had obviously decided that the Law of Divorce would appear on their papers.

'The first principle,' continued Mara unrolling the scroll of vellum that she held, scanning it rapidly and then rolling it up again before anyone could notice that it was blank – exhaustion had prevented her from filling it up the night before – 'the first principle in divorce is that both shall depart as they came; whatever is still left from the goods that each brought to this marriage will be retained by that person.'

Both heads nodded. Mara noticed a flash of amusement in the blue eyes of sixteen-year-old Enda as he glanced at the solemn faces of his fellow scholars. Enda would be taking his final examination to qualify as a lawyer this summer. He would undoubtedly pass, she thought. She would miss him and his quick brain.

'After that, this is the position: Ryan, of course, retains the clan land and the flock of sheep that he possessed, but Cliona, who shared in his work, especially during lambing time, will

16

be allocated one ninth of the lambs dropped during the year of marriage. In addition, she must be paid half the price obtained from any articles of clothing made by her from the wool and sold at the market place. If there is clothing or woven cloth in the house, she must also receive one half of it. This is because these are the fruits of her labour.'

She paused, looking around at the crowd. There was a lot of interest on all of the faces in front of her. Divorce because of a new relationship was reasonably common, though most men seemed to be content with just acquiring a wife of the second, third or even fourth degree – and most wives accepted the situation as long as their own position was unaltered. But divorce where there was no fault on either side was quite uncommon. Still, it was good to have the possibility if a couple wished to part. In England, where no divorce existed, an unhappy couple were locked together for life.

'In the case of any wool or fleeces, not yet combed nor spun, then Cliona's share is just one ninth. In addition, Ryan must supply her with a sack of oats for every month that remains until the end of the year to come – that is until the first of May,' she continued and then hesitated.

She had already pleaded with the young couple to reconsider but her words had not borne any fruit. She would try once more before the final words were spoken.

'That is the legal position and this is where the

law finishes. The last step is for you to take, Cliona, as I understand it is your desire for this marriage to be dissolved. Before you take this step then I would ask you to think that you are depriving your child of his father and that perhaps with a little understanding on both sides this marriage can still be saved.'

A low hum of approval came from the crowd and Mara could see faces, both of men and women, turned eagerly towards the young couple.

Cliona hesitated. Her face flushed a deep red. She looked at her husband and then at the crowd and suddenly she climbed on top of a low, flat clint and held out her child, facing, not Mara, but the relatives, friends and neighbours that thronged around her.

'Do you see this child?' she demanded passionately. 'A lovely, healthy boy! All who know me know that he is the light of my eyes and the joy of my life. Well, if I had done what this man, my husband, wanted me to do, this child would not be here. As soon as he knew that I was expecting a baby, what does he do but go to the physician and come back with some medicine for me to take. As soon as I smelled it, I knew what it was. Anyone who works with lambing sheep has to know about herbs and their effects. I knew what that one was! It was pennyroyal! He wanted me to miscarry his own child so that I would go on working up the mountain and earning more silver for him.' She stopped and then said, 'I wanted my child; God only knows how much I wanted him. I threw the mixture in his face and I swore to myself that once I was delivered safely and had recovered from the birth, then I would divorce this man.' She drew a deep breath, kissed her baby passionately and then climbed down. This time she did not stand near to her husband but deliberately moved to the other side, turning her face away from him.

'This was very wrong!' Mara addressed Ryan so sternly that he wilted and looked uncomfortably at the ground beneath his feet. 'It is one of the great tenets of Brehon law that a woman's right to have a baby is absolute. She may even leave her husband, if he is unable to give her that baby, go to another man to become pregnant and then return to her husband – and no reproach may be made. You endangered the life of your wife and sought to kill her child. A case may be brought against him if you wish, Cliona. What do you say? The decision is yours.'

The woman shook her head. 'Give me what is rightfully mine,' she said still in loud, clear tones. 'Let me walk away from this marriage with that I have brought to it and with the fruit of my labours, and I ask no more.'

'Then,' said Mara gravely, 'the next step is yours.'

Cliona stood very tall, looking across at her husband and holding her baby high in the air. 'I divorce you, I divorce you, I divorce you,' she said clearly and steadily.

A low murmur came from the crowd. There was a note of approbation in it, thought Mara and waited patiently until it had died down. Justice under the Brehon law system was a communal matter so the courts were always held in the open in order that all could attend. There were no savage punishments, no prisons, no force was used so the judgements and the retribution for any crime committed had to be reinforced by the clan of the guilty person. In this case, the O'Connor clan had heard the reason for Cliona's desire to part from her husband and had approved.

'As the three-fold repudiation has been spoken,' said Mara, 'I now pronounce you, Cliona O'Connor and Ryan O'Connor, to be no longer man and wife.'

Now the murmur swelled. All heads turned towards the young mother. No one moved; they would wait until Mara dismissed them, but smiles of sympathy lit up the faces. Cliona would find that she would not be alone in her struggle to raise a child without a father. The O'Connor clan – the clan of her father as well as of her husband – would come to her aid whenever it was needed. Ryan O'Connor turned away and began to walk through the people who parted to allow him to pass. His head was down and with his stick he struck viciously at the nodding heads of the yellow-centred moon-daisies in his path.

Mara suddenly felt very weary. This, she

hoped, would be the last judgement day before the birth of her own child. Another few weeks now, she said to herself. She could hardly get out the traditional words wishing the presence of God in the people's lives and that they might live in peace with their families and neighbours.

'You go back to the law school,' she said to her young scholars as the crowd started to move away. 'Brigid will have your supper ready. I'll walk back slowly.'

She sighed as she turned to go down the road that led to her home. She needed some time to think about what she had heard today, she thought as she watched them running lightly across the stony fields, leaping from clint to clint, soaring over the deep grykes with the agility and energy of wild goats. She would not have made them walk at the slow pace of a heavily pregnant woman, but in any case she was glad of some time to herself. She would have to talk to Malachy the physician. This was a terrible story that had been revealed, she thought as she passed the small ancient church of Kilcorney and automatically made the sign of the cross. She was filled with anger against the young husband, but even more so against a man who would betray his profession and seek to kill instead of to heal. She had a lot of thinking to do and the silent presence of Cumhal, her farm manager, would not stop her doing this.

The problem of Malachy would have to be solved.

Two

Bretha Nemed Déinenach

(The Last Book of Laws)

It is the law that every pregnant woman should have whatever food that she desires. She may even enter the king's house and ask for something from his table.

If a woman craves beer, the brewer must give her some, even if his casks have already been sealed.

Every physician must cultivate the herbs that will give relief during childbirth.

The first signs of grey dawn on that June night had just arrived when Mara woke. She sat up in bed gasping. A terrible pain gripped her – a pain so bad that it seemed as if some monster had invaded her stomach and was desperately twisting within. Her face was soaked in sweat and her nightshift was saturated. Every fibre of her logical mind tried to tell her that it could not be the baby – that the baby was not due for another month, but her body knew the truth. Inexorably, the body was pushing aside the bones within her; inexorably, the pain pulsated. Keep calm, she told herself. This will pass and then we'll see. It was twenty-two years since the birth of her daughter Sorcha and her memory of that night was vague. There would have been pain, of course, but nothing like this, she was convinced. Of course, Brigid had been with her; that would have made a difference. Then, as now, she trusted implicitly in Brigid who had been nurse and mother to Mara from the time of the death of her own mother. Breathe in deeply – she seemed to remember Brigid saying those words and she tried to follow the advice, but it was different when she was alone and somehow she had lost her courage, or perhaps trim young muscles had made a difference. She had been fifteen years old when her daughter was born and now she was a woman of thirty-seven.

After what seemed like an hour of agony, the pain seemed to subside. Slowly and carefully, unwilling to rouse the sleeping dragon within her stomach, Mara got out of bed. The sky was brightening towards the east. A blackbird trilled from outside her window and another replied. Then a chaffinch and his mate. And soon the whole medley of singers began. Mara smiled wryly at the jubilant note. Judging by the last pain, she had hours of agony before her; she wished they would keep their joyful dawn chorus until all was over. She selected a clean shift from the wooden press in the corner of the

23

room and added a nightgown over it. Then she went to the door and called out: 'Áine!'

Áine was one of the two girls who worked in the kitchen at Cahermacnaghten law school. Brigid had insisted that this girl sleep in the Brehon's house during the last few weeks – almost as though she had foreseen that an emergency might arise. However, Áine seemed to be a sound sleeper and there was no response to the increasingly loud calls.

How long was it since the last pain? wondered Mara. If the baby was really arriving a month early, these would come at regular intervals. And if the next one was as bad as the first, she would not be able to call for assistance while she was in the grip of the pain. 'Áine,' she screamed again and again with no result. And then in desperation, she picked up the brass candlestick from the shelf by her door and threw it violently down the stairs, aiming for the door of the small room beside the kitchen.

It hit the door with a crash and Mara screamed the name again. After a minute, Áine peeped out, looking quite scared.

'Get Brigid, tell her the baby is coming.' Mara was barely able to gasp the words as the pain was coming back. Now she began to feel quite frightened. Surely she had never suffered anything like that before. She would have remembered agony like this. This pain was beyond the limits of imagination, certainly beyond the limits of memory. Bent over and helpless, she

24

stumbled back into her room and managed to climb on the bed, before the worst of the pain immobilized her again.

After that she lost track of time. Nothing but pain filled her world.

And then Brigid was in the room, snapping orders to Áine and Nessa, her other helper. There was little comfort, though, this time, from her presence and the intervals between the pains were filled with anxiety. Something was badly wrong. Brigid was an experienced midwife – always in demand for difficult births – she was trying to sound cheery and confident, but Mara could read the truth in her eyes. Brigid was frightened.

'Drink this, *allanah*, this will help,' the old endearment was a measure of Brigid's anxiety. Although Brigid had been Mara's nurse from the time of her mother's death until she had reached adulthood, she always gave Mara the title of 'Brehon' since the day that she had qualified and inherited her father's post as judge and lawgiver to the people of the kingdom of Burren.

Obediently, Mara drank the potion. It tasted bitter, but anything that held the slightest promise of alleviating the pain would have been welcome. Brigid, always well prepared for everything, must have brewed the medicine well ahead of time, in readiness for the birth.

Once again, the pain racked her. She was barely conscious of Brigid peering between her legs, and she was past caring for the worried expression that her housekeeper wore when next she saw her hanging anxiously over the bed. The potion had not diminished the agony, but had added a nightmarish quality to it. It seemed to paralyse her tongue and confuse her brain, leaving nothing there but the huge swelling consciousness of pain.

Brigid was shouting an order at Nessa now. The words blurred in Mara's mind – all but one word and that was *Malachy*. They were sending for Malachy, the physician. They must not! Malachy must not come near her baby. The narcotic pressed heavily on her mind and on her tongue. She could not articulate the words; she could not even remember why she did not want Malachy, but she knew that he must be stopped. Someone must stop him coming up the stairs. She lost all control of herself, screaming in agony as the pain racked her body, but never lost that conviction.

But somehow she could not get the words out – just the one word, repeated over and over again. Just the name, *Malachy*.

'Drink some more! Come on, *allanah*, it will do you good. Just try some.'

Mara tried to resist, but the bitter potion went down her throat. Before it took effect, she tried again to speak, tried to convey her fears of Malachy to Brigid. Somehow she could hear her own voice, as if it belonged to someone else, and it came to her as an echo bounces back from a stony cliff. *'Malachy,'* it said, and then again, just the one word; no other would come.

'He'll be here soon, *allanah*, we've sent for him, he won't be long now.' Brigid's voice penetrated the wall of pain, but brought no comfort.

But he did not come and the sun moved away from the window of the east-facing bedroom and still he did not come.

And then – it seemed like days later to Mara – the pain subsided. The terrible, racking contractions ceased. She shook her head fretfully when Brigid offered another drink. It was not needed now. There was no more pain. Her body was shutting down.

'I'm dying,' she said, and heard her voice quite clearly in the suddenly silent room. Her eyes filled with tears. This meant that the baby would die too, this so-desired child, the son of a king. She had been waiting for his birth and now it would never happen.

She lay there for some time and none of the women in the room spoke. They were busy when the pain was there, tearing her apart, but now it seemed that they did not know what to do. Her body had given up. There was no pain, no urge to push, nothing.

She closed her eyes and then opened them. There were footsteps on the stairs, someone running up – not Malachy – he would have sounded much heavier, not her husband, Turlough – he, too, was a heavy man, and in any case was busy with his war – and then the door swung open with a rush and Malachy's fourteen-year-old daughter and apprentice came in.

Mara watched her sleepily. 'Poor Nuala, she looks very white,' she said, or thought, blinking the tears from her eyes.

Faintly, and from a great distance, she heard Brigid. No words could be distinguished. Nuala had turned her back. Mara could see her delving into the medical bag – Nuala was proud of her medical bag which had belonged to her grandfather.

Mara closed her eyes again. Dying was easy, she thought. There was just a gentle, floating sensation. She wanted to be left alone, was barely conscious of Nuala examining her, but then someone was shaking her arm, shouting in her ear. She opened her eyes, 'My baby,' she tried to say.

Nuala was speaking now, slowly and distinctly in her ear. 'Mara, listen to me, listen, you're not going to die. The baby is lying the wrong way, but he's small. I'm going to draw him out with grandfather's birthing tongs. It will hurt, but I'll save the baby. I promise you, Mara. I will save your baby.'

Three

Bretha Crólige

(Judgements of Bloodlettings)

The fine for a secret and unlawful killing is three-fold. First there is the eric, *or the body fine, then there is the* lóg n-enech *'the price of his face', the honour price of the victim.*

Thirdly, there is an extra sum for the secrecy and this doubles the honour price.

A killing is declared 'secret' if the murderer does not acknowledge the deed within forty-eight hours.

'Dead! Malachy! He can't be. I saw him yesterday. I saw him pass the law school. What happened?' Mara's body ached from the long hours of childbirth, but her mind was as alert as ever. She stared at Fachtnan, the eldest scholar in her law school.

'Brigid told me not to tell you,' he said. As usual, when agitated, he ran his right hand repeatedly through his thatch of rough, curly hair.

'What nonsense. Tell me everything straightaway,' she said firmly.

29

He looked at her and hesitated, but he had been a scholar at the Cahermacnaghten Law School for over ten years and the habit of obedience to his *ollamh* (professor) was deeply ingrained.

'He was poisoned.' Fachtnan spoke in a whisper, almost as though he feared to disturb the sleeping child in the basket beside the bed.

'Poisoned!' Mara lay back on the pillow and took a deep breath. 'Could it have been an accident?'

'Nuala thinks not.'

'Poor Nuala.' Mara now realized that even through the mists of her own terrible agony, she had noticed Nuala's very white face. Then her mind went back to the suspicious death. As Brehon of the Burren, it was her responsibility to find the truth and bring the culprit to justice.

'Where is Nuala?' she asked urgently.

'She's with Brigid and your daughter. She thought I should tell you. Do you want to see her?'

'No, you tell me. I won't distress her just now.' Nuala adored Fachtnan. Mara hoped that he would have been able to help to comfort her; he would undoubtedly have heard the details. Her mind went back to the moment when Nuala had come into the bedroom and had, with huge courage and huge skill, managed to drag the baby from her womb. Without Nuala, both she and the baby sleeping beside her would be dead. 'Poor child,' she said aloud.

'Apparently, it was Caireen who found him. He was in agony. Nuala was working at the far end of the herb garden. Caireen came out and shouted for her. He was quite dead by the time Nuala came in.'

'What happened?'

Nuala would have told Fachtnan everything; she would have turned immediately to the kind young scholar – from the time that she had been a small child, Nuala had trotted after Fachtnan and he had never repulsed her. Since Malachy's second marriage to Caireen, Nuala had been at odds with her father and had turned even more towards Fachtnan. It was good that he had been there – she was sure he had been able to comfort the girl at this terrible moment in her life.

'Well, apparently, Caireen persuaded Malachy that he should drink some French brandy every morning before he mixed his medicines. She always filled his cup and left it for him on the table in his study.'

'And something was put into the brandy?' Mara knew that table, set just under the window. On a hot day such as this, the window might have been open. Someone could have passed by and seen an opportunity. But who would want to kill him? Malachy was not liked on the Burren and was considered to be a poor physician. The story she had heard yesterday had confirmed that he was corrupt and willing to sell his knowledge to help young Ryan O'Connor to abort his own child.

31

But did he have any enemies who hated him enough to kill him? Except his own daughter, perhaps, thought Mara involuntarily, and then shied away from the terrible idea. There would have been others, she told herself and her mind went again to the story that she had heard at judgement day in Poulnabrone. Were there other cases of Malachy playing God and administering death instead of healing?

'And that's not all.' Fachtnan spoke hesitantly. 'Apparently, Caireen screamed at Nuala and accused her of murdering her own father.'

The baby woke and cried, and Mara turned to it immediately. She hadn't enough strength to lift him; even leaning over to the side of the bed made her head dizzy.

'Lift him up, Fachtnan, give him to me.'

'What are you going to call him?' Fachtnan was surprisingly competent at lifting the baby from the basket and placing the swaddled bundle in her arms.

'I've thought of Cormac – for the last five hundred years, everyone in the O'Brien royal family is either Turlough, Conor, Donal, Teige or Murrough. Cormac will be a change,' said Mara. She spoke automatically, though. Her mind was on the murder. What a terrible thing, especially for Nuala. How had she reacted to that accusation flung at her by Caireen?

Everything had been arranged for this birth. The law scholars would have finished the Trinity Term and gone to their homes. If war had not occurred, King Turlough Donn, her husband, would have been back from his yearly tour of the southern part of his domain, around the city of Limerick. It had been decided that Mara would go to the Thomond for the birth in order to be under the care of Turlough's own physician, Donncadh O'Hickey; and Fergus MacClancy, Brehon of the neighbouring kingdom of Corcomroe, would look after the legal affairs of Burren for a couple of months while Mara cared for her baby.

Everything had been arranged, but everything had been arranged for July. This baby boy had come early and had disrupted all plans. Now, above all, she needed to deal with this murder and to find the truth about Malachy's murder, and, if possible, to protect Nuala who had always been dear to her and now was even more dear.

And then the baby was in her arms, nuzzling at her. Mara patted his little back and felt weak with love for him. He needed her now. She could not deal with him and deal with this murder. Someone else would have to take over and do the investigating.

'Fachtnan,' she said. 'Ride over to Corcomroe. Tell Brehon MacClancy what has happened and about the baby. Ask him if he will take over this case. Send Brigid in to me, will you.' Fergus would have to cope, she thought.

And then when Fachtnan had gone out she settled herself to feed the hungry baby.

But little Cormac did not seem to want to feed. After a minute he turned his head away and cried, first a whimper and then a fully voiced cry. Again and again Mara tried the baby at her breast, but each time he rejected it.

'I have no milk,' said Mara starkly when Brigid came flying in, her ginger hair looking as untidy as Fachtnan's. Too much was happening, she thought, feeling tears flow down her cheeks.

'Is it any wonder,' scolded Brigid, taking the baby from her arms and rocking him gently. 'That stupid boy; I told him to say nothing. I felt like boxing his ears when I heard that he had told you. Murder, indeed! And you just awake! And the time that you had! Give it a day or so and just relax, and don't ask for any news from outside. Just eat and drink and sleep and rest. God knows that you need it – the way you work.'

Mara smiled. Brigid's vigour was doing her good. She dried her face with a corner of the sheet and endeavoured to think. She had to do the best for everyone now. Hopefully, Fergus would take charge of that murder investigation, but there was no denying that the Brehon from Corcomroe was not of the brightest and quickest wits. He would be continually consulting her, continually asking for advice.

And then there was her baby. Mara looked at the tiny infant with concern. Could a baby as small as this survive?

'Unwrap him, Brigid,' she said.

34

'Now, stop worrying. You don't want him to catch cold.'

'The sun is pouring in through the window,' said Mara. 'Go on, unwrap him, Brigid. I want to see him properly.'

The baby was tiny; tiny and very fragile. Thin little arms, stick-like legs – like those of a little frog, eyelashes not yet grown. This baby has come before his time, thought Mara, looking at him in a worried way. He needed feeding. Perhaps Brigid was right; perhaps she was too tense. It had been a shock to hear of Malachy's murder. After all, the man was a relative of her own. But of course it had been even more of a shock to hear of the accusation that his wife had flung at his daughter.

'Send Sorcha in for a few minutes and the children – they can see their new little cousin,' she said to Brigid, doing her best to keep her tone of voice light and relaxed. Although Sorcha was her daughter, she was probably much more knowledgeable about babies, having had three children in the last few years. I was only fifteen when she was born, thought Mara. How full of confidence I was then! I don't remember worrying about her at all.

Sorcha's wide blue eyes were shocked and her face pale when she came in. Obviously she had heard the news. Of course Malachy was not only a distant cousin on Mara's side, but was also very nearly related to her husband, Oisín.

'Has Oisín heard the news?' Mara thought that

35

she had not heard his deep, melodious voice for a few hours.

Sorcha shook her head. 'He went off for a long walk this morning,' she said. 'I have no idea where he is.'

'I see.' Mara rocked her crying baby. Her son-in-law would want to be off soon, she thought. Already he was quite bored by life in the country and missing the hustle and bustle of the city of Galway.

'He's very small.' Five-year-old Domhnall bent over the baby with an appraising look.

'You were as small as that when you were born, Manus, weren't you?' said Aislinn, reaching up to pat the little boy in her mother's arms. She knelt adoringly in front of the cradle and tried to interest her younger brother in his tiny cousin.

'Manus wasn't as small as Cormac when he was born,' contradicted Domhnall.

'Yes, he was,' said Sorcha hurriedly. 'You've just forgotten.'

'No, I haven't. *Mamó*'s baby is much smaller.'

Mara winced. Her grandson had a calm, logical mind and once he had decided on a matter no one could argue him out of a statement. He was right, of course. Even on the day he was born, Manus had been a fine bouncy baby with the dark hair and brown eyes of his father. She gazed at little Cormac; he looked as fragile as a windflower, she thought.

'He's hungry,' said Sorcha. She popped Manus

down on the floor and took her newborn brother from her mother's arms. He nuzzled into her, crying fretfully.

Mara saw Brigid frown thoughtfully and a quick glance passed between her daughter and her housekeeper.

'Come on, you two,' said Brigid to the two older children. 'Let's see if the brown hen has hatched out her chickens yet.'

'*Mamó* has hatched out her chicken, hasn't she, Aislinn? That's supposed to be a joke,' added Domhnall in exasperated tones when his sister stared at him in a puzzled way.

'He does look a little like a newly hatched chicken,' said Mara trying to sound amused, but despite her best efforts tears leaked out from her eyes and began to run down her face. She dashed them away impatiently. New born chicks often died; she knew that.

'I have no milk,' she said once more when the children had gone out.

'Let me feed him,' said Sorcha in her practical way. 'I have plenty of milk for two. I'll feed Manus at the same time and then he won't get jealous.'

No, but I am, thought Mara, though she knew that she was being stupid and childish. She shut her eyes. She would have to find a wet nurse, she thought, unless this was just temporary due to her long and difficult labour.

'Try to rest now. Close your eyes. Don't worry about the milk. It was the shock of hearing of

Malachy's death; you should never have been told,' said Sorcha, sounding motherly and concerned.

'Perhaps,' said Mara. She shut her eyes obediently, but her mind went on working.

Was she shocked by Malachy's death? She thought not, in a way. He wasn't a popular man, not esteemed in the kingdom. Not very much liked, either. Although he was Mara's cousin, she wasn't sure that even she had liked Malachy for some time. He had not been behaving in a very likeable manner. His lack of care for his patients, his obsession with obtaining silver for his service, his behaviour to his own daughter, his effort to seize her property some months ago and his ridiculous preference for his new stepsons – all these had exasperated her.

Mara's eyes snapped open.

'I must talk to Nuala,' she said urgently. 'Don't try to argue me out of it, Sorcha, you're as bad as Brigid. I promised Malachy over a year ago that if anything ever happened to him then I would look after Nuala. I must see her.'

'Quarter of an hour won't make a difference,' said Sorcha firmly. 'Let me feed these two hungry children and then I'll get her. Now do try to rest. You can't be doing ten things at once when you are just after having a baby. You should have a sleep after I put Cormac back. You look terribly tired.'

It was the early afternoon before Mara woke.

38

She felt a little better and instantly sent Áine to fetch Nuala. Brigid would be busy with the scholars' dinner and Sorcha would be feeding her own brood. Now was the moment to see the poor girl who had not only lost her father but had also been accused of the murder by her step-mother.

Nuala had just arrived in Mara's bedroom when the clip-clop of horse hoofs outside signalled the arrival of Fergus MacClancy, Brehon of Corcomroe. Mara gave an exasperated sigh. Now, just when she needed time to talk to Nuala, Fergus would be there, fussing as usual. However, she and the girl would have a few minutes of privacy as the visitors would need to take the horses up to the stables at the law school.

'Come and sit by me,' said Mara softly with a quick eye at the peacefully sleeping baby. 'How are you, Nuala?'

'I'm all right,' said Nuala. Mara studied her. She had known Nuala from the moment that she was born, the only baby to survive from Malachy's first wife, the beautiful Mór, who had struggled with ill-health for years and eventually died from a lump in her breast. Mór had been the dearest friend that Mara had known and, for her sake initially, she cherished the daughter. Love for the intelligent, determined, passionate Nuala had grown, though, and now she was as dear to Mara as her own daughter, Sorcha.

'Am I going to be a suspect?' As usual Nuala was direct and uncompromising.

'No, of course not,' said Mara hastily.

A wry smile twisted Nuala's mouth and for a moment tears softened the direct look from her dark brown eyes.

'Why not? I quarrelled with him. He tried to take my inheritance away from me. He banned me from his house. Replaced me with the sons of that woman that he married. He tried to deny me the possibility of being a physician when everyone knows that it was my dream since I was a child.' Nuala enumerated the facts in a dry, hard tone and then dashed the tears impatiently from her eyes. Her tanned skin had a faintly sickly tinge and her eyes were deeply shadowed. 'And I hated him,' she finished, staring desolately out of the window towards the distant blue terraces of Mullaghmore mountain.

'And you loved him,' said Mara softly, and when Nuala said nothing, she stretched out and took the girl's cold hand within her own two.

'You've said all this to me, now,' she said firmly. 'You've said it to me, Mara, friend of your mother and cousin to your father. What do you say to me, Mara, Brehon of the Burren?'

Nuala pulled her hand away and walked to the window. She stood there for a minute and then came back. The tears were gone now, but her brown eyes were wary.

'What can I say?' she demanded angrily. 'I suppose that I should say that I had nothing to

40

do with this death, and that I ask you to investigate the murder of my father and to bring the culprit to justice in front of the people of the Burren at the judgement place at Poulnabrone. That's what you want me to say, isn't it? But will I be believed? Do what you are supposed to do, but don't ask me to help you.'

Nuala's voice rang out and Mara put a hasty finger to her lips, however, her eyes went not to the sleeping baby, but to the open window. Voices could be heard and heavy footsteps echoed from the paved path outside.

'That's enough, Nuala,' she said softly, but with a note of authority in her voice, 'go now, but ask Brigid to fetch the baby before she shows Fergus up here.'

It wasn't just Fergus, though. Brigid had barely removed the baby when the footsteps sounded on the staircase. Mara shut her eyes and groaned softly as the voices floated upwards. Siobhan, Fergus's wife, a woman of unsurpassing dullness, was on her way up, also. Her voice, with pauses to recover from the steepness of the stairs, was as loud as always.

'Poor thing ... what I always say is ... no life for a woman ... and the king, too ... of course, he is always away ... these terrible battles...'

And then there was a silence. Mara grinned reluctantly. Fergus, no doubt feeling embarrassed, poor man, had probably put a finger to his lips. Then her eyes sharpened. Someone else was coming up the stairs behind the MacClancy

41

couple – a heavy footfall. Odd. Who could it be?

'Ah, Mara. Good to see you looking so well.' Fergus's over-hearty greeting immediately convinced Mara that she was looking terrible. She sat up a bit straighter and wished that she felt able to get out of bed and be her normal self.

'But where is the darling little baby?' Siobhan looked all around the room as if expecting to see an infant concealed under some piece of furniture.

Mara didn't answer – her eyes were fixed on the man who had followed Fergus into her bedroom. He was of squat stature, quite young, but with a huge stomach, imperfectly concealed by an over-large *léine* and carefully draped cloak. He had a short, sparse red beard and a pair of small green eyes twinkling from under his sandy-coloured eyebrows. He didn't appear disconcerted by entering a strange woman's bedroom, and beamed happily at her before plumping himself down on the most comfortable chair in the room.

'Ah,' said Fergus apologetically, seating himself on the window seat, 'Mara, this is my young cousin, Boetius MacClancy. Just walked in the door half an hour ago. He has just passed his final examinations at the MacEgan school in Duniry and is now an *ollamh*.' He beamed proudly at his relation and Mara murmured some congratulations, while wondering irritably why Fergus had seen fit to land his cousin on her the very day on which she had given birth.

Pompous name, Boetius; suits him, she thought, while studying the young man with a professional smile still nailed to her face. He had probably been christened Baothglach, but had Latinized the name to make it more acceptable to English ears.

'Does King Turlough know the happy news yet?' enquired Fergus.

'No, not yet,' said Mara briefly.

'You haven't told your husband!' Siobhan almost fainted with shock.

Mara gazed at her irritably. Really, Fergus was a fool, she thought. Why on earth did he think it was a good idea to bring along his stupid wife and his cousin to visit a woman who had given birth only a few hours previously.

'It was very kind of you to visit, Siobhan,' she said keeping her voice as bland as she could manage. 'And very nice to meet you, Boetius. Unfortunately my energy is limited so perhaps, Fergus, you and I could have a few minutes alone while we talk of legal matters. Would that be all right, Siobhan?'

'Oh, the death of Malachy. What a terrible thing,' shrilled Siobhan. 'Don't you worry your head about that, Mara. We've got just the solution. Boetius here will investigate the murder. He will take over your legal work as well as your teaching duties – after all, he is a qualified *ollamh* so he is perfectly able to teach. He is young and strong, and he will manage everything beautifully. I'll have a word with your

43

housekeeper about a room for him so that he won't have to waste time riding between here and Corcomroe. He will keep your lads in good order and take no nonsense from them.'

'I'll soon sort it out for you. No need to worry about a thing.' The large young man beamed at her happily. His voice was as pompous as his name, thought Mara, wondering how to get out of this unexpected turn of events.

'We thought that would be the best thing, especially in view of the murder,' Fergus chimed in. 'You see, I would not be able to give it my full attention. Like you, there are examinations coming up and I have a case of shipwreck to deal with, and...' He tailed off looking at her anxiously.

'I don't think that will be possible,' said Mara hastily. 'My daughter, her husband and my grandchildren are already here. We will have no spare accommodation, especially as I have invited Nuala to stay here, also, as her uncle Ardal has accompanied the king into battle.'

'Of course, you know your own business best, Mara.' Siobhan's voice betrayed a deep doubt on that subject as she continued. 'But I'm surprised that you, the Brehon, should harbour someone who has been accused of the crime.' She nodded her head wisely and added, 'We met Sadhbh, Malachy's housekeeper, and she told us what occurred. Poor Caireen; what a terrible thing to have happened to her. We're on our way over to see her, after we leave here. Poor

44

woman! Her husband poisoned and his own daughter accused of the terrible deed.'

'Who accuses Nuala?' Mara sat up in bed. A rapid surge of blood flooded out and drenched the sheet beneath her. She felt her head become dizzy; suddenly she was hot and soaked with sweat; and then, just as suddenly, icy cold. The three figures in front of her shifted in and out of focus. She tried to say something more but she couldn't. There was an odd smell in the room and a deadly faintness seemed to be paralysing her. The last thing that she heard was a shrill, high-pitched shriek from Siobhan.

'I don't care what you say, you lie there and think of nothing. You can see that Cormac is getting on fine. There is nothing at all for you to worry about. God is up there in His heaven keeping everything going; no need for you to be bearing the world on your own shoulders.'

'The boys?' queried Mara. Cormac was tucked into bed beside her and yes, he did look a little less fragile. She herself was feeling better. The haemorrhaging had stopped thanks to Nuala and her skill. And the alarming fits of faintness had not occurred for the past few hours. The fever that had followed them had now subsided and her head was clear. How long had she lain there, drifting in and out of consciousness? It must have been days.

'Everything is fine,' scolded Brigid. 'And I've told you that six times already. That young man,

45

Master MacClancy, he's in there with them now.'

'How is he getting on?' asked Mara anxiously. Her mind went to her six scholars. Would this young Boetius MacClancy make allowances for Fachtnan and his memory problems; be tactful with the brilliant but opinionated Enda; understanding with the adolescent humour of the two fifteen-year-olds, Moylan and Aidan; patient with twelve-year-old Hugh who was finding the work of the law school difficult, and then there was eleven-year-old Shane, clever and needing new challenges to avoid boredom – how would the young man cope with her scholars?

'He's getting on all right.' Brigid's sniff always spoke volumes. Mara waited; more would come, she knew that.

'He's too familiar with them,' said Brigid eventually, with a toss of her head. 'Larking around with that Aidan.'

'Oh, is that all?' Mara felt relieved. This was a young man and young men are exuberant and fun-loving – perhaps he had only appeared pompous and self-satisfied in the presence of his elderly cousin.

'I don't like him.' Nuala had been silent up to now. She had hardly left the bedchamber for the past two days, sleeping in the bedroom on a truckle bed, busying herself around Mara, checking that everything was in order and that there was no recurrence of the drastic bleeding. Between Sorcha, Nuala and Brigid, Mara was

46

beginning to feel stifled. Her suggestion that she should get up from her bed seemed unpopular with them all, so she lay back of the pillows and busied herself in examining her son's tiny fingernails. She would not enquire any more about Boetius, but make up her own mind.

'Any word from Turlough?' she asked, and again a quick glance passed between the three nurses.

'Don't worry about him,' said Brigid heartily. 'We haven't sent a messenger, as you ordered, so there is no reason for him to send a messenger here. You know what King Turlough is like, God bless him, he'll ride up here one morning or one evening and give us all a surprise.'

There is news, and it's not good, thought Mara. However, she had long decided that what she could not influence, she would try not to worry about, and she turned her attention back to her child.

'Nuala, is there any chance, at this stage, that I will be able to feed Cormac myself?' It seemed strange to be asking a girl still two months from her fifteenth birthday a question like that, but Nuala had kept mother and son alive during the long and difficult labour, and during the last days had probably once again saved Mara's life. In fact, for the last year she had been tending competently to the people of the Burren. One of the reasons why Malachy had been so angry with his daughter had been jealousy over the fact that so many people preferred her ministra-

47

tions to his.

'I would say that it is unlikely at this stage.' Nuala was, as usual, honest and direct.

'Try again, Mother.' Sorcha had a softer nature. Not as intelligent as Nuala, Sorcha's life had been easy and straightforward. She had been adored by Mara and by Brigid, had lived a happy life at the law school, learning to read, write and add up, to spin, weave and sew, but showing little interest in the law and with no inclination or ability to undertake the long years of intense study that would be required for qualification as a lawyer. When she was sixteen she had married Oisín, a distant cousin of her mother's.

Once again Mara tried, but once again Cormac turned away fretfully. The decision had to be faced. It wasn't fair to expect her daughter to go on feeding Cormac when she had her own little Manus to care for, and would soon need to return to Galway where her husband had a prosperous business. In any case, thought Mara, trying to look on the bright side, she had planned to engage a nurse to look after the child while she was teaching and looking after the legal affairs of the kingdom.

I must find someone, she thought, as the faintness began to well up again. Little Cormac must be well fed and well cared for. And I'll give Boetius MacClancy one week to solve this murder investigation, she thought, and if he hasn't solved it by then, I'll take matters into my own hands.

Four

Urcailte Bretheman

(The Forbidden Things of a Judge)

1. A judge shall not come to a decision before the chaff has been blown from the corn; that is to say, all evidence has to be carefully sifted.
2. No one person should influence a judge; all must be equal before him.
3. He must not be slow or negligent in the seeking-out of the facts.
4. He must never accept bribes or show favour.
5. He must never allow his knowledge of the law texts to fade.
6. He must not make up his mind too quickly, but must challenge all his decisions as if he were his own enemy.
7. He must never utter a lie at a public judgement.

'I have everything under control. There's no need for you to worry your head about anything, *Mamó*.' Young MacClancy gave a roguish grin and Mara scowled. She had made a big effort to dress in her most dignified gown, a magnificent

49

garment made from flowing black silk, its colour relieved by the white lace at the wrists and neck of the linen *léine* that she wore beneath. Brigid had washed her dark hair and coiled the thick braids at the back of her head. A quick glance at the looking glass had confirmed to Mara that, though pale, she was looking well. Who was this bumptious young man to attempt to tease her by pretending to be one of her grandchildren?

'Brehon,' she said coldly and with emphasis. Then before he could respond she said swiftly. 'Just make your report to me, please.'

He swept her a playful bow, but when she didn't respond he arranged his face in solemn lines.

'Well, of course, the murder was a very easy matter to solve...' he began, but upon seeing her expression he added kindly, 'coming fresh to the situation I could see the truth of it. More difficult for you, of course.'

Mara stared at him frostily. 'I have never come to any conclusion about a murder before I investigated the matter fully,' she said emphatically. 'Nor would you, I am convinced,' she added in a manner that belied her expressed conviction.

'Oh, I've done a bit of poking around,' he said airily. 'Youthful energy, you know, *Ma* ... Brehon. I do my bit of teaching, set those lads of yours down to work, conduct their examinations and then I go and have a few chats around the place, do a bit of poking around, you know. There are no flies on me.' He tapped a finger to one side of his broad nose.

'Examinations!' exclaimed Mara, distracted from her thoughts about Malachy's murder. 'The boys have done their examinations!'

'Done, marked, moderated by my cousin Fergus, and they all know their results by now,' said Boetius complacently. He combed his red beard with his podgy fingers and beamed happily at her.

'B – but ... how ... what examinations?' Mara realized that she was stuttering with rage and pulled herself together. Her voice was cold and hard as she said firmly, 'I have my own examination papers which are based on the work that my scholars have done here at Cahermacnaghten. It was kind of you to endeavour to test them, but I would prefer to do that myself.'

'Don't you worry about a thing,' said Boetius. 'These were your own examination papers. I took them from the wooden press in the schoolhouse. Your daughter, Sorcha, found your key and gave it to me.'

Now, how do I get around this? thought Mara. There was something about this young man that she disliked very much. On the other hand, there was no denying the fact that between fever and haemorrhaging she had been incapable of any effort for the last week. She couldn't blame Sorcha – only wished that Boetius had asked Brigid for the key. Her daughter did not have a

51

suspicious nature; her housekeeper would have been very sure that no other than Mara, herself, should handle that key.

'Two failures, I'm afraid.' Boetius smiled gently. 'Still, four passes! Not bad for a small country place like this,' he said patronizingly.

'Aidan and Hugh,' Mara said the words more to herself than to him. Hugh was a sensitive boy and would have been thrown off his stride by her unexpected absence, and she herself had often threatened Aidan with failure if he did not work a little harder.

'No, Aidan did all right – especially in the *viva voce* – I flatter myself that Aidan has responded very well to my teaching. He likes someone young, someone who will have a laugh with him.'

'So who failed then?' Mara decided that she would ignore this young man's annoying habit of trying to tease her.

'Fachtnan, of course,' said Boetius. 'And Hugh, as you guessed.'

Mara stared at him with consternation. Fachtnan had made enormous progress in the last few months. She had been certain that he would pass. He had some memory problems, but he and Mara had worked on a set of visual memory prompts and mnemonics – something she had read about in a text relating Greek scholastic methods. This would be a crushing blow to the poor lad.

'And my cousin, Fergus, fully agreed with

me.' Boetius chuckled at her expression. 'No really, I know what you're thinking. Dear old Fergus is not too bright, but even he could see that this lad could not qualify as a lawyer. He's not suitable in any way, you know. He forgot some elementary facts in the *viva voce* and his Latin is poor. No, no, he could not have been passed. It might be best for him to give it up completely. I understand that he has already had an extra year.'

'Fachtnan has an excellent understanding of the duties of a lawyer and will make a superb Brehon,' said Mara curtly. 'I would like to see those examination papers, please.'

Boetius laughed heartily. 'You don't trust me, do you?' he said wagging a finger at her, his small green eyes twinkling merrily. 'Well, I'm afraid that they are no longer here. I'm not one of those people who sit around and let grass grow under foot. I've already sent a messenger with the papers over to the Brehon in Thomond.'

Mara was silenced. There was nothing she could do. This obnoxious individual was a fully qualified teacher. If Fergus had not weakly sign-ed the moderation papers she might have been able to hold new examinations. If the papers had not been sent to Thomond, she could have double-checked to make sure that the marking was correct, but she was now left with no way out of the situation. In a moment of weakness, she had tacitly agreed to Boetius MacClancy taking over her duties and she would have to put up with the consequence. It would not do twelve-year-old Hugh too much harm to have an extra year, though she was sorry as the child had little confidence and had been badly affected by the death of his mother eighteen months ago. Fachtnan, however, was a different matter.

This would be a terrible blow.

Mara glared at Boetius. 'I would have preferred if you had waited,' she said in tones that would have made the most troublesome adolescent shiver, but had little effect on the self-satisfied individual opposite.

'No trouble at all, I assure you,' he said cheerfully. 'Now let me tell you about this murder. It's a sad case, but justice must be done.'

'You haven't summoned the people of the kingdom to the judgement place at Poulnabrone and told them of your conclusions?'

'Oh, no, I thought I would leave that for you to do.' Boetius had not picked up on the irony, or else decided to ignore it. 'There is no hurry,' he said condescendingly. 'It's not yet two weeks since the poor fellow was murdered.'

'And?' Mara was determined to say as little as possible. To her annoyance she began to feel slightly weak. Little Cormac cried from the room above and she half-rose and then made herself sit still. Brigid was with him. Between Sorcha and Brigid her child would be well looked after.

'It's a delicate matter, you see,' continued

54

Boetius. 'I've been looking up the law books and, to give you your due, you do have a fine collection...' he paused to be thanked for the compliment, but after a quick, keen glance at her face he continued.

'I never remember reading of a case like this; and I must say it for myself that I have a great memory. The thing is that there is plenty said about what must happen if a son kills his father, but nothing is said about what should happen if a daughter kills her father.'

And now it was out. Mara had suspected it.

'What do you mean?' she asked grimly.

He raised his sandy eyebrows. 'It's obvious, surely,' he said with a light laugh. 'Motive, opportunity, means. Young Nuala had them all. According to her stepmother, Caireen, who seems a very nice woman, Nuala hated her father and often told him that she wished that he were dead. She had some idea that if he were out of the way, she could set up as a physician in the Burren. Ridiculous, of course.' He gave another light laugh and looked at her enquiringly, but still she said nothing so he continued.

'Nuala had the opportunity to kill him; she was actually working in the herb garden at Caherconnell when Malachy died, and of course she could have found the means. Apparently, according to Caireen, Malachy was poisoned. Nuala, of course, would have known where all Malachy's poisons were kept. Caireen told Siobhan that.'

'What!' Mara was jolted out of her resolution to say nothing.

He beamed at her. 'Yes, I think I've got it all worked out – motive, means, opportunity,' he repeated.

'You mentioned a discussion between Siobhan and Caireen. Surely that is not evidence.' With an effort Mara kept the lid on her boiling temper. How dare this young man try to patronize her! However, that was a small matter compared to the danger he represented to Nuala unless she got on her feet quickly and took back her position from Boetius MacClancy.

'Yes, Caireen has been a great help to me in solving this murder.' He waited for a question and when none came he exclaimed, 'But I'm tiring you. Look, why don't you go back to your bed and leave everything to me.'

'Go on,' said Mara. 'I am perfectly well, thank you. You were saying that you consulted books to no avail. What exactly were you looking for?'

'What is the correct penalty for a daughter who has murdered her father, of course.' Boetius nodded his head wisely and raised his sandy eyebrows at her pityingly, as one who is making all possible allowance for the defective memory of an ill person.

'I must seem very old-fashioned and out-of-date,' said Mara with false humility, 'but I normally look for evidence before speculating on the penalty.'

'The evidence is obvious.' Boetius was begin-

56

ning to sound a little impatient now. 'There is no doubt at all in my mind that Caireen is correct. Nuala murdered her father, Malachy. She was working in the herb garden, she slipped over to the window when no one was looking and put some poison into his drink, then back to the weeding again. The question is what penalty should be awarded? I know there is all that old-fashioned business about putting someone guilty of patricide into a boat without oars and setting them afloat on the ocean, but I can't find if that has ever been done to a woman.'

'So, what is your solution?' enquired Mara.

Boetius flashed a smile at her. 'Fergus's lady wife, you know Siobhan, don't you? Well, she came up with the solution. She and her friend, Ailse, they talked it over with Caireen. Caireen did not want the ultimate penalty – as she truly said, Nuala's death would be of no use to her. So Siobhan suggested that Nuala should enter a convent, become a nun and spend her life praying for forgiveness. And, of course, her property at Rathborney should be given to Caireen to recompense her for the death of her husband, Malachy.'

'What! Nuala be forced to enter a convent!' As soon as the exclamation left her lips Mara felt annoyed with herself. It would have been more dignified to ignore the malice of stupid people.

'A very humane suggestion.' Boetius beamed at her condescendingly. 'As Caireen remarked, if the girl was in Galway she would be hanged.'

'With no trial! Is that the custom under English law?' Mara raised her eyebrows mockingly.

'Well, as I said to Caireen, the judge would be certain to bring in a verdict of guilty.' Boetius was not disconcerted by her question.

'So you have discussed the matter with all of these people?' The baby cried again from upstairs, but Mara's attention was concentrated on Boetius MacClancy. The baby would be well looked after; little Cormac was gaining weight visibly from Sorcha's rich milk; Sorcha herself was well and happy, enjoying outdoor meals and fun with her three children who were all growing tanned and rosy in the Atlantic air on the Burren. But Nuala was as dear to her as any of them, and Nuala was in grave danger from this ignorant, opinionated young man.

'The matter of Malachy's murder and your surmises should not have been discussed with anyone,' she said hotly.

'Oh, I didn't mention it to any of the scholars,' he said reassuringly.

'That was not what I meant. My scholars are trained never to mention any legal matter to outsiders; that would not be true of a gossip party at the MacClancy household.' And if that observation made its way back to Fergus – well, that was too bad, she thought. What on earth did he mean by allowing that conversation to take place? She rose to her feet.

'Where are the scholars?' she asked.

'I left them some work to do.' He looked a little bewildered at her question as he, too, rose.

'Let's go over there.' Brigid would fuss, but that could not be helped. The sooner Mara took matters back into her own hands, the greater the chance of preventing irrevocable harm to Nuala's reputation and her future happiness.

Mara said no more until they had walked the few hundred yards between Cahermacnaghten and the Brehon's house. In the distance she could hear her grandchildren playing and then a shout of 'Bran', and her beautiful white Irish wolfhound came soaring over one of the stone walls and joined her. She patted him and he leaned his muscular body against hers. He would have missed her badly during the last week.

'It's all right, Sorcha,' she called. 'Bran is with me.' Hurriedly she turned towards the law school enclosure. Neither Brigid nor Sorcha would dare interrupt once she took her position in front of her scholars. Stiffening her spine and trying to ignore the jelly-like state of her legs, she walked through the gate.

The law school at Cahermacnaghten was built within the enormously high and thick walls of an ancient enclosure. There were five small thatched, stone houses there: the schoolhouse, the scholars' house, the farm manager's house, the kitchen house and the guesthouse. They all had been newly limewashed and gleamed a brilliant white in the sunshine.

There seemed to be a certain amount of horse play going on inside the schoolhouse, judging by the noise. Mara could hear Aidan's loud adolescent voice, a raucous laugh from Moylan and an exclamation of pain from Hugh. She moved swiftly across the cobbled yard in front of her companion and threw the door open dramatically.

To her amazement the noise did not instantly stop once the door was pulled open. Aidan and Moylan continued their game which seemed to involve rubbing handfuls of ash into Hugh's red curls. There was no sign of the two oldest boys, Fachtnan and Enda, but eleven-year-old Shane was doing his best to save his friend.

'Well!' exclaimed Mara and suddenly the noise stopped. Every head swivelled towards her. The boys quickly moved to their desks and sat very straight and very upright, looking ahead. She moved to the top of the room and took up her accustomed place beside the large desk. Boetius followed her.

'So this is how you behave when you have been trusted to work alone,' said Mara, and proceeded to read them a lecture. Where were Fachtnan and Enda? she wondered, and then became conscious that, instead of being subdued by her words, Aidan was sniggering behind his hand and Moylan, who had fixed his eyes on the ceiling with an expression of carelessness, glanced, from time to time, at something behind her. Going on with her lecture she swung around and surprised a large and sympathetic grin on Boetius's face, who was winding his finger around and around – presumably in some sort of signal that her lecture was going on and on. The man was actually having the temerity to mock her behind her back. Instantly she stopped and stared hard at him. He immediately rearranged his features into an exaggerated expression of disapproval, but his small green eyes twinkled and Mara heard a stifled giggle from Aidan.

'Could you kindly fetch Enda and Fachtnan to me. Presumably they have gone to work in peace in the scholars' house.' She spoke to the man with elaborate politeness, but did not give him his title and kept her eyes fixed intently on him until he went through the door. Then she sat down in her usual chair and looked seriously at her pupils. Every eye fell before hers and she remained seated, hoping that Brigid would not follow her and insist on her going back to bed.

A long silence, Mara had always found, reduced the rowdiest adolescent to good order and this was a silence that she had no intention of breaking until the two senior boys arrived.

Enda and Fachtnan greeted her with such pleasure that she began to feel a little better. Boetius made little attempt to hide his impatience, asking her if there was anything else that he could do for her.

'Bring a stool for *Ollamh* MacClancy, Hugh,' said Mara authoritatively. 'Yes, put it there, just beside Shane.' Now the young man was seated facing her, almost part of her scholars.

'Let's discuss this murder of Malachy the physician,' she said.

There was a look of surprise from Fachtnan and of pleasure from Enda, and the younger boys sat up very straight and tried to look responsible.

'My scholars are well used to the procedure that we employ when we go about solving a secret and unlawful killing,' she said condescendingly to Boetius.

'And we understand that we are all under a sacred oath not to say anything about our deliberations to anyone outside this room,' said Shane rapidly.

'I'm sure that *Ollamh* MacClancy knows all about this; it would have been part of his training,' said Mara sweetly, and saw Enda give her a long look.

'May I write on the board, Brehon?' Aidan raised his arm politely.

But Mara said coldly, 'I think on this occasion, I will choose Hugh. His handwriting is very clear.'

Hugh's delicate white skin turned slightly pink as he came out to the whitewashed board and picked up the stick of charcoal.

'Any comment from anyone?' Mara looked around the room.

'I think we should make a list of reasons why anyone might want to kill Malachy,' said Enda, with a quick glance at Fachtnan. 'It seems too early in the investigation to start writing down names.'

'My own feeling exactly!' Mara beamed at him. 'This is just the beginning of the enquiry. It would be a great mistake to rush towards picking out something obvious, wouldn't it? What should we do first?'

'Explore the means to commit the murder,' said Shane tentatively. 'But perhaps you could tell us the facts, first, Brehon. No one has talked to us about the murder. We haven't had any discussions about it or anything.' He cast a sidelong look of dislike at the man sitting on the stool beside him and then turned an attentive face towards Mara.

'Well, the facts are that on the morning of June 11, the physician Malachy was found dead in his stillroom by his wife, Caireen. On a table was a half-emptied glass of French brandy. It is presumed that some poison had been put in the glass – I'm not sure what—'

'Impossible to tell,' interrupted Boetius. 'Could be anything, according to Caireen, the man's wife.'

Fachtnan raised his hand politely and Mara nodded at him.

'Nuala, the physician's apprentice, has told me that she can guess which poison was used.' Fachtnan tried to keep his voice unemotional, but his dark eyes were worried.

'Could you fetch Nuala, please, Fachtnan,'

said Mara politely.

'Interesting that she knows...' commented Boetius, but Mara ignored him and nodded toward Shane who was waving his hand in the air.

'Should Hugh put a drawing of the stillroom on the board while we are waiting,' suggested Shane. 'We've all been in that stillroom, so we should be able to remember between us.'

'Good idea,' said Mara.

'Draw a square,' ordered Moylan. 'It's a square sort of room.'

'D for door,' said Aidan.

'W for window,' said Enda. 'The window could be important. It looks over the road, doesn't it, Brehon?'

'And the door is next to the stairs, isn't it?'

'And that sort of couch thing where he examines his patients – that's over against the wall opposite the window.' Now the suggestions were pouring in as fast as Hugh could draw.

'Shelves on either side of the door.'

'Poisons on that top shelf, by the fire – mark in the fireplace, Hugh.'

'And the table!' Enda was as sharp as ever. 'Does anyone remember where the table was in that room? My own feeling was that it was next to the window. If that's right, I think that is very significant.'

'You're quite right,' said Mara triumphantly. Suddenly back with her sharp-witted boys, she felt a surge of energy and well-being. 'And why is it significant, Enda?' She gave a triumphant glance at the puzzled frown on the face of the stout, self-important figure of Boetius Mac-Clancy, but managed to refrain from suggesting that Enda might explain the significance to the young man.

'Because the window is by the roadside and anyone, with very little risk, could drop poison into the brandy.' Enda addressed his words to Hugh, thinking that only to him would this need to be spelled out.

'Ah, here is Nuala,' said Mara, as Bran got up with a wag of his long muscular tail and went towards the door.

Nuala looked wretched. Always very slim, she had lost weight in the last week and now appeared quite thin. Her tanned face had a sickly, yellowish tinge and her brown eyes had dark shadows beneath them. Mara greeted her with a brisk, matter-of-fact manner and respectfully asked for her opinion as to the poison.

'I have been thinking about that.' Nuala's voice was dry and her manner professional. Mara turned a composed, interested face towards her, but her heart ached to listen to the child calmly and dispassionately account for her father's death, and explain about poisons to her audience.

'I thought of digitalis, made from the seeds of foxgloves. This would cause death by excessively speeding the heart beats until the heart collapses, but there were signs of acute vomiting, burns around the mouth and the dead man

65

had sweated badly – his clothes were quite damp with sweat, so I came to the conclusion that the most likely poison was aconite, wolfsbane it is known as.'

'And is that a poison that you grow in your herb garden?' Boetius asked the question in a mild tone of voice, but his green eyes were keen and he raised his sandy eyebrows with an air of mock innocence. 'Something perhaps that you have handled, made medicines from, is that right?'

Nuala faced him. 'My father's herb garden has a section for poisonous plants. But most of them, including digitalis, can be beneficial if given in tiny quantities. Aconite, wolfsbane, was only introduced recently from the garden in Galway belonging to Caireen's first husband. It was not something that I would have chosen to grow as its only medicinal use is when it is used with goose grease to rub into rheumatic joints – and even then there are better herbs. Aconite is a deadly poison and to my mind the dangers outweigh the benefits. I have never made any medicines from it and I never shall.'

Well done, Nuala, thought Mara with a feeling of pride.

'But you knew where it grew,' stated Boetius.

'It could not be missed,' said Nuala briefly. 'It has tall, blue, hooded flowers at this time of the year.'

'So anyone could have picked them?' asked Fachtnan, gravely.

66

'The poison is made from the root, not from the flowers – in any case, I think that it is unlikely that someone took some from the herb garden,' said Nuala. 'It would not be necessary. My father had a large jar of aconite poison which he sold to farmers and shepherds to get rid of wolves. This is why he had it.'

'And you knew where it was kept?' asked Boetius.

Nuala nodded in a perfunctory manner and turned to Moylan who was waving his hand in the air.

'Could you test the brandy to see whether it held aconite, Nuala?' he asked.

'No,' Nuala's voice was expressionless. 'Caireen poured out the brandy and rinsed the glass with water from the jug. She said she wanted to give him a drink. Apparently,' the girl's voice was dry, 'Caireen did not realize that he was dead.'

There was a silence for a moment. All the boys looked sympathetic. This was desperately hard for Nuala, Mara knew, but she also knew that nothing would be as hard as brooding silently and not knowing what was going on.

'Do you know whether any other accidental deaths occurred from farmers putting aconite around their farms? Or from the misuse of medicines?' asked Fachtnan.

Mara looked at him with interest. He had a fine, intuitive intelligence. He had gone straight to the heart of the matter. Of course, there had been several deaths in the kingdom during the last couple of months and rumour had it that relatives had blamed Malachy's poor doctoring for these.

However, this was not a matter to discuss in front of Malachy's daughter.

'As far as I know, not from the use of aconite,' said Nuala briefly. 'That is, not humans, I mean.'

Mara rose to her feet.

'I fear I must leave you now, boys. I am not fully recovered as yet but I hope to be back at work with you quite soon. Fachtnan, could I ask you to continue with this investigation? Aidan, will you make notes and bring them over to me after dinner?' She turned to the young Boetius with a smile which she strove to make friendly.

'Perhaps I could ask you to go across to Caherconnell and to make an inventory of all the medicines on Malachy's shelves. It is not a task which I would like to entrust to any of my scholars when it's a case of handling jars containing poisons.'

And that, she thought, as he bowed without comment, should keep him busy for the rest of the afternoon.

'Come with me,' she said to Nuala.

Five

Córus Fine

(The Regulation of the Kin Group)

The possessions of an individual are divided into two categories. First, there is the land that he inherits through his membership of a kin group. Secondly, there is the wealth that he accumulates by virtue of his own endeavours. Land can be included in this category if it has been bought and not inherited.

On the death of the individual, inherited land is divided equally between the sons of all marriages. If there are no sons of the blood, then the land is divided between the brothers; in the case of no brother, the land goes to the eldest male descendent of his great-grandfather. Failing that the land reverts to the clan.

A female heir will receive the house that she lives in and enough land to graze seven cows.

The sun shone with the intense heat of mid-June as Mara and Nuala walked together down the road towards the Brehon's house. The day was hot with that particular scent which was, in Mara's experience, found only in the Burren. It was a scent of damp vegetation mixed with the clean, slightly acrid aroma of baking limestone. The clints that paved the fields as far as the eye could see sparkled almost silver in the sunlight, and the deep grykes, or cracks between the slabs, were filled with bright colour from the clear, intense magenta of summer flowering cranesbill and the delicate pale blue of the fragile harebells.

'So it was just Caireen that was there when your father's body was found, is that right?' Mara kept her voice unemotional and matter-of-fact.

'That's right.' Nuala used the same tone. She stared across the grykes towards the distant pale blue swirls of Mullaghmore mountain.

'No sign of Ronan or of any of his brothers, then,' stated Mara, and then when Nuala did not reply she said quietly, 'Just tell me everything that you remember about that morning.'

'I know what you're thinking—' began Nuala.

'No, you don't,' interrupted Mara. 'No one, but I, knows what I am thinking. Now come on, Nuala. Just start at the beginning and go through it again. You left here quite early, walked across to Caherconnell. And then?'

'And then,' said Nuala with an impatient sigh, 'I went into the little stone shed where the gardening things are kept – I didn't want to see any of them at the house, so I just took out a basket for the weeds and a small fork, and I set to work. Nobody had bothered doing anything so there were weeds everywhere.'

'Which part of the garden were you in?' asked Mara.

'I started off at the far end with the bed of woundwort and then I had just moved down to work on the camomile when Caireen screamed. I don't want to talk about it ... shouldn't you go indoors and rest?'

'I can't bear to go on into the house again,' said Mara. Nuala was stubborn; there would be no point in pursuing the questioning for now. 'Let's go and join Sorcha and the children,' she suggested. 'They're having their dinner over there on the field. It's such a treat for them to have meals out-of-doors. Collect Cormac, will you, Nuala? Brigid is looking after him. The sunshine won't do him any harm, will it?'

'I'll bring a piece of linen to shade him and then he will be fine,' said Nuala running down the road, her long legs covering the hundred yards' distance in the same time that it took Mara to open the gate and start to cross the field.

'*Mamó, Mamó*,' shouted Domhnall and Aislinn as they came running towards her.

'May I come into your dining hall?' Mara asked politely. A large clint had been spread with a piece of linen, and wooden plates and wooden goblets had been laid out on it. In the centre were flat baskets of food and a big flask of milk for the children. Mara smiled when she

71

saw the milk. It had been coloured pink. This was Brigid, she knew. When she herself had been young, Brigid had coloured the milk with a few raspberries and had persuaded her that it came from a magic pink cow, owned by the fairies. The same story had been told to Sorcha, and now Domhnall and Aislinn were the latest believers. Would little Cormac grow up to enjoy this same treat, she wondered, her eyes going to the Brehon's house where Nuala was walking carefully down the path holding a heavily swathed bundle in her arms.

'Thank goodness this fellow's not crawling yet,' said Sorcha with a glance at plump little Manus in her arms, 'these two have me worried enough, leaping from stone to stone.'

'I should get Cumhal to drive you to Fanore beach one day. It would be lovely for the children to run around the sands. I meant to arrange it, but the baby coming so early put everything askew.' Mara watched her grandchildren with a smile. Sorcha had no reason to worry about them. They were as sure-footed as the wild goats that roamed the High Burren and the mountain sides. Both looked very well, she thought; the pure Atlantic air of the Burren had tanned their skins to a gorgeous shade of deep brown which went so well with their short white *léinte*.

'Yes, that was a shock. A whole month early! Never mind, it's all for the best; now you can enjoy him for the two months of the summer holidays,' said Sorcha, who had a happy nature that always saw the bright side of everything.

'Here's a plate for you, *Mamó*, but you'll have to share with Nuala.' Aislinn arrived back with some harebells and carefully arranged the flowers around a plate for her grandmother, and placed a wooden cup beside it. 'That was *Dat*'s plate but he didn't stay for the meal.'

'Where is Oisín?' asked Mara, admiring the nodding heads of the harebells.

'Oh, you know Oisín,' said his wife tolerantly. 'He can never sit still for long. After five minutes he was off, striding across the fields to Kilcorney. He wants to look at those oak trees in Malachy's woodland.'

'Why?' asked Mara casually. Her attention was on the bundle in Nuala's arms. She held out her own arms, a slight ache of love trembling through her whole body. She curved around the light weight and held the tiny baby against her cheek for a moment.

'He's making plans to fell the trees and use them for making wine barrels,' said Sorcha. 'He's been thinking about that for years. I used to laugh at him and tell him that Malachy would probably outlive him, but there you are! Oisín always get what he wants, sooner rather than later.'

'Of course,' breathed Mara. 'He's Malachy's heir, isn't he?'

Almost absent mindedly she held out a finger for the baby to clutch.

How could I have been so stupid, she thought, exasperated with herself. Of course, under Brehon law, Malachy's heir was neither his daughter Nuala, nor his wife Caireen. No doubt Caireen, who had lived under English law in Galway, expected to inherit, but Brehon law, though making provision for a daughter (and not a widow, who was expected to return to her own family), firmly gave the inheritance of the clan land to the nearest male relative if there were no sons nor no brothers to inherit. The Davorens had been a clan where males were in short supply. Her own father had just a daughter to inherit, but she had been lucky enough to keep his farm because the land at Cahermacnaghten had been presented directly to her father by the king as part of the payment for his services as Brehon of the Burren, and so was not clan land.

Malachy, on the other hand, had no official status as a physician and possessed only a small amount of clan land. And of course, clan land in Malachy's case was not farmland, but a woodland comprising twenty acres of mature oaks.

'Nuala, did you know that Oisín was Malachy's heir?' She asked the question casually, arranging the linen folds above the baby's face to protect his delicate skin against the intensity of the sun's rays.

'No, I didn't.' Nuala sounded hostile. It was impossible to speak to her of anything to do with Malachy. She immediately seemed to assume the air of suspected person, and turned sullen

74

and uncommunicative.

If Nuala did not know, then Caireen did not know either, thought Mara, tenderly exposing her son's stick-like legs to the air, and then carefully draping a piece of linen so that the sun did not burn his delicate skin. It had never been mentioned, she suspected. Malachy had no interest in that oak woodland. He sold the odd tree to Blár O'Connor, the wheelwright, or had one of his men cut up a few fallen trees after a storm, but that was all.

So it was likely that Caireen, new from Galway and used to English laws, thought she would inherit all. Mara disliked Caireen immensely, but, still, was it even sensible to suspect her of murdering her husband?

Probably not. Malachy alive was at least making money and could sponsor her three sons through to physician status. Suddenly a thought came to her.

'Do you know when Ronan, Caireen's son, will qualify as a physician?' she asked Nuala.

'Ronan is already a qualified physician,' said Nuala in a surly manner. She looked away from Mara, but not quickly enough to hide the expression of rage on her face. She picked up a honey cake that Aislinn had put on the shared plate and snapped it in half with her strong white teeth, staring across the stony fields with an expression that she strove to make indifferent.

'That was quick!' exclaimed Mara. 'I thought he had another year to go.'

Nuala shrugged her shoulders and then turned away from Sorcha's curious eyes. Mara knew why her daughter looked puzzled. Nuala acting as physician was mature, poised and communicative. Nuala speaking of her father turned into a rude, angry adolescent.

'It just happened a couple of weeks ago,' she said.

'So that's why I didn't know about it. I should have been informed. Did Malachy feel that he was ready?'

'He examined him, got a physician from Galway, a friend of Ronan's late father, to moderate the results; Ronan was declared a full physician two weeks ago.' Nuala's voice was toneless and lacking in any emotion, but Mara could imagine how she felt. Malachy was doing his best to deny his own gifted daughter the opportunity to achieve the ambition that had possessed her since she was a child, and yet he had gone to great extremes to rush forward the appointment of his stepson. Mara gave a quick glance at the tight-lipped face as she patted the girl's hand with unspoken sympathy.

'He probably faked the result. Ronan isn't that good. Malachy would do anything to please Caireen,' remarked Nuala, still in a dry, toneless voice.

Mara saw Sorcha look slightly shocked. The way Nuala referred to her father as 'Malachy', the detached way that she spoke of him, the depth of bitterness in her voice would create a

76

bad impression on anyone, even someone as good-natured and unsuspicious as Sorcha. Mara hoped that Nuala would not talk about her father in front of too many people. Had she spoken of him like that in front of Boetius? There was an uncomfortable silence for a moment, and then Sorcha exclaimed, 'There's a horse coming down the road. Look, it's stopping at your house, Mother.'

'Visitor!' shouted Domhnall.

'Cumhal will say that we are over here, Domhnall. Look, he's coming out of the school. Don't shout any more. You'll wake the babies,' said Sorcha, watching Brigid's husband, Cumhal, the farm manager, leave his task of making room for the sweet-scented hay in the huge barn and come out to meet the woman on horseback.

'It's Teige O'Brien's wife, Ciara, from Lemeanah Castle, you know.' Mara gave the explanation to Sorcha while endeavouring to look hospitable. Teige was chief of the O'Brien clan in the Burren, a cousin and friend of her husband, King Turlough.

'Let me hold little Cormac while you talk to her. Manus is fast asleep.' Sorcha laid her sleeping son on a folded sheepskin on the ground beside her, and took the baby from her mother's arms. Mara gave him up reluctantly. He was so tiny and so fragile that she hated letting him go.

'Don't worry, he'll soon be as strong and healthy as these three,' said Sorcha, sensitive to her mother's moods.

'Brigid says that Cormac is our uncle.' Aislinn cast a dubious look at Cormac. 'He's too tiny to be an uncle.'

'Let's play a joke on the visitor.' Domhnall was going through the painful stage where he insisted on telling jokes to everyone. He ran off instantly and waited by the field gate.

'Would you like to meet my uncle, *bhean usail* (noble lady)?' his voice floated back as he greeted Ciara and escorted her over the clints towards where his mother and grandmother sat. 'He's got a big black beard and he is as tall as the gable of a house ... and there he is sleeping on my mother's lap!'

'God please him; isn't he beautiful,' said Ciara fervently, but Mara was not deceived. Ciara had been shocked by the baby.

'He arrived a month early, gave us all a surprise,' she said trying to sound like her usual competent, cheerful self.

'He's looking wonderful, all the same, God bless him,' murmured Ciara. She appeared to be struggling to think of something else to say, but then gave up and started to admire Sorcha's three children and to exclaim over their size and beauty, and resemblance to their father Oisín.

'Any news from Teige?' asked Mara.

'Only that they were camped near to each other at O'Briensbridge, just outside Limerick – so near that they could hear each other drinking,' said Ciara promptly. 'Each side are waiting for the other to move first. I came to see if you

78

knew anything else.'

'No, we haven't heard,' said Mara catching a worried look from Sorcha. So this was the news that they had been keeping from her. Turlough and his forces were drawn up in battle formation. Perhaps the battle had already taken place. That wretched bridge! Turlough and his brothers had built it some years ago and it had been his pride and joy ever since. The Earl of Kildare would have known that any threat to O'Briensbridge would bring the warlike king of Thomond, Corcomroe and Burren marching into battle.

'Very likely nothing will come of it,' said Ciara hastily, and fell to admiring Cormac again. Aislinn and Domhnall wandered off on one of their daily optimistic excursions to find the chuckling cuckoo that woke them every morning with its echoing call, and was still shouting after their bedtime. Looking bored and unhappy, Nuala moved a little aside, squatting down and examining some plants in the small raggedly rounded holes where rainwater had dissolved the limestone. The three women left behind turned their attention to the the tiny premature baby.

As if Cormac felt their eyes on him, he woke and cried.

'He's hungry again,' laughed Sorcha, bending over her little half-brother. Instinctively his mouth turned towards the source of milk, and Mara winced as Ciara glanced at her and then at the baby in her daughter's arms.

'Sorcha is feeding him for me. I have no milk,' she said in tones that she strove to make matter-of-fact and commonsensical.

Ciara nodded in a perfunctory way.

'Are you looking for a wet nurse?' she asked, and Mara responded gratefully to the lack of fuss or false optimism.

'Yes, do you know of anyone?'

'I do indeed. The wife of Teige's chief shepherd, a very good fellow, Teige says he never had a man as good with the sheep and all their ailments, a very nice family; well, his wife lost a baby last week. He died from a fever, poor little fellow. It would be an act of kindness to give work to poor Eileen. She's all alone at the moment as the husband will be very busy up the mountain with the sheep shearing.'

'How old is she?' Mara was cautious. A girl who had lost her own son might not be careful enough of this very, very precious little fellow. She would have preferred someone who, like Sorcha, was nursing her own child and had enough milk for two.

'Oh, she's not a young girl. She has been married for over twenty years. It's very sad because it looked as though she were barren. This was the first child. You needn't think that she is a heedless young thing. That child was always beautifully cared for and looked as strong as a young horse. It was just one of those things! Children die easily. Poor little fellow, he died of a fever. You'll like Eileen. She's a very nice woman, very good with her hands, and we always have her at the tower house whenever we need extra staff for a party or a festival. She'll do some lovely stitching for you; I think that you would like her. I've never seen such a good seamstress, though she's left-handed and they are not usually so good, are they? She gets quite a bit of silver for her work at Noughaval market. Would you like me to ask her to come to see you?'

'Yes, do.' Mara had a quick, inward struggle, but it was no good trying to evade facts; she was not able to feed her son and Sorcha would be returning to Galway in a week or two. She had to have a wet nurse, and this Eileen, at least, was no giddy girl, but a woman of about Mara's age, or more. She watched resignedly as Sorcha fed the baby; no matter who it was, she was going to be jealous. She just had to put up with it, and get on with solving the murder and sorting out the problems that Boetius had left her with after failing two of her scholars in their important summer examinations.

'Here's Oisín!' exclaimed Sorcha, and a minute later, to the accompaniment of joyful squeals from the children, Oisín came into view; Aislinn riding high on his shoulders and Domhnall clinging to one hand.

Baby Manus woke and howled, his large brown eyes surveying the company indignantly. With one arm Sorcha reached out for her own child, slipped him under the linen shawl that she wore around her shoulders and allowed him to feed from her other breast.

'Now we'll have peace all around,' she said.

'Aren't they the image of their father,' said Ciara looking at the three dark-haired, dark-eyed children.

'The living image,' said Sorcha.

'All descended from Dubh (black) Daibhrean himself,' said Mara. 'My father used to tell me about him. I remember him telling Ardal O'Lochlainn and myself the story of the different races that came to Ireland. Ardal with his red hair and his white skin was a descendent of the Celtic race, and me with my dark hair and dark eyes was a descendent of the Firbolg race.'

'It's true,' said Ciara. 'Sorcha is the only one of the O'Davoren clan without the dark hair and eyes. Look at Nuala, the image of Malachy, of course.'

'Sorcha takes after her father Dualta,' said Mara briefly. 'Oisín is a true O'Davoren.' She hoped that this talk about the O'Davoren clan would not lead to talk about Malachy's murder. He, of course, like his daughter, had been O'Davoren in looks, but he had missed out on the brains that the O'Davoren family seemed to possess. Malachy had been a poor physician. Somehow he had lacked the ability or the application to do justice to the people of the Burren who had sought his help and advice.

Mara surveyed her handsome son-in-law,

admiring the adroit way that he managed to greet Ciara and herself, kiss his wife, stroke the rosy cheek of his youngest child, accept a bunch of tiny pimpernel flowers from Aislinn, admire Domhnall's prowess at jumping across grykes, at the same time as stretching out on the warm surface of the clint and exposing his tanned bare legs and arms to the heat of the sun.

Oisín was Mara's second cousin. He had come from an obscure branch of the O'Davorens – there were neither physicians nor Brehons in his immediate family. His father, his grandfather and his uncles had all been coopers and had been content to live out their lives in the useful trade of barrel making. Oisín, though, had been ambitious. In his teens, he had visited Galway to sell some barrels there and had decided that the life of a merchant was the one for him. Though still a young man of just thirty, he had done so well that he now had a fine stone house as well as a shop in the city of Galway.

Sensitive as always, Sorcha waited until Nuala had got up in a bored way and sauntered back towards the house before questioning him.

'Well, what was Malachy's woodland like?'

Instantly he sat up, full of energy. 'I couldn't have believed it,' he said enthusiastically. 'That place is a goldmine. The trees are magnificent. It's only twenty acres, but it must be worth more than a farm of two hundred acres.' He beamed at his wife. 'I must get my brother over here to pick out some of the best trees for felling. I'll save a fortune if I have my own oak for storage barrels. I could never, in my wildest dreams, have guessed that I could have inherited so much from Malachy.'

Was that true? wondered Mara. Had he not estimated the value of that woodland before now? Oisín was shrewd and knowing. And surely oak trees do not change much in five or six years. In fact, as far as she could remember that piece of woodland in Kilcorney looked much the same in her own childhood as it was now. Oisín had spent weeks staying with Malachy when he was courting Sorcha and had never failed to visit him whenever he was in the Burren. He must have seen that woodland hundreds of times. It was a favourite walk for courting couples. There was, perhaps, something slightly artificial in the way he laid so much emphasis on not realizing its value.

'I think this little fellow has had enough,' said Sorcha. She peered down at the tiny baby and then smiled at her mother. 'He's fast asleep; do you want to take him?'

'Could I hold him?' asked Aislinn wistfully.

'When we are indoors,' promised Mara. 'I just want to have a turn holding him myself now. I didn't see too much of him while I was ill.' She saw Ciara give her a long look and busied herself with her baby, averting her gaze. Did she sound as jealous as she felt? she wondered.

'You'll be making wine barrels with it, will you?' Ciara turned her attention to Oisín.

84

'I've got a brilliant idea,' he said, his white teeth flashing in a brilliant smile. 'You'll be interested in this, Mother!'

Mara turned her face towards him, wishing that she had stopped this 'Mother' business when he first asked Sorcha to marry him. There was less than seven years in the difference between herself and her son-in-law, so it was all rather absurd. However, she guarded her tongue very carefully. Sorcha's affection was hugely important to her and she would do nothing to imperil relationships.

'Yes?' she queried.

'Well, you know you have always said that you mostly use the last quarter or so of the cask just for cooking or mulling – and you wouldn't be the only one. True wine lovers all do the same thing. And of course, no matter how careful you are with the tap, sooner or later air gets in and then the wine starts to spoil.'

'That's true,' said Ciara. 'Teige always complains that we are feeding him the dregs of the barrels and that we should reserve these for the hot wine at night for the men-at-arms.' Her face clouded suddenly and Mara knew that her thoughts had gone to her easy-going, affectionate husband, now in the company of his men-at-arms, fighting for his lord, face to face with the Earl of Kildare and his English troops. Would it end in tragedy?

'Well, tell us your idea,' said Mara hastily. She could not bear to allow her thoughts to dwell on

Turlough out there, leading his kingdom's forces, and perhaps never having the opportunity of seeing his new born son.

'I suddenly thought of this idea a few weeks ago.' Oisín, as always, was fluent and confident. 'I thought: why not make half-size barrels, or even quarter-size barrels? I could make this my speciality. O'Davoren wines for wine lovers! I could, very likely, sell some to the people in all parts of the country, not just here in the west of Ireland. Perhaps even the Earl of Kildare himself.'

'It's a good idea,' admitted Mara. 'Will your brother be willing to leave Thomond, though, in order to work for you?'

'Oh, I just want some advice from him and then I'll set up my own operation. Build a few houses for the tree-fellers and a few shelters where the wood can season. After that I'll think about employing some coopers to make quarter-size barrels.'

'Well, it does sound a brilliant idea,' said Ciara rising to her feet. 'I shall have to tell Teige about it. He's very fond of a good cup of wine in the evening. I must go now, Brehon. It's been wonderful to see you and the baby, but I must get back to Lemeanah Castle and see what my young people are up to.'

'Won't you come into the house and have some refreshment?' asked Mara. 'Brigid will kill me if I allow you to go without anything to eat or drink.'

'I won't,' said Ciara firmly. 'You stay where you are and enjoy the sun. I'll call in on Eileen when I get back, and I'll ask her to come and see you tonight if she is interested.'

'I'll go to the gate with you,' said Sorcha, rising to her feet and depositing her plump baby on her husband's lap.

There was a moment's silence after she left. Mara held her sleeping son and admired the red and gold colouring of a tiny firecrest who was flashing in to peck the tiny oval seeds from the pink-flowered herb Robert plants in the grykes, and then flying away triumphantly. The man beside her sat very still, rocking his baby son. She glanced at him curiously and saw that his eyes were not on the child, but gazing across the clints as if he was viewing, in his mind's eye, the unseen woodland that was going to bring him prosperity, or perhaps even riches. He felt her glance and turned to smile at her.

'So, Mother, the sooner Malachy's affairs can be wound up, the better for me.'

'The murder has to come first,' she said firmly. 'There will be certain complications about Malachy's affairs. You do realize that, although you are the heir to clan lands, under Brehon law his daughter must get land to graze seven cows and the house that she lives in – that is the house that she used to live in with her father.'

'No problem about that,' he said easily. 'I've been thinking and I had a look around Caherconnell. The herb garden stretches to about two acres; the house meadow where Malachy had his cows and his hens should be another four or so, and then there is the big field where he kept his horse. All of that should amount to enough – and, of course, there is the property at Rathborney. I understand that the property was for Malachy's use until Nuala comes of age, I suppose that will be for Caireen, will it? That's what I was told, anyway.'

'I'm not sure who gave you to understand that, but it is incorrect,' said Mara emphatically. 'The property at Rathborney was left to Nuala by its owner, Toin the Briuga. I drew up the will myself and these were the terms, as well as I can remember them.' She half-shut her eyes and recited.

'"*And I bequeath to Nuala, daughter of Malachy O'Davoren, physician in the kingdom of the Burren, my house at Rathborney and all the revenues from the farm situated in this place.*

'"*This gift,*"' continued Mara opening her eyes and looking very directly at her son-in-law, '"*is for her to have and to hold without conditions.*" And the will went on to say, if I remember rightly: *"However, this testator would like to express a hope that the gift will enable the said Nuala, daughter of Malachy O'Davoren, to fulfil her ambition to have a school of medicine and also to enable her to pursue her studies in that subject."* I may have misremembered some of it,' she concluded, trying to sound modest, 'but I would say that it was the gist of the matter.'

'I'm impressed by your memory, Mother.' Oisín didn't sound too put out and he spoke lightly, his tone casual. 'Still,' he added, 'I'm sure that you will do your best for me, and of course, for your daughter and grandchildren.'

'I do my best for everyone in my interpretation of the law,' said Mara serenely. Suddenly she began to feel better. She enjoyed pitting her brains against a worthy adversary. Oisín was bright and clever, but he underestimated his mother-in-law if he thought that he could bribe or bully Mara, Brehon of the Burren.

Six

Cáin Íarraith

(The Law of Fosterage)

The fee for fosterage ranges from three séts, one-and-a-half ounces of silver, for the son of a small farmer, up to thirty séts, fifteen ounces of silver, for the son of a king. The fee for a girl is higher than for a boy because a girl is less likely to be of benefit to her foster parents in later life.

Triad 249

There are three things in life where the outcome is dark:
1. Depositing an object into somebody's custody.
2. Going surety.
3. Fosterage.

Rather to her surprise, Mara saw no more of Boetius on the day that she sent him off to record the names and amounts of poisons on Malachy's shelves in Caherconnell. She was just as glad, as it gave her an opportunity to have a long talk with Fachtnan and to assure him that she would be delighted to employ him as an assistant for the coming year.

'I'll need help in the school, what with the baby and everything,' she told him, 'and I can think of no one that I would be more pleased to have and who would suit me better. You will be of great assistance to me. So don't worry about a thing. Nothing has changed. Now tell me, what do you think that we should do with Hugh?'

'He's upset,' said Fachtnan sympathetically.

What a nice boy he is, she thought. He is able to put aside his own bitter disappointment and enter into the feelings of the younger boy.

'Perhaps you could give him a bit of extra help over the next few days,' she suggested. 'It would be good for Hugh and good for you also. While you are going over the early stages of law and Latin and poetry, you will be improving your own memory as you are trying to help Hugh to memorize everything. I'll ask Enda to take over Moylan and Aidan. We mustn't take up any more of young MacClancy's time. I think that you and Enda can manage, do you think so?'

Fachtnan was a little hesitant and said eventually that Aidan might be a bit difficult. 'He got on very well with *Ollamh* MacClancy and I think that has gone to his head a little.'

Things must have got quite bad, thought Mara, for Fachtnan to say that. He was a boy that never liked to tell tales. Aloud she said, 'I'll be in and

91

out. I think you'll find that Aidan will soon settle down again. Enda can be quite firm when he wants to be.'

After supper Eileen arrived. Mara was quite astonished when a grey-haired woman with lined skin followed her housekeeper into the room. She had not expected Eileen to look so old. She looked far older than Mara, whose black hair was still without any grey and whose skin was still plump and fresh.

The woman was well spoken, though, intelligent and alert. She looked very clean and her *léine* was snowy white.

'I think it is best if the baby feeds whenever he wants to feed,' she said, proffering her opinion without apology. 'I know some people like to keep to set hours, but I will be with the baby every hour and minute of the day and I have plenty of milk. I'd like to feed him as often as he will take the milk and certainly whenever he cries.'

And then she took the tiny Cormac from Brigid's arms with such an expression of tenderness and love on her face that Mara was quite won over. However, she forced herself to be practical. She knew very little about this woman, apart from Ciara's recommendation. The money aspect was easily settled. Eileen was well satisfied by the fee she offered, and it was a generous one as the woman would live in the house and get all of her meals cooked for her. However, it was a very responsible position and

Mara hesitated slightly before engaging her.

'Would you mind if we said a month's trial?' she asked apologetically. 'I know that your husband will be away for a month, so that will give us all the opportunity of seeing how this will work out. You might wish to return to your own house at the end of that time.'

'Whatever suits you, Brehon. We'll see how he looks at the end of the month and you can tell me if you are satisfied with me.' Immediately she settled herself to feed the baby, murmuring a soft old Gaelic song into the ear of the child.

'What do you think, Brigid?' asked Mara, when Eileen had taken the child up to the little bedroom beside Mara's own. Nessa, Brigid's assistant, was sent up the stairs with a jug of hot water for the baby's bath. Mara watched for a while and then, when she was sure that Eileen was competent, she beckoned to Brigid and they both left the room.

'I think she will suit fine,' said Brigid immediately. 'She seemed able to soothe him well and I liked the way that she bathed him. He was quite happy, even kicking his little legs, God bless him. What he needs now is lots of care and that's what I think that Eileen will give him. That's a sensible woman, no silly girl. She'll suit us fine.'

'I think so, too,' said Mara, conscious of great weight of responsibility passing from her shoulders. Oddly enough, she was not unhappy to see the elderly-looking Eileen feeding her baby, whereas the sight of the blooming figure of her daughter, giving the breast to Cormac, had filled her with jealousy. What an odd person I am, she thought and turned to Brigid.

'Has the young MacClancy returned from Caherconnell?' she asked.

'Not a sight or a sound of him, Brehon,' replied Brigid. 'But don't you fret. Cumhal is keeping an eye on the scholars. Young Aidan won't know what hit him if he tries any of his cheek on Cumhal.'

Boetius did not come back to the law school that night, reported Brigid. Mara thought of sending out a search party, but decided not to bother. He was a grown man; he could look after himself. From her point of view she would be just as pleased if he never returned.

However, when she got up in the morning and looked out from her bedroom window she saw him crossing the clints. It was just about time for school, so at least he had not missed that. Still, she expected him to come and explain his absence.

When he had not reported back by mid-morning, she lost all patience and summoned him. The scholars had all been playing hurling for quite some time so presumably he was at leisure.

'I expected to hear from you yesterday evening,' she said mildly when he arrived.

'It was late so I stayed the night.' Boetius, she

was glad to see, had given up trying to charm her. He spoke quite abruptly.

'Oh,' she said and raised an eyebrow at him. 'I wondered where you were and asked Cumhal, the farm manager, whether you had asked him to supervise the scholars in your absence. Cumhal, of course, has a great sense of responsibility and when he realized that you were not present, he immediately took the lads into his charge.'

He was a little taken aback and, meanly, she was glad of it.

'You yourself sent me on an errand,' he said sullenly.

'Just past noon,' she reminded him.

He flushed an unbecoming, blotchy red. 'Caireen asked me to stay to supper,' he said stiffly. 'I thought it was the least that I could do after she had been so helpful in the matter of these poisons. Afterwards she had various legal questions, matters which she had not liked to bother you with,' he amended hastily. He took a sheet covered with neat handwriting from his satchel and handed it to her, muttering 'Here is the list that you asked for.'

'No aconite,' said Mara after rapidly scanning the list. 'Wolfsbane,' she added as he looked puzzled. To give him his due, he had written the poisons in an alphabetical list which did make it, much easier to find what she was looking for. 'This list is very helpful,' she said, unbending a little, 'it's strange, though, isn't it, that the aconite is missing? You would think that the

95

murderer would just take some and put it back on the shelves. Nuala was quite certain that her father had made up a large quantity of it.'

'Probably young Nuala doesn't know as much as she thinks,' he said complacently. Mara would have forgiven him that if he had not immediately added, 'Unless, of course, she was careful to remove the jar in case her step-brother, who seems an able young man, would have found an antidote for aconite and thereby saved her father's life.'

What nonsense, trembled on Mara's lips, but she swallowed the words and said with stiff politeness, 'Anyway, I wanted to thank you for all that you have done for me and the law school.'

'That was nothing to me,' he said compla-cently. 'I'm one of those people who can easily do two or three jobs at the same time.'

Mara sighed inwardly. It was probably going to be quite difficult to get rid of him.

'I'm very thankful for your services, *Ollamh* MacClancy,' she said slowly and clearly, 'how-ever, I am happy to say that I am quite well now, and getting better every hour. I won't keep you any longer. Could you tell me how much I owe you for your services?'

He looked very taken aback at this plain speaking. 'I can easily stay another week,' he protested. 'I'm enjoying it very much.'

'I'll be fine, now,' she said, glad to find how firm her voice sounded. She went to her desk drawer, unlocked it and took out a small box.

'No, no,' said Boetius, though his small eyes were fixed covetously on the silver. 'I don't need to be paid. That was just an act of charity for someone I hope will be a neighbour – in the near future, please God.'

I suppose he is hoping that Fergus will retire and hand over to him, thought Mara with an inward shudder. Outwardly she kept the smile fixed to her face. 'No, I insist,' she said firmly.

'Well, what about ten ounces of silver? Would you think that correct? Or anything that you fix upon will be agreeable to me.'

'Ten ounces of silver, then,' said Mara. Inwardly she was astonished. This was a huge sum of money for just over a week's work for a man who had just qualified. And I didn't even ask him to do it, she thought bitterly, as she carefully weighed the silver on her little scales and then handed it to him. Still, it would be worth it to get rid of the man, she thought grimly. What a pity I didn't get him out before he failed poor Fachtnan and Hugh, though.

'Oh, one thing more ... when are the examination papers expected?' she queried. 'I would like to see them.'

'As I told you, I sent them to Thomond. I sent your own man, Seán,' said Boetius. 'I gave him instructions to go and to return as quickly as he could.'

Mara suppressed a groan. Seán was her slowest and most unreliable servant. Brigid and

Cumhal, both efficient and hard workers, were always dying to be rid of him and had probably suggested him for Boetius MacClancy's errand – not realizing its importance.

'Let me see you to the door,' she said hospitably, as he put the silver into his pouch after a careful scrutiny of the pieces. 'Don't worry about the boys; they will be fine. Fachtnan is used to acting as my assistant. He and Enda are excellent with the younger scholars.'

At the door he hesitated. His small eyes looked into her with a shrewd, knowing expression.

'Of course, it must be very tempting for you to overlook certain matters, given that you are just after having a baby...' He smiled suddenly, his red beard jerking forward. 'I understand that is an emotional time for ladies, but the scales of justice, you know ... a Brehon must be impartial—'

'Thank you for your professional advice,' interrupted Mara frostily. 'I think that I can handle this affair.'

'What I wanted to say,' he continued imperturbably, 'is that I feel very sorry for Caireen, and think that she should not be denied her right to receive a fair and just compensation for the death of her husband because of any scruples that you, as Brehon, might harbour about convicting young Nuala.' His light green eyes met her dark hazel ones and there was no mistaking the challenge in them.

Mara stood very still and was glad to see, after

a moment, his eyes falter before hers.

'I shall walk down with you to the law school and find a man to fetch your horse while you are packing your things,' she said after a pause. She hoped that her remark was made in the spirit of hospitality to a guest, but she was conscious of a desire to know what he meant.

Did Boetius mean that he was going to act for Caireen at judgement day?

Or was he going to complain about Mara's conduct of the case? If so, the only resource was the king himself, at the moment absent fighting against the Earl of Kildare and his English troops. Even this bumptious young man could not be opinionated enough to think that this complaint would be successful.

Mara gave him a few minutes to think about the matter before she resumed speaking.

'So, what are you going to do with yourself now – after you've had a rest from your studies and had time to look around?' she asked lightly as she went ahead of him through the gate. She did not look at him but fixed her eyes on a large, furry bumble bee exploring the yellow heart of a sweet-scented woodbine flower that twined around the stone pier.

'I shall stay with Fergus and help him to manage the affairs of Corcomroe,' he said genially. 'Between ourselves, I think that Fergus is looking forward to taking life easily and leaving things to a younger man. The office of Brehon of Corcomroe would be a good experience for me – for a few years, at least, while I was fitting myself for better things.'

'That is, of course, if King Turlough Donn is willing to ratify your appointment,' said Mara. She was slightly ashamed to hear the undertones of a threat in her words. Still, Boetius would be very lacking in intelligence if he had not considered the possibility of the king asking his wife's advice – and prejudiced though she was against him, she was certain that he was not stupid.

'Of course,' he said easily, and she had to be satisfied with that.

She had been so anxious to get rid of him that she had not asked him to explain his remark about Ronan. Did that mean that the newly qualified physician was in the house when his step father died? And if he were, why was he not there in the stillroom, making efforts to revive Malachy when Caireen screamed for Nuala?

The boys were working well when she went into the schoolhouse. Fachtnan was sitting beside Hugh patiently going through some Latin clauses with him. Shane was busily making notes from *Corus Fiadnuise*, the cumbersome text about the regulation of evidence. And sharp-witted Enda was laying bets on whether Aidan or Moylan would be the first to find the penalty for an incompetent physician. Each of the boys were allowed a turn, strictly limited by Mara's precious sand timer, to look through the enormous medical tome *Bretha Déin Chécht*.

What a great teacher that boy will make, thought Mara, impressed by her scholar's cleverness. It was seldom that Aidan, in particular, took much interest in his law studies. *Bretha Déin Chécht* was a difficult, rather boring book, but at this moment the two boys were having to scan each page in order to find the information and win the contest. She had always thought very highly of Enda's brains, but now he looked as if he also possessed the skill to get the most out of people.

Fachtnan, a very different person, was showing great patience with Hugh and that pairing seemed to be working well. It would give Fachtnan a chance to lodge facts more securely into his uncertain memory and would provide Hugh with extra tuition, and hopefully ensure that he would pass his examination next year.

Giving the boys an approving nod, Mara said, 'Well, as a reward for such good work, I think that you could all have a couple of hours off for Midsummer's Eve, or St John's Eve, I should say. I suppose there will be the usual bonfire at Noughaval market square.'

There was a cheer at that and Mara regarded them with a benevolent gaze. It would be quite in order for her scholars to attend the bonfire. She made up her mind to suggest that Sorcha should take her two eldest there. Perhaps even Oisín would attend. St John's Eve was a fun festival for all, quite approved by the church once it had been tagged on to St John, though Mara suspected strongly that it had its origins in pre-Christian, druidic fire ceremonies.

Mara left her scholars to their studies and wearily she made her way back to the Brehon house. She was getting stronger every day, though the conversation with Boetius Mac-Clancy had somewhat drained her. It was a weariness of the spirit, rather than of the body, she acknowledged to herself. She would have to face facts and talk to Nuala, and, yes, to bear in mind that this girl, as dear to her as her own daughter, and nearly as dear as her tiny baby son, should be considered as a suspect in her father's murder.

Nuala was with Eileen, talking about medicines and remedies, when Mara tracked her down. Eileen was listening to her attentively and nodding in a knowledgeable way as Nuala described the plants. It was a shame about Nuala; there had been an attempt to get her taught by an elderly physician when she had left Caherconnell, after the huge row with her father last March, but the man had died after a few weeks. Nuala had gone on living with her mother's brother, Ardal O'Lochlainn, trying to study on her own – caring for the herb garden at Caherconnell, earnestly adding to her own store of medicines. Ardal, to give him his due, had given her a stillroom of her own at Lissylisheen tower house, and encouraged his workers to consult her about various minor cuts and illnesses. Nuala was finding the time long at the moment, Mara suspected, wandering around the law school with nothing to do, but Ardal had not wanted her to be alone while he and his men-at-arms were with the king.

'How is my little fellow?' Mara leaned over and picked up the baby.

'Doing well,' said Nuala in her best professional manner. 'He is making good use of his food. Look at him.'

Mara peered into the baby's face. She had feared to hope too much, but now there was no doubt that the infant was beginning to look less fragile. The transparent look was beginning to go and his skin was creamier, with even a slight suggestion of plumpness about the cheeks. She pressed her lips to his tiny face and smiled as his fingers closed around her thumb.

'He's going to be like Turlough,' she said with satisfaction. 'He's got the very same shape of eyes and, yes, I think they are beginning to turn green. Got the same chin, too.' Immediately she was filled with longing for Turlough to come home soon and to see his baby son. What was keeping him?

'No one is keeping any news from me about Turlough?' she asked, and Nuala shook her head firmly.

'No messengers have come in the last week.'

'I'll send someone if we haven't heard by tomorrow,' said Mara decisively, knowing inwardly that it had been a weakness on her part not to have done that before now. 'Seán should be back by then,' she said aloud. She met Eileen's eyes. The woman was looking at her with curiosity. Mara looked back with interest. It was not often that one of the farm workers on the Burren looked at her like that. To them she was something apart – Mara, Brehon of the Burren, judge and lawgiver – something immoveable and unchanging, like the huge boulders that lay here and there, perched on the stone pavements of the rocky fields. Eileen, however, looked as though she were weighing her up. Mara winced slightly. Perhaps Eileen thought she was a poor mother.

There was no doubt, though she tried to disguise it, that she was jealous of Eileen, who had nothing to do but feed the baby – her baby – and cradle him in her arms for as long as she wished. This reminded her of something and she turned to Nuala.

'Walk down with me to Blár O'Connor's place,' she said to the girl. 'He was making a cradle for me. Of course, no one expected this young man to arrive in the middle of June, but I'm sure that news has reached the wheelwright's place. We'll see if he has it ready.'

'Why go to a wheelwright for a cradle – Cumhal or one of the men on the farm could have made one for you?' Once medical matters were no longer under discussion, Nuala's mood turned sour and argumentative, again.

'It was Turlough's idea. A wheelwright had made a cradle for his eldest daughter and Turlough swore that no cradle ever rocked better. He came with me to Blár O'Connor last Easter and we planned it together.' Mara decided to ignore Nuala's moods and to talk naturally and cheerfully.

Blár O'Connor was a highly qualified wheelwright, skilled not just in wheel making but also in wagon building. He lived and worked within the walls of an ancient enclosure called Lios na Binne Roe, a small farm not far from Cahermacnaghten, near the Kilcorney crossroads. It was easy to see why the enclosure was named 'Binne Roe' (red cliff) as it was just beside a steep cliff face whose surface was covered with the orange-red, jelly-like mass that oozed from iron deposits in the soil.

'I always think that this place should be in Corcomroe, not in Burren,' said Mara as they turned off the road and went down the lane to the wheelwright's home. 'What is it in that old poem? – doesn't it go like this – *"Burren's stone is light and bright; Corcomroe is black and red"*, something like that anyway, isn't it?'

'I wouldn't know. I hate poetry,' said Nuala moodily. 'Ardal is always trying to suggest to me that it would be better to be a poet like my mother, than a physician like my father.'

Mara laughed. 'And poor Mór, your mother, was never allowed to be a poet, except in secret.

She badly wanted to go to Bard School, but your grandfather was completely against it, and she was married off to your father by the time that she was fourteen years old.'

'And then she had me the following year. What a disaster to have a child like me!' Nuala sounded so miserable that Mara was relieved when there was a shout from the enclosure.

'You're very welcome, Brehon, I was just going to send a lad up to you to tell that all was ready. Come and look at your cradle.'

Blár O'Connor was a small man – surprisingly small for a man who lived by the labour of his hands. He was a clever man, though. Mara's nearest neighbour, Diarmuid O'Connor, had once remarked, in his quiet way, that since Blár O'Connor was the smallest in the family he had to have brains to survive. 'You watch him,' Diarmuid had said. 'While everyone else is wasting time fussing and flexing muscles, Blár has worked out the neatest and quickest way to move a piece of wood, or which part to saw that needs the least labour.'

He came forward now, moving lightly and quickly, and said in his quietly confident way, 'I think you'll be pleased with it. We made it from oak as the king, God bless him, ordered.'

'The oak tree is a special symbol for the O'Brien clan; the O'Brien king is always named under the oak tree at Magh Adhair,' replied Mara, still trying to interest Nuala and distract her from her gloomy thoughts. It didn't work.

106

Blár O'Connor, though courteous, looked surprised as this was something that everyone knew, and Nuala just stared straight ahead, her black eyebrows contracted to a straight line, her brown eyes wary and opaque.

Even Nuala unbent a little when she saw the cradle. It had been exquisitely crafted, the curved hood scalloped with a tiny carved creature at the inside edge of each of the four scallops. Mara could just imagine the delight of any baby who discovered these tiny companions – there was a fox, a cat, a hare and an owl – and she made up her mind that she would not point them out to her little son, but allow him to make his own discovery.

'The rockers are perfect,' she said aloud, stroking the carefully waxed wood, planed to a satin-like smoothness. 'My lord will be pleased by these. He knew that you would do this wonderfully.'

Blár O'Connor's face clouded over. 'It was Bláreen, God have mercy on his soul, who did these, poor lad. He was a great workman, God be good to him. He had these oak felloes laid by for over a year – all ready they were to make a set of wheels, but nothing would suit him but to take two of them for the cradle. "It'll be something to have made the cradle where the king's child will lie", that's what he said. It was he that carved those little creatures too. I can just see him doing it with a smile on his face, he was a handsome lad, Brehon, as you know...' He shot a quick glance at Nuala's averted face and then shut his mouth firmly.

Mara, also, glanced at Nuala. For a moment she hesitated, but then laid her hand on Blár's arm and said the words that had come into her head. 'The kingdom will be a poorer place without your son, Blár. He was a craftsman and an artist and I never knew a single person to say a bad word about him. His memory will live on as long as the carts and wagons that he made with such skill roll down our roads. Every time that I rock my baby in this cradle I will think of him. I can't wait to put him in it,' she finished in a lighter tone of voice. 'I'll send one of my men with a cart to fetch it before the evening.'

'He was the light of his mother's eyes,' said Blár O'Connor, his face still dark and brooding. 'Still "the Lord giveth and he taketh away"...' He paused but did not finish in the usual fashion with the phrase 'blessed be the name of the Lord'. He was gazing at the dense woodland that lay between him and the sea, his pale blue eyes filled with rage and his mouth was tight with anger.

And then he looked at Nuala and an expression of embarrassment came over his face.

'Don't you trouble yourself, Brehon. I have a cart going that way this afternoon. One of my men will drop the cradle off for you. The wife wants to give it a last polish – great woman for making polishes. Gets the beeswax from the beekeeper Giolla at Rathborney and she mixes it with some lavender.'

'I can smell it,' said Mara burying her nose in the scented wood. She was glad, for Nuala's sake, that the interview was ending on such an amicable note. It was hard on the girl to be made to feel responsible for her father's sins and at the same time be suspected of causing his death.

Bláreen O'Connor, the only son of the wheel-wright, had been a magnificent son. He had the height and breadth of shoulder that his father lacked, but was blessed with a happy, easy-going temperament that meant, unlike most young men in their early twenties, he never got into fights or drank too much. Everyone liked the lad and his father and mother were reputed to adore him.

And then, one day in the middle of last month, Bláreen had taken a short cut home through one of Lorcan O'Connor's fields. Unknown to him there was a particularly vicious bull there and the boy had been tossed. When he managed to get home he was bleeding severely. His father immediately sent for Malachy, but Malachy did not come, instead sending a message that he was owed money by the household and was not going to attend before his fee was paid. Almost immediately after the messenger returned the young man had died.

'I shouldn't have gone there with you,' said Nuala abruptly as they walked back down the long avenue to the gate.

Mara looked at her. The girl's cheeks were

flushed and her eyes were full of tears.

'You're upset to hear your father spoken of, is that it?'

Nuala's mouth twisted in a wry grin, making her seem older than her fourteen years.

'I suppose it would be nice to hear him spoken of, as you spoke of Bláreen. But you know yourself that the kingdom won't be a poorer place without Malachy O'Davoren. Do you know why Blár didn't pay his bill to my father?'

Mara shook her head, but Nuala wasn't even looking at her; she was still staring ahead with that flush of anger – or was it shame? – on her cheeks.

'Blár O'Connor did not pay his bill because Malachy had been treating a cut on his arm for months with the wrong ointment. The cut had gone bad. It needed to be opened to allow the sepsis to escape and then kept open until it was clean. Malachy had been treating it with comfrey...'

Mara turned an attentive face towards the girl. Comfrey, she knew well. It was a herb that grew on damp meadows – in fact she could see some of its tall, pale pinkish-purple flowers in the field on their left-hand side. Nuala, herself, had often gathered some from the meadows near Cahermacnaghten.

'And was treating it with comfrey correct?' she asked.

Nuala shook her head vigorously. 'No, it was the wrong thing. Comfrey is good for healing, but it is too good. What was happening was that the wound was healing superficially but leaving all of the bad stuff inside. It was absolutely the wrong herb to use.'

'And Malachy did not realize that?'

Once again Nuala shook her head, the black braids flying out at angles from her head. 'He did,' she said bitterly. 'I found one of my grand-father's medical notes open on his stillroom table – just at the page where he had written: "Comfrey may be used externally to speed wound healing and guard against scar tissue developing incorrectly. Care should be taken with very deep wounds, however, as the external application of comfrey can lead to tissue forming over the wound before it is healed deeper down, possibly leading to abscesses." And beside it was a small jar of paste made from comfrey – I knew it was comfrey when I smell-ed it. And then Malachy came rushing in and took the jar, closed the book, put it back on the shelf, asked me what I was doing there and then rushed out again. I followed him and saw him give the jar to Blár's man and tell him to remind his master that he owed him two pieces of silver.'

'So what did you do?' asked Mara.

'Took a jar of St John's wort from the shelf – I, myself, had made most of these ointments and pastes, so I didn't bother to ask for permission – and that afternoon I called on Blár's wife and asked her to try this out on her husband's cut.

She did and it healed up fast. Blár is clever and he realized that Malachy's medicine had been worse than useless – and that's probably why he decided not to pay the latest bill.'

'So Malachy gave the wrong medicine – and knew it was the wrong medicine – and this kept the wound from healing. But why?' Mara had begun to understand.

Nuala shrugged. 'Didn't much care. Just grabbed a jar of comfrey – perhaps he didn't read all of my grandfather's notes. Or perhaps...'

He probably did read the note, thought Mara sadly, suspecting that Malachy had deliberately kept the wheelwright's injury from healing so that he could continue to get silver from him. Blár O'Connor must be one of the richest workers in the kingdom. He would be able to afford to pay a physician any fee that was requested. Money had been Malachy's god ever since he had made his second marriage a few months ago.

But did Blár realize the full extent of Malachy's treachery?

And would he have been prepared to kill one whose greed for silver had allowed a boy to bleed to death while he waited for the father's payment?

The talk with Nuala could be postponed. There was an urgent question to be asked and she could find the answer to it at her own law school.

'Go in to the baby,' she said to Nuala when

they arrived at the Brehon's House, 'I just want to ask the lads a question.' And then she sped down the road to the law school

Everyone was busy when she opened the door. Bran was on his feet in an instant, greeting her with a violently wagging tail. The boys turned smiling faces towards her as she struggled for breath.

'Fachtnan and Enda,' she said urgently. 'When you go on wolf hunts with Donogh Óg O'Lochlainn, have you ever gone to Binne Roe? Recently, I mean.'

'Blár O'Connor's place,' asked Fachtnan in puzzled tones, but Enda was quicker. His very blue eyes blazed with excitement as he replied.

'Not recently, Brehon. Blár O'Connor poisoned all of the wolves around his place.' He stopped and then said dramatically, 'He poisoned them with wolfsbane, aconite, I should say. He showed me the great big jar of the stuff that he got from Malachy O'Davoren.'

Seven

Bretha Déin Chécht

(The Judgements of Dian Cecht)

The physician's fees are fixed by law, according to the rank of the patient as well as the gravity of the case. For a death wound, the fee is four cows and a three-year-old heifer from a king; three cows and a two-year-old heifer from a chieftain. If, however, he is not a professional physician and has failed to disclose that fact, he is liable to a fine if his treatment is unsuccessful.

When the physician attends a patient, he and up to four of his pupils are entitled to their food at the house of the patient, but if the wound was inflicted maliciously, the offender has to supply the cost of the food. If the wound heals in an unsatisfactory way, the physician might have to refund his fees unless a certain stipulated time has elapsed between the healing and the wound breaking out again.

Instantly the books were closed. Mara moved to her desk, followed by her faithful Bran, and

114

faced her scholars.

'And we do remember that everything said here is sacred to this law school and not to be spoken of outside,' recited Hugh.

'Never mind about that,' said Enda impatiently. 'Brehon, do you think that Blár O'Connor could be a suspect?'

'I think he could be,' said Mara. 'Nuala realized that Malachy was treating an injury of Blár incorrectly. She gave the correct ointment to Blár's wife. He's a clever man and I think that he may well have suspected Malachy of prolonging treatment in order to get more silver, so he refused to pay him – which, under the law, he was quite entitled to do. If he had consulted me, I would have backed him up. However, he did not and Malachy, when he got the message about Blár's son being gored by a bull, instead of coming instantly, just replied that he would come as soon as he was paid. In the meantime, of course, the young man died of loss of blood.'

'And Blár regarded Malachy as the killer of his son.' Fachtnan said the words thoughtfully, his dark eyes full of sympathy.

'And as he happened to have a whacking great jar of wolfsbane there, he decided to give Malachy a taste of his own medicine.' Moylan chuckled at his wit.

'And of course, we know that the flask of brandy was on the table beneath the window.' Mara decided to ignore Moylan, though the joke was in poor taste.

115

'And the morning was hot,' said Hugh. 'The window would definitely have been open.'

'I'll make a note of that, shall I, Brehon?' said Enda, writing busily. 'We can easily find out that for certain once we get to work.'

Mara smiled. Her scholars were obviously keen to get started on investigations. She had always involved them in the legal work of the kingdom, feeling that practical experience was an essential part of their education.

'Brehon, is Nuala really a suspect? She seems to think that she is,' asked Fachtnan. Mara gave him her full attention. He had a worried look in his honest brown eyes.

'I think she has to be, Fachtnan,' she said. 'After all she did have the means, the knowledge, of course, and also perhaps a motive since her father had rejected her and was doing his best to stop her from becoming a physician.'

'And, of course, he also was trying to take away the Rathborney property that should be hers,' said Aidan, proving that the boys had been talking over Nuala's affairs among themselves.

'And she would be a female heir to Malachy – get the land fit to graze seven cows and the house,' mused Enda.

'So that's two reasons to suspect her,' mused Hugh, 'though I don't believe that Nuala did it.'

'A lawyer has to weigh all of the evidence,' reproved Shane. 'No personal feelings should be allowed to interfere with this.'

'Very true,' said Mara with a sigh. 'You re-

116

mind me of my duty, Shane.'

'So who else disliked Malachy the physician enough to kill him?' Enda held the quill poised in his hand and looked around the schoolroom.

'And had access to his medicines,' added Moylan.

'I think we must add to that who had knowledge of the medicines,' said Mara. 'You see, a few days ago, I would not have known what aconite is – would not even know what it was made from.'

'I came across a description in *Bretha Déin Chécht*,' said Shane. 'Just a minute, I have it here somewhere.' He delved into his satchel and then took out a piece of vellum, covered in his small, well-formed handwriting. Quietly he read it aloud: '"Aconitum is a handsome plant with dark green leaves and bright blue flowers which are shaped in a distinctive hooded shape from which it gets one of its many names: monkshood. It is also called wolfsbane as it is very poisonous and often used to rid a land of wolves. The poison is made by pounding the roots of the plant. Great care should be taken in the handling as it is a deadly poison."'

'And Malachy, according to Nuala, had a large jar on his shelf, labelled aconite,' commented Mara.

'But most people around here cannot read,' objected Hugh. 'And even if they could, would they know that aconite is just another name for wolfsbane?'

117

'Yes, but you must remember all the farmers who had got it from Malachy,' said Aidan. 'I think that wolfsbane is one medicine that many people of the Burren would know about. And would know how deadly it was.'

'This is the next task,' said Enda, writing busily. 'We must conduct a door-to-door search of the farms to see who had bought wolfsbane from Malachy.' He laid down his quill. 'And, of course, this brings us to the next point. What about Murrough? He lost his favourite wolf-hound. You remember how it happened?' He looked around at his fellow scholars and continued fluently, 'Malachy had baited his own woodlands with the stuff – had put it into a dead hare. Murrough walked his wolfhounds through those oak trees and his dog Rafferty cleared off – you know what Rafferty was like – anyway, he didn't come back when Malachy called him, and eventually one of the other dogs found him and he was dead. Had died in agony, too, poor dog. Vomited up his guts! The whole ground was covered with it.'

Mara swallowed, feeling almost sick to think that the same thing could have happened to her beloved dog, Bran. She, too, had often walked with her dog in the oak woodlands, and had allowed him to run ahead of her and to enjoy himself chasing hares and squirrels. One would almost feel that the man had been struck down by the hand of God. Her lips tightened as she remembered the handsome, good-natured, much-

118

loved Bláreen who had bled to death because Malachy had been more interested in silver than in saving lives. Were there others that this man had so injured that they had been moved to take his life? Her mind turned to Cliona. Thank God, the girl had known enough to reject the potion that Malachy had supplied to her husband. Was there anyone else who might have been injured? She turned to her scholars.

'Any more ideas?' she asked. 'Anyone who might bear a grudge against Malachy?'

'There have been a couple of deaths in the last few months,' said Fachtnan thoughtfully. 'It's hard to say, though, that these people would not have died if they had had a better physician. Mostly they were very old or very young.'

'Perhaps we could make enquiries as we go around the farms,' said Aidan. 'The important thing is to find someone who feels that the physician was the reason why that member of their family died,' he added shrewdly.

'That's a good idea,' praised Mara. 'As you say, Aidan, we are looking for someone who would want to kill Malachy, not investigating his cases. Make a note of that, Enda.'

There was a moment's silence as Enda's quill scratched busily over the surface of the small sheet of vellum. He replaced the pen on the inkstand and looked up, his face alert.

'Brehon, what does Malachy's wife get after his death?' he asked. 'Not land I know, but...'

'Under Brehon law,' said Mara carefully, 'she

119

gets nothing, as you say, Enda. And to be honest, I doubt that Malachy had much savings from his profession. He seemed to be spending very freely during the past months – he had that new wing built on to his house for one thing.' She paused for a moment, but then thought that these scholars of hers always had to know the whole truth. 'I'm not sure that Caireen knew that she would not get the house nor the land – the position is different under English law and Caireen would have known that law in Galway.'

'Not enough to kill a man for,' stated Moylan.

'Ah, but you forget the business,' said Enda. 'After all, the house is not just a house. It's a physician's house. It has the stillroom full of medicines, it has Malachy's medical scrolls, his bag full of instruments. Everything is there—'

'And,' interrupted Mara, 'Caireen's son, Ronan, has just been declared a qualified physician. He has been certified by Malachy himself and a physician in Galway. Nuala told me that.'

'Was Ronan there at the time?' asked Aidan.

'I'm not sure,' said Mara. 'At least Nuala said that he wasn't. She and Caireen were the only ones of the family present.' She noted that Aidan gave a disappointed sigh and then brightened up.

'Wait a minute,' he said then. 'Don't Ronan and his brothers inherit Malachy's property? After all, the sons of all marriages, even those of the fourth degree, inherit, don't they?'

'No, at least, yes ... you are right about the

120

sons of other marriages, but remember Ronan and his brothers are not of Malachy's blood – this is what I always tell you – the laws of inheritance are there to safeguard clan land,' explained Mara.

'They probably don't know that,' muttered Aidan, looking unconvinced.

'But Ronan was not there so that's off the point,' said Enda impatiently.

'Mother love,' said Fachtnan with a quiet smile.

'What do you mean?' queried Moylan, looking puzzled.

'Well, do you remember that mare belonging to Ardal O'Lochlainn? That blonde mare with the four dark socks? She was such a gentle animal. Anyone could ride her. Do you remember when she had a foal? Liam ... remember Liam, everyone? Well, when Liam came into the stable in the early morning, he found a dead wolf lying by the doorway. The wolf must have come to attack the foal and the mare killed it.'

'I see what you mean, Fachtnan,' said Mara. 'You think that Caireen might have killed Malachy in order to allow her son Ronan to inherit the position of physician. Ronan, as far as we know, was not in the house at the time – do put that on your list of things to investigate, Enda – but Caireen was the one who discovered the body, so we must have her, at least, as a suspect. That was a very good point, Fachtnan – like you to think of it.' Mara noted how Fachtnan looked pleased at her praise. Poor lad, his confidence must be at a very low ebb after the blow dealt to him by that dreadful Boetius.

'Though I would not have called that awful woman, Caireen, a lovely, gentle mare,' joked Aidan, but the two older boys both turned impatient, frowning faces towards him and he hastily said, 'it's a very good analogy, Fachtnan.'

'I agree,' said Mara, concealing her surprise that Aidan would know a word like analogy. 'I do think that this is a better reason than my original speculation that Caireen may have done it in order to inherit the property. Even if she did think that her inheritance would include the oak woodlands...'

Immediately, six alert faces stared at her.

'That would be clan land, of course,' said Enda.

'Who does inherit the oak woodlands, Brehon?' asked Hugh.

'My son-in-law, Oisín,' said Mara casually and watched their eager faces look suddenly embarrassed.

'We must consider everyone,' she reminded them.

'It's only a few acres,' said Moylan.

'And he lives in Galway.'

'It wouldn't be any use to him, would it?'

'I think that it might,' said Mara. 'He has plans to use it for barrel making and I understand that oak is a great wood for barrels. This could be quite valuable to Oisín.'

'He sounds innocent if he told you what he was going to use it for,' said Hugh reassuringly.

'That's a point,' said Mara, amused at their concern. 'Still, I do think that he has to go on our list for the moment.' She rose to her feet. 'Now I must go back to my house. Come over to the Brehon's house for your supper. We'll have it in the garden. I'd like you all to meet my new son.'

'Will little Cormac become a king or a Brehon?' asked Shane with a glint of mischief in his dark blue eyes.

Mara laughed. 'I hadn't thought of that,' she acknowledged. She considered the matter for a few minutes. 'A Brehon,' she said decisively. 'He looks clever!'

Leaving them laughing, she strolled back to her own house with a smile on her face. It was only as she entered through the gate that the smile disappeared. She had suddenly remembered something.

Oisín had not told her that he had a use for the oak woodland; it was Sorcha who had innocently betrayed her husband's plans.

Nuala was not with the baby. She was on her knees feverishly plucking out weeds from a bed of summer flowers. Mara had made that a few years ago, designing it to be like a stained glass window with the diamond-shaped beds of purple flowers and the blue flowers separated from each other with narrow strips of limestone.

123

During the last few months it had been neglected – increasing girth made weeding impossible for Mara – and buttercups had started to spring up, introducing a rather discordant note of brassy yellow.

'Cormac's fine; he's fast asleep.' Nuala spoke without looking up. 'That Eileen is very good with him, I think. She seems to know a lot about different potions and salves. I was quite surprised. I think you will have no worries about him now. He's looking well.'

'Were there worries last week?' said Mara, seating herself on a stone bench and bending over the baskets of lilies that stood on either side of it. She had planted these lilies last spring when they were just dry, papery bulbs and now they were tall white scented flowers. What a difference a few months made. Cormac had just been an unknown stranger in her womb, then, and here he was already putting on weight and becoming more boy-like all the time.

'I think I'll send a man towards Limerick if we hear nothing of Turlough by tomorrow,' she said without waiting for Nuala to answer her question. She knew the answer to it anyway. That tiny baby's life would have been in extreme danger from the moment that he was dragged from her womb. And, of course, without Nuala, he would undoubtedly have died. She looked thoughtfully and lovingly at the girl. There was an air of heavy sorrow and despair about her. There was no doubt that she knew herself to be under suspicion. Or was it something worse? Did Nuala have something on her mind? Mara pushed the thought away. Surely this girl could not have killed her own father?

'I've been reading about the ancient physician Dian Cecht laying down strict laws for a house where sick people should be nursed. I think he called it a hospital. I was thinking of making one there at Rathborney.' Nuala spoke suddenly, her eyes on Mara. 'I was wondering if I could take a few slips from your herbs here – I want to make a start down at Rathborney.'

'I know what you mean,' said Mara. 'It's in the Brehon laws.' She thought for a moment and recited: 'The house must have four doors, so that one could always be open no matter what the direction of the wind. It must have running water beneath it, so that it must either be built over a stream or on the banks of one.'

'That's right. You know the way that little stream flows through the garden of Rathborney. I could get Donogh Óg to build a small house across that stream – with four doors so that it would be filled with fresh air. This could be a place for a very sick person. And then I could use the main house for a school for physicians. That's if I ever manage to qualify.' Nuala's face clouded over again, but she added, 'It is a good idea to start on the herb garden, though. I was almost afraid to even think of Rathborney in case it was taken from me. Father seemed to be determined to keep it for himself. I hardly dared to hope that I would ever live there.'

'Well, it depends on your father's will,' said Mara in a matter-of-fact tone. 'I'm not sure whether he made one or not. In any case, I think Ardal will probably be your guardian.'

'Until I get married,' said Nuala sharply.

'Yes, of course,' said Mara peaceably. 'Now, come and sit by me. I really must get this terrible murder of your father solved and the culprit brought to justice at Poulnabrone.'

'And you think it might be me.' Nuala got up and took her place on the bench beside Mara. Her face darkened again.

'Let's not talk like that.' Suddenly Mara felt confident about how to handle this matter. 'Just think of me as Brehon of the Burren and I am asking you to tell me about that morning when Cormac was born. Just start at the beginning and go on from there.'

'Well...' Nuala seemed to be taking time to think, to turn over the events of that momentous morning. She turned her dark eyes towards Mara and they were wary. The girl seemed uneasy. Her voice was strained and monotonous. 'As you remember, Ardal, Turlough and all the other chieftains went off at dawn on Friday. I came over here – you remember we spent the evening together. You went off to bed early saying that you were tired after the session at Poulnabrone. I went to bed at the same time as I did not know what to do with myself.'

'Yes?' Mara was listening attentively.

126

'So having gone to bed early, I got up early – before dawn. I know it sounds strange, but that's what I did. I couldn't sleep any longer and I felt restless. I dressed and I got a piece of bread and a drink of buttermilk from the kitchen house, and decided to walk across to Caherconnell and to do some work at the herb garden there. The sky just began to turn grey when I got down as far as the Kilcorney Cross and then dawn came when I was about halfway across. Funnily enough, I thought I saw a man on a horse come out of the stable at Caherconnell just when I was on the top of the hill near Kilcorney church. I was probably mistaken. Anyway, there was no one around when I got there. I worked for a few hours, I suppose, and then I heard Caireen screaming.'

'Had you heard anyone else go to the house before then? Seen anyone?'

'I think, looking back over it, that your man Seán had come – just before Caireen started shrieking. Presumably to tell Malachy that you had gone into labour. I'm not sure about that. Everything was so confused.'

'Never mind about Seán now. I can find out about that when he comes back from Thomond. But did anyone else come? Did you hear anyone?'

'I think I might have heard a step,' said Nuala after a minute. 'It's difficult to tell. Perhaps I am just imagining it.'

'Go on,' said Mara with a sigh. It was always

the same when gathering evidence after an accident or a killing. Memories were always overlaid by the dramatic or tragic events that followed.

'Anyway, I was working away, weeding the clump of clary, as it happens – I suppose I had you in the back of my mind and I knew that clary would be useful when you went into labour.'

'And you heard Seán? Or did Caireen scream first?'

'No, I remember now,' said Nuala after a pause. 'I heard Seán and this was a while after I heard some footsteps.'

'And then?'

'I suppose it must have been three or four minutes later. I heard the scream.' Nuala stopped. 'Everything was very confused,' she said apologetically. 'I had to try to revive him ... to try to decide what killed him ... Caireen kept on screaming ... and she was shouting at me that I had done the murder...'

'And Seán was still there?' Mara wished that she could offer sympathy, could put her arm around the child and tell her to forget the terrible occasion, but the truth had to be sought. She had to remain neutral.

'Yes, I think he stood around all the time, with his mouth open,' she added with an attempt at a smile.

'And what about Caireen's sons? What about Ronan?'

128

'They didn't appear.' Nuala frowned. 'Odd, because I was fairly sure that I heard Ronan's voice earlier.'

'And then?' asked Mara, making a mental note to interrogate Seán when he returned from Thomond – perhaps others in the household at Caherconnell, also, if only she could find an occasion when Caireen was not around.

'After a minute or two – at least I suppose it must have been that, though it seemed longer – well, I knew that he was dead and that nothing more could be done for him. Caireen was having a hysterical fit and Sadhbh was fussing over her – you know what Sadhbh is like?'

Mara nodded. Sadhbh was Malachy's housekeeper and certainly a woman who liked to make a drama out of everything. She would have been in her element in this situation, rushing around fetching drinks for Caireen, exclaiming in horror at the death. Mara didn't care for Sadhbh too much, thinking that Sadhbh, who had brought up Nuala, should not have taken her father's part so firmly in the differences between him and his daughter. When Nuala had needed her, the girl had been repulsed by a woman who was only thinking of her own future in Malachy's household.

'Anyway,' continued Nuala with a shrug, 'I asked Seán what he had come for. He told me about you. Brigid had told him to tell Malachy that you were very bad. So I packed a bag with everything that I thought I might need – thank

God I remembered the birthing tongs – and I borrowed a pony and came across to Cahermacnaghten.'

'It was a good thing for me, and for Cormac, that you kept your head so well,' said Mara rising to her feet. 'Without you, we might neither of us be alive. I shall never forget that.' For a moment she rested her hand on the slim brown arm and then said in a lighter tone. 'Now, I will leave you to your weeding and go to see my baby. Don't work too hard. I have invited the lads to supper here this evening. Perhaps when you get tired of the weeding you might stroll down the road and ask Diarmuid O'Connor to join us. He will be interested to see the baby. He and I have been friends since we were children. I'm going to ask Cumhal to send a man to invite Murrough of the Wolfhounds and Blár O'Connor, also, so that we have a few neighbours to drink to the baby's health.'

Nuala, she thought, as she went indoors, had given her plenty to think of.

The girl had been unconcerned and very open in her evidence. This was not proof, of course, but somehow Mara felt sure that Nuala had not been responsible for her father's death.

But if that was true – who was the guilty person?

Caireen was the person who had placed the brandy in the glass on Malachy's table. Did she, also, add some of the deadly aconite to the drink?

130

Whose feet had made that step on the path about half an hour before Malachy's death?

And why, if he was in the house earlier, was there no sign of Ronan when his stepfather died in agony?

Eight

It was ordained in Cormac's time that every high king of Ireland should keep ten officers in constant attendance on him, who did not separate from him as a rule, namely, a prince, a Brehon, a druid, a physician, a bard, a seancha *(storyteller), a musician and three stewards:*

1. The prince to be the body attendant on the king.
2. The Brehon to explain the customs and laws of the country in the king's presence.
3. The druid to offer sacrifices, and to forebode good or evil to the country by means of his skill and magic.
4. The physician to heal the king and his queen and the rest of the household.
5. The file *(poet) to compose satire or panegyric for each one according to his good or evil deeds.*
6. The seancha *to preserve the genealogies, the history and transactions of the nobles from age to age.*
7. The musician to play music, and to chant poems and songs in the presence of the king.
8. And three stewards with their company of

attendants and cup-bearers to wait on the king, and attend to his wants.

This custom was kept from the time of Cormac to the death of Brian son of Cinneide without change, except that, since the kings of Ireland received the Faith of Christ, an ecclesiastical chaplain took the place of the druid, to declare and explain the precepts and the laws of God to the king, and to his household.

The supper was a success. Brigid, as usual, after a few exclamations, had risen to the occasion, and the long trestle tables were covered with shallow baskets woven from willow and piled high with honey cakes and crisp bread rolls. Bowls of whipped cream brimmed over with tiny wild strawberries, and bitter-sweet raspberries were sandwiched between layers of Brigid's special white-of-egg and honey cake.

The cradle was the showpiece of the evening. Little Cormac slept soundly within it, dwarfed by its splendid proportions. Eileen and Brigid had filled it with a mattress stuffed with sheep's wool and covered with crisp white linen sheets, and with a couple of woollen blankets, woven from the finest wool, folded up at the end of the cradle, in case the evening should turn cold.

'A little prince!' Diarmuid kneeled awkwardly on the ground and stared at the child. Nothing else seemed to occur to him, so he repeated his phrase and then got to his feet with relief and

133

embarked on a discussion of the cradle with Blár O'Connor.

'Great piece of work, that,' he said stroking the satin-smooth wood. 'Where did that oak come from? I think I can guess. Not far from here, isn't that right?'

'That's right. Kilcorney,' said Blár O'Connor with a hasty glance towards Nuala.

Diarmuid nodded his head with a smile. 'I knew it,' he said with triumph. 'Grand trees these – must be about two hundred years since they were planted – been well looked after in the past, too.'

Mara left them to their discussion of how to look after forestry, and their lamentations that enough people did not think of the future and plant trees for their future heirs, and went to greet Murrough.

Murrough O'Connor was a breeder of wolf-hounds, who lived at Cathair Chaisleáin, on the steep cliff behind Poulnabrone. He was a small, round man, good-natured and well liked by all. He made a good living by breeding and selling his handsome dogs. Mara's wolfhound Bran had come from there and King Turlough himself owned a few of the hounds. The dogs were Murrough's livelihood. He was good with them and fond of them. However, nobody could have predicted that a man like that, after half a life-time of rearing and selling animals, would have suddenly fallen violently in love with one dog.

Rafferty had been the pick of the litter, a

magnificent puppy, huge even when he was only a few weeks old. Murrough would have got a great price for him. Several offers had been made and when they were rejected the surrounding chiefs had reckoned that Murrough was saving the dog for a client in England. Perhaps even for King Henry VIII himself.

However, time went on and the dog was not sold. There had been something about Rafferty – perhaps it had been his exuberance, the depth of his affection for every human being – something which rose to the level of idolatry when turned upon his owner, but Murrough turned down every offer for the dog who continued to worship him. In turn, Murrough had adored Rafferty. He slept by Murrough's bed, was fed from Murrough's table and everywhere Murrough went, Rafferty accompanied him. He was quite untrained, but luckily possessed a sweet nature and was friendly to smaller dogs as well as people. Everyone on the Burren got to know Rafferty and he was greeted wherever he went. The law school boys loved him too. His exuberant high spirits matched their own and Bran, though a very well-trained dog himself, seemed to be amused by his young cousin's antics and they played great chasing games around the fields of Cahermacnaghten.

And then came the tragedy. Rafferty was poisoned and died a terrible death because of Malachy's action of putting wolfsbane into the carcass of a hare in the oak woodland. Murrough mourned his beloved dog as if he had been a child of the house. Even now, two weeks later, thought Mara, he was full of sorrow. His round cheeks seemed to have fallen in, and his small frame seemed to have shrunk.

Why had Malachy laid that poison? What reason did he have? Even if wolves did go through there at night, they would cause no harm. There were no animals in the wood. The few cows and chickens that Malachy possessed were all in the fields around his house. On the other hand, he must have known that many people walked through the woodland, often accompanied by dogs, and that young children came to pick bluebells and primroses there. He must have realized that he was taking a great risk.

Diarmuid and Blár were still discussing the oak woodland, so Mara quickly steered Murrough away once he had admired the baby. Eileen was sitting with Shane, who was engaged in teaching her to play chess, and Fachtnan was sitting beside them, overseeing the tuition.

'Bring Murrough a cup of wine and some food, Fachtnan,' she said as she watched Murrough sit beside Shane. Her boys got on very well with Murrough and loved to plan elaborate wolf hunts with him. These wolf hunts, even if they seldom resulted in any capture of their prey, gave the boys great exercise and excitement and made the weekends fun for them. Mara made a slight face as she thought of

136

the alternative. She, like everyone else, hated wolves who could do such harm to the young lambs and calves, but this poison, this wolfsbane, was such a terrible way to kill any living creature compared to an instantaneous death from the powerful jaws of the wolfhounds.

As the evening wore on, the guests continued to eat and drink. Mara surveyed the scene. Everyone was enjoying themselves – even Eileen, who seemed to be quite animated as Shane explained the moves of the castle to her. Murrough had left the chess players and was wandering around in the little hazel woodland looking at the white windflowers, Bran, the wolfhound, at his heel. Brigid was enjoying the compliments on her cooking; young Nessa, her assistant, was giggling with Aidan about a large dab of cream on his chin; and Cumhal, Brigid's husband, who was himself a good carpenter and wood turner, was showing Blár the wooden wine cups that he had made from an old apple tree that blew down in the storm. Nuala and Fachtnan were organizing races up and down the path for little Domhnall and Aislinn, while Sorcha played with her baby Manus, swinging him up to look at the tiny apples forming on the old Bramley tree and then lowering him down again quickly when he tried to grab one.

And then suddenly there was a sound that made Mara's heart stop.

The marching of feet, the smart click of metal horseshoes on the paved road.

And then the triumphant toot-toot of a bugle.

'It's the king!' screamed Shane, abandoning the chess game and racing to the gate.

'The king!' echoed the other boys, and in a minute they had joined him, the six of them forming a sort of guard of honour, lining both sides of the road.

Mara stood very still for a moment. Tears flooded into her eyes and her legs trembled. Only now did she realize that she had been quietly preparing her mind for bad news. A warrior's life was only as long as the distance between battle and battle.

Turlough Donn O'Brien had inherited the three kingdoms of Thomond, Corcomroe and Burren from his uncle eleven years ago and those eleven years had been spent fighting. He believed passionately in the old Gaelic ways and hated the new order of Earls, such as the Earl of Kildare and the Earl of Ormond, who had surrendered their birthright and paid obeisance to the king of England.

And now he came into sight, flanked by two of the chieftains of the Burren: the O'Lochlainn and the O'Connor. The MacNamara and the O'Brien would have dropped off from the cavalcade near to their own castles, but these two lived nearby.

King Turlough Donn was a heavily built man of fifty, with brown hair, which had given him the nickname of 'Donn', just turning grey, light green eyes and a pleasant open face. A pair of huge moustaches curving down from either side of his mouth gave his face a warlike look, which was denied by the gentle amiable expression in his eyes. He and Mara, the Brehon of the Burren, had been married the preceding Christmas.

'Safe and sound,' he shouted boisterously, as she forced herself to go to the gate. He urged his horse forward, swung himself down from the saddle before any of his men could grab the reins and then stopped, mouth wide open at the sight of her slim figure.

'Whaaat!' he shouted out in a long-drawn note of exclamation, and she smiled quickly and reassuringly.

'Your son was in a hurry,' she said. 'Come and see him. Come in, come in,' she invited the two chieftains. 'Come and see the latest O'Brien.'

This time she did not care whether she woke the baby. She leaned over the cradle and lifted the warm little bundle out of it. He woke, but did not cry. Eileen had fed him less than an hour ago and just recently his little stomach seemed to have expanded enough to retain milk for longer periods. He opened a pair of slate-blue eyes and stared mistily at his father. Turlough held out his arms and Mara placed the baby in them.

'Hold your finger out. See how he will grasp it!' Mara caught a grin on Sorcha's face, but she did not care if every baby in the world did this – it still seemed a miracle to her that such a tiny baby would have such strength.

'And he is well, strong?' Turlough surveyed

his son with a fond smile on his face. 'And you, all went well?'

'Very well, and very strong, both of us,' said Mara firmly. She hoped that no one would bother Turlough today with the story of Cormac's birth. Now was celebration time. She quickly whispered in Fachtnan's ear and he and Enda went into the house and reappeared a few minutes later with a large cask of wine. Brigid sped off to get more cups and more platters. Nessa was sent over to raid the stocks of the kitchen house in the law school, taking Aidan and Moylan with her to carry the provisions back, and Oisín broached the cask in a professional manner, filling up jugs for Shane and Hugh to take around to the guests. Mara handed the baby to Eileen who was at her elbow.

'Malachy not here?' Turlough had a special smile of welcome for Nuala who was always a great favourite of his. He did not wait for the answer.

'Who wants to hear about the battle?' he roared.

'Us, us,' shouted the boys, and the rest of the guests added their pleas.

'Wait until everyone is sitting down, my lord,' said Ardal O'Lochlainn. 'This is a story that is worth the telling.' He gave a puzzled glance at Eileen and she looked back impassively. Of course, thought Mara, the O'Brien and the O'Lochlainn ran sheep together on the Aillwee mountain. Ardal was a man who took an interest

140

in every animal on his land and he would have known; probably have met both Eileen and her husband when the time came for the clans to separate the sheep. Ciara had mentioned what a good shepherd the man was.

'Fill up everyone's cups, boys,' said Mara hastily. 'I think we will all need to drink a toast after this.' She nodded at Eileen and glanced towards the house. A slight breeze was stirring from the west; the baby would be better indoors. Eileen herself would have little interest in hearing about an event at which her husband was not present and Mara did not wish to run any risk that this tiny baby would get chilled.

'We heard that you came up to them when they were camped near to your bridge,' said Diarmuid O'Connor.

'Why did they camp there? Why not attack the bridge straightaway?' asked Murrough eagerly.

'Or better still, cross the bridge over towards the east – nearer to Kildare for them – and once they were safely across, they could have destroyed the bridge behind them,' put in Oisín.

'Well, that's easy. They were waiting for the cannon – you've never seen a cannon, boys, but it's a huge, big, metal thing like a pipe, the size of a cart and it spurts great balls of hot metal out of it – enough force in those things to knock down a wall the size of that.' And Turlough gestured towards the massive, ancient wall around Cahermacnaghten law school.

'So it would make short work of a wooden

bridge.' Enda's blue eyes were filled with excitement. Mara shuddered inwardly as she reflected how much harm to living flesh and bone a deadly instrument of war like that could do, but she kept an interested face turned towards her husband. This was the moment of his glory and she would not spoil it.

'What about guns, my lord?' asked Moylan. 'Did the English troops have guns this time, just like they had at the battle of Knockdoe? You remember you told us about them and how they would kill a man who came near enough to them.'

In answer, Turlough looked at Ardal and they both began to laugh, Ardal quietly amused, Turlough roaring and slapping his thigh.

'That was the joke of it.' Turlough began to recover and looked from face to face. 'They had their guns and when morning came we all lined up against them. There was no sign of the cannon arriving – these things are so big and heavy that it takes them a day to do a few miles – well, of course, because they had their guns they thought they could beat us.'

'Wish I had been there,' said Aidan wistfully.

'You'd have enjoyed it,' Turlough assured him. 'There they were and the men with guns were in front of the others, and there we were facing them: the men on horseback with their battle axes and their throwing spears, the men on the ground, the kerns, with their darts – well, you know what these are like, Fintan, don't you?'

The blacksmith nodded. 'Yes, my lord,' he said happily. 'And I'd bet that three-pronged iron top against any arrow – but against guns...'

'Ah, but we had a secret weapon!' Once again, Turlough laughed and Ardal joined him. The boys moved even closer, their eyes shining with excitement. The neglected girls began comparing their garlands.

'They were between us and the river so the sun was in our eyes.' One of Turlough's men joined in the recital.

'And then the good old west of Ireland weather took a hand,' said Turlough, resuming the story. 'It all happened in a moment. The clouds blew across the sky and the next thing was that it began to rain.'

'Poured down,' supplemented Turlough's bodyguard, Fergal.

'And there were all those English troops standing there, pointing their little guns at us and nothing happened.'

'But why?' screamed Shane. 'But why, my lord, why didn't they fire at your men?'

'Because,' said Turlough, 'because...' He was laughing so hard that he couldn't continue for a moment and even after he resumed, he had to keep stopping to laugh again, 'Because these guns work by setting fire to gunpowder inside the barrel – the little pipe – and it ... it explodes and spits the ball out – that's how it works, I think – and the ball comes out with such force that it can break a man's arm – but the rain came down and every one of their matches, their lights, every one of them were quenched and ... there they were just standing there with their silly, little useless pieces of metal in their hands, and my brave lads sending across their darts and the horsemen throwing their spears and the gallowglasses with their battle axes ... and...'

'Go on, go on,' screamed Aidan, his eyes shining.

'Please, my lord, go on,' pleaded Shane.

'I need a bard,' said Turlough, ruffling his greying hair with one hand and then pulling at his moustaches with the other. 'I can fight, but I'm no storyteller. Ardal, you do it for me.'

Ardal O'Lochlainn rose to his feet. A ray of sunlight shining through the holly trees to the west of the garden shone upon him as if to pick him out. He was a fine figure of a man, with his tall athletic frame, his eyes as blue as the sky above their heads and his red-gold crown of hair. He waited like a true artist until every eye was upon him and then began to speak clearly and plainly, and yet with a hint of the rhythmic speech of a bard.

'The Earl of Kildare, whom men call the Great Earl,' he said in his musical voice, 'had mustered a great army. All men who paid court to the English king had joined with him. And among that vast army were his cousins the Geraldines of Munster, under the conduct of James, son of the Earl of Desmond, and there came to the gathering also all the English of Munster, and McCarthy Reagh (Donald, son of Dermott, who was son of Fineen), Cornlac Oge, who was the son of Cormac, son of Teige, and many more of the English and Irish of Leinster. This great army proceeded into Limerick, murdering and pillaging as they went. And all men feared their passing.' He paused and looked around, holding the glances of all. Even little Domhnall, sitting on his father's knee, leaned forward, fascinated by the tale.

'And then,' said Ardal dramatically, 'there came to challenge him Turlough, the son of Teige O'Brien, Lord of Thomond, descendent of Brian of the Tributes, and he came with all his forces. And with him was Ulick Burke, he whom men name the Clanrickard, and then there was MacNamara of Clanmullen, the *Siol Aodha*. And there came also the lords of the kingdoms of Thomond and Corcomroe, those who had sworn to bring their own warriors to each *slógad*, and from the kingdom of the Burren there were O'Briens, MacNamaras, O'Connors and O'Lochlainn.

'The Great Earl marched with his army through Bealaeh-na-Fadbaigh and Bedach until he arrived at the bridge of Portcroise, that mighty monument to O'Brien power which had been constructed over the Shannon. And when he came to there, Kildare and his troops encamped for the night, waiting for the morning light to continue the spoil and pillage. Their goal was the great bridge across the River Shannon, but they waited for their cannon to arrive, and that was the mistake.

'For the mighty O'Brien left him not in peace, but hurried to the spot. Well-tried in arms, and well-knowledgeable about battles, the O'Brien did not engage in battle straightaway. Stealthily, he and his men crept along until they were within arrow-fall of Kildare and his men. They encamped so near them, that both armies could hear each other's voices during the night.

'On the morrow, the Great Earl mustered his army, placing the English and Irish of Munster in the van, and the English of Meath and Dublin in the rear.

'And,' finished Ardal, his triumphant voice ringing out like the clash of brass cymbals, as he raised his wine cup with his left hand, 'the O'Brien attacked the army of Kildare, and slew many of them. They escaped by flight, and the army of O'Brien returned in triumph with great spoils.' Ardal paused again, once more looking around to survey his audience, before saying in a low and triumphant voice,'There was not, in either army that day, a man who won more fame than King Turlough Donn O'Brien, king of Thomond, Corcomroe and Burren.'

The cheer that rose up then was loud enough to be heard across the Burren. Everyone was standing now and the filled wine cups were raised towards the king, and all voices echoed as Ardal shouted: 'The king! May God bless him and protect him.'

'And keep him safe for his wife and child,' whispered Mara in Turlough's ear. He nodded, smiled, pressed her hand, but she could see that the great victory still filled his mind. She left him with his men and went to talk to Brigid who was busily directing her workers to place fresh food on the table.

The wine, from the new barrel, was perfect, thought Mara, sipping it. It was smooth with an exquisite flavour of blackcurrants and none of that slightly burned taste that began to affect the wine at the bottom of the barrel. This was superb. She looked for Oisín to congratulate him, but he had gone back to join in the conversation between Blár O'Connor and Diarmuid O'Connor. She could only just overhear, but smiled when she realized that Oisín had managed to turn the conversation from the Kilcorney oaks to France. Her son-in-law imported vast quantities of wine from France and was quite an authority on that country. He spoke fluent French and liked nothing better than a trip there on one of his boats carrying merchandise from Ireland to the west coast of France. Mara would not have minded to join in a conversation about wine, but casks did not interest her greatly so she moved across the garden to find Murrough sitting on an iron bench in front of her holly trees, with Bran's narrow muzzle on his knee and tears pouring down his face.

'You still miss Rafferty,' she said gently as she

147

seated herself beside him. With another man she might have pretended not to have seen the tears, but Murrough was as simple and as unaffected as his own dogs.

'I miss him every hour and minute of the day,' he said, taking out his linen handkerchief and mopping his wet cheeks.

'I can understand,' said Mara softly. 'I was just thinking today that I could not bear to have something like that happen to Bran.'

'Please God that you won't have to bear that grief,' said Murrough, a sob tearing his voice. 'The man is dead now – but the evil lives on. Who knows how many people, how many places, have a hidden store of that cursed wolfsbane? Still, at least there will be no new supplies of it now that Malachy has gone. Poor Rafferty. He was such a lovely dog.'

'He was,' said Mara softly. 'I don't think that I have ever known a dog so full of life and spirits. He never grew up, did he? Except in size, he stayed a loving, playful, mischievous puppy.'

'He did indeed,' said Murrough and this time a laugh broke through the sob, 'Every piece of mischief that he could get into, well, head first, in he went! I used to say to him, joking like, "Rafferty, you have my heart broke" – I never thought that these words would come true.'

Mara turned to look at him. This man had an open and child-like nature. If he had done the deed, killed Malachy the way that his own beloved dog had been killed, it was possible that he could, even at this stage, be brought to admit the murder. The fine would not be a problem for him. He was reputed to get vast quantities of silver from English purchasers of his magnificent dogs.

'Murrough,' she said, laying her hand on his small, slightly womanish hand, 'Murrough, did you kill Malachy? Were you the one that put the wolfsbane poison into his brandy?'

He stared at her for a minute and his reddened eyes suddenly grew large and fixed. Eventually, his gaze broke contact with hers, almost with an effort. His eyes were now back on Bran and he stroked the narrow forehead, and then ran his hand along the long back, caressing the thin, whip-like tail with two fingers and then returning again to the neck. Again and again, he stroked her dog and then, eventually, he looked up and met her eyes.

'Brehon,' he said and then hesitated.

'You can tell me, Murrough,' she said reassuringly 'Tell me the truth and together we will work out what is to be done.'

He looked away from her, turning his face from the setting sun and towards the east. It seemed to her that he was looking for the oak woodland of Kilcorney, seeking to see the place where his beloved dog breathed his last. As she watched, she saw his face change. It hardened, closed up and the eyelids seemed to droop over the vulnerable eyes.

149

'Brehon,' said Murrough, and his tone was cool and remote, 'I am saying nothing. I do not want the murderer of Malachy the physician to be found. Suspect me if you please. Set those bright lads of yours to work investigating where I was and what I was doing on that morning. I don't care! Let them ask here and there. Let them question neighbours, friends and relations, but don't expect me to tell you anything.'

He put his arms about Bran's neck and then with a little push moved him away and stood up. 'I'm off home now, Brehon. My dogs will be expecting me. I wish you, the king and your little baby every good that life can bring to you. I would do anything for all three of you – anything, except one thing. Do not ask me to aid you in solving the question of the killing of Malachy O'Davoren, physician in the kingdom of the Burren.'

Nine

Maccslechta

(Son Sections)

The father or the foster father of a child normally bears responsibility for a child under the age of fourteen.

An offence by a child of a fuidir *(a tenant at will) is paid for by his lord.*

A child between the age of twelve and seventeen is called a 'thief of restitution'.

This means that if he or she steals something, the object or its value needs to be restored, but there is no other penalty.

'Nuala was very quiet last evening, wasn't she?' Turlough had slept late, and now sauntered into the room where Mara was rocking little Cormac in her arms and singing an old lullaby to him.

Mara raised her eyes from the baby. She had avoided talking about the affairs of the kingdom yesterday but it had to be done today. Turlough was not just her husband, but was also the king and thereby responsible for law and order in the

151

Burren.

'Let me look at him properly.' Turlough bent over the baby. 'Looks like you,' he pronounced.

Mara smiled. 'He's the image of yourself,' she said with conviction. 'Look at those eyes and that chin. And the fair skin. He's definitely an O'Brien. Nothing of the "black" O'Davorens about him.' And then suddenly she thought of Sorcha's children, and of their inheritance of the dark eyes, hair and skin from their father Oisín. Perhaps sensing a change, the baby cried, the pale cheeks reddening. Turlough took a step backwards in alarm.

'He's just hungry,' reassured Mara. 'Eileen will feed him. Ah, there she is. I hear her coming down the stairs. Just open the door, will you, Turlough.'

Eileen bowed respectfully to the king, but her eyes were on the little baby. Mara firmly repressed a feeling of jealousy as the woman held out her arms with such an expression of love. Almost as soon as the baby was handed over he stopped crying and nuzzled into his wet nurse. As Eileen carried him back up the stairs to her bedroom, Mara could hear her murmuring the same lullaby that she herself had been singing. Could Cormac tell the difference? Or, in his eyes, was Eileen the real mother? Nothing in life is ever perfect, she reminded herself sternly, and moved her thoughts towards the story that she had to tell about the secret and unlawful killing in the kingdom of the Burren. She would say nothing of her feelings of failure that she had not managed to feed her baby. Turlough had not questioned Eileen's presence or the fact that she was the one to feed the baby. No doubt, his first wife had routinely engaged a wet nurse and little was seen of a new baby until it was three or four years of age.

'Come out into the garden and I'll tell you about Malachy,' she said. 'Brigid will bring your breakfast out there.'

The garden had that lovely freshness of a June morning. The grass was still damp from the night's dew, but the flowers blazed in the bright sunlight. The air was filled with the scent of the lilies in their baskets and of the gillyflowers that lined the pathway. Mara and Turlough made their way across to the bench in front of the holly trees and sat in silence for a few minutes, gazing at the delicate blue spirals of the path that led up Mullaghmore mountain at the eastern fringes of the kingdom.

'Well,' said Turlough. 'It's good to be back. Now tell me about Malachy. What's he doing? Trying to thwart your little friend Nuala in her ambitions?'

'He's dead,' said Mara. 'He died, rather terribly, by drinking a dose of wolfsbane, or aconite, as Nuala calls it. It had been put into the brandy glass and he drank it – you remember the way that Malachy drank – just opening his mouth and throwing the liquid down his throat.'

'I can't believe it!' But Turlough did not sound

that upset. She had to remind herself that he was a warrior and that death was a familiar occurrence. No doubt, despite the celebrations and the triumph, there had been many deaths during the past week. 'Was it an accident, then?'

'No accident – Malachy was not very bright, but he would not have put aconite in his own glass – one of his best glasses. In fact, it was one of the glasses that my father brought back from Italy. It was just like my own Venetian glasses. My father gave it as a present to Malachy.' She stopped and thought for a moment. It had never occurred to her that Malachy's death could have been an accident. A moment's reflection was enough, though. There was no possibility of a careless mistake. All of those poisons were clearly labelled.

'No, it was murder,' she said. 'The killing has not been acknowledged,' she added, and saw him look at her with sympathy.

'What a nuisance for you, just out of childbirth. Don't say that you are trying to manage everything yourself. Why can't Fergus Mac-Clancy of Corcomroe do it? We arranged that, didn't we? I'll send for him immediately and tell him to take over matters. Perhaps we could go and stay in our castle at Ballinalacken for a few days and let him carry on.'

'It's not the fault of Fergus that I am taking charge of this matter,' said Mara firmly. 'He sent his cousin, a most bumptious young man called Boetius MacClancy, to take over the affairs of

154

the kingdom and of the school. I'm afraid that I sent him off with a flea in his ear. I didn't care for him and his methods.' And then as she saw him look doubtful, she added, 'His idea of solving a murder was to say instantly that Nuala must be guilty.'

That diverted him as she had intended. 'Nuala,' he roared. 'What nonsense! That little girl!'

'She's over fourteen, unfortunately. Otherwise she would not be liable for any punishment for a crime. Of course, she is still under seventeen so if she stole something, she would be deemed to be a "thief of restitution". There would still be no penalty, but the stolen property would have to be returned. However, I'm afraid that murder cannot fit into this category. The life taken cannot be returned. Certainly, Boetius was correct to consider Nuala. She benefited from his death – she is his heir and also Malachy was trying to take the property at Rathborney from her – and, as you know, she and her father were on bad terms. No, Nuala must be considered. What I objected to was that she was the only one to be under suspicion. He made no attempt to find out anything else. And also he gossiped about her possible guilt with Caireen and that stupid wife of Fergus's.'

'The man must be a fool,' said Turlough emphatically.

'Dangerous, I think,' said Mara thoughtfully. 'He is very much under Caireen's influence.'

155

She told him about Caireen's plan to force Nuala to enter a convent, and for the valuable property at Rathborney to be confiscated and given to the wife as recompense for the loss of her husband. 'You can see,' she finished, 'I must take this matter in hand and solve this crime. Otherwise these accusations will be hanging over Nuala for the rest of her life.'

He nodded reluctantly and then brightened. 'At least you have the lads.'

'That's right,' she said. 'They can do all the donkey work. They love riding around the Burren and gathering evidence. And, of course, their brains are sharp and their knowledge of the law is excellent. Now, here comes Brigid with your breakfast. Tell me some more about that great victory, the battle of Limerick.'

It wasn't just Brigid who was coming down the path, though. Turlough's two bodyguards, Conall and Fergal, were at the gate with three horses.

'Oh, bother, is it that time already! I have to ride to Thomond, Mara. I haven't been there yet and I must bring tidings of the victory. The clan will expect it.' He put a large arm around her, saying, 'I hate to leave you so soon, and the baby. You do understand, don't you? I'll be back in a few days.'

'Of course I understand,' said Mara serenely. She had understood all of this when she had eventually made her decision to agree to marriage with a king. They both had their tasks to

156

do, their obligations to meet, but that almost added to the sweetness of the times when they could be together. Four or five days might give her time to sort out the murder. Sorcha and Oisín would be leaving at the end of the week and the boys would be off on their summer holidays. That would be the time for Ballinalacken, the beautiful castle standing high above the Atlantic Ocean which Turlough had recently rebuilt for her.

'Ballinalacken will be for him, won't it?' said Turlough watching her tenderly, almost as if he could read her thoughts. 'That will be his inheritance from his father. That is mine to give as I choose. I'll get all that fixed up while I am at Thomond.'

'Eat your breakfast,' said Mara. 'I don't think Cormac wants a castle just now. His needs are simple.' Her eyes went to Eileen who had emerged from the house carrying the baby. After his meal, Eileen always carried him for a while, rocking him gently in her arms as she paced between the Brehon's house and the law school. Then when he slept she would put him into a basket, either in Brehon's garden, or in the law school yard, and watch him sleep. Cormac's needs were simple, but they were being met with unremitting care and dedication. It was lucky, thought Mara, that Ciara had arrived that morning; Eileen, quiet, unobtrusive and devoted, was the perfect nursemaid for the little prince.

* * *

Turlough and his men-at-arms had just departed when Nuala came drearily into the garden. Her usually glossy hair looked untidy and dull – almost as though she had slept in the braids. Her white *léine* was crumpled and had grass stains on the back of it. She had certainly not changed it today – perhaps had even slept in it overnight. Mara looked at her sharply.

'Nuala, in your profession as well as in mine, personal feelings have to be put aside. You must not let the world know what is wrong with you. You must hold your head high and show a brave face.'

And then, when the girl just glared at her impatiently, Mara said, 'Shouldn't you be over at Lissylisheen? Ardal is back and will be needing you. After all, you are his woman of the house, as he calls you. He will want to give a celebratory dinner to his men-at-arms, and, if I know Ardal, no doubt the workers will join in with the celebrations.'

Nuala shrugged sulkily. 'He doesn't want me. He managed without me before.'

'He's been far more cheerful since you were there. For a while I thought things might work out between him and his wife of a fourth degree, but Marta went back to Connemara and took little Finn with her, so you are his hostess and you must act as such. Now, go and wash your hair and have a bath. There is water heating down there in the bathhouse. Oh, and do find a

158

clean *léine*. If you haven't one of your own, Brigid will find you one of mine.'

'If I'm a nuisance to you, I'll go,' said Nuala in a tragic manner, and Mara's heart melted.

'You know you are not a nuisance to me; you know you are as dear to me as my own child, but this is no place for you now. Your father's murder must be solved and I don't want you involved in the case.'

'All right, I suppose I might as well go.' Nuala got to her feet with a sulky expression and then said irritably, 'I suppose I had better change that *léine* before Ardal sees it. He would die of shock. He keeps talking about buying me silk for a gown.'

'Let him do that,' said Mara serenely. 'Men enjoy spending silver on women that they are fond of – and Ardal is very fond of you. Your mother was always his favourite member of the family. Oh, and Nuala, before you go, could you tell me something? You said that Caireen discovered your father's body about ten in the morning. How did you know the time, or were you just guessing?'

'Guessing, I suppose,' replied Nuala with a shrug. 'Not really, though. I remember now. The cows were being brought into the milking parlour. That is always at ten in the morning.'

'I see,' said Mara. That was reasonably good evidence, she knew. Cows were fussy creatures. She had often heard Cumhal scolding Seán for being late with the milking and telling him that

159

the cows would hold back their milk if he didn't keep to the same time every day.

The boys were all working so quietly when she went into the schoolhouse that for a moment she thought they were not there. Enda was sternly supervising Moylan and Aidan, who were writing down everything they remembered from their studies of *Bretha Déin Chécht*, Fachtnan was going through the regulation of the kin group from *Córus Fine* with Hugh and Shane was wrestling with a passage from the works of Horace, the Latin poet.

'I'm sorry to interrupt you all, but I am anxious to solve this murder,' said Mara with false concern, smiling as books were shut and six bright faces turned towards her. She laughed then. It was obvious that her scholars were eagerly awaiting her arrival.

'Let's plan this well,' she said perching on the edge of her desk. 'I can't do much walking and certainly no riding so you must be my eyes and ears.'

'And carry your knowledge of the law,' said Enda with a grin.

'And make careful notes,' said Shane, lifting his dark eyebrows.

'Have you found out any more information, Brehon?' asked Hugh.

'Well, I found out from Nuala that she thinks the body was discovered at about ten o'clock in the morning. It was just about milking time, anyway, so that's a valuable piece of information as people tend to remember seeing cows driven along the road towards the milking parlour.' Mara decided that she would not mention Murrough's defiant statement for the moment. Other suspects needed to be investigated first.

'What would you like each of us to do, Brehon?' asked Fachtnan.

'I was thinking, Fachtnan, that you could go over to Caherconnell. See Caireen. Be very polite and respectful – I don't need to tell you how to behave. You are very good at this sort of thing – probably better than me! Try to find out whether she was alone in the house – except for the servants, of course. I really want to know whether Ronan was present – the other boys are spending the summer in Galway with Caireen's sister, but, in any case, Ronan is the one that I am interested in. Fachtnan, you will have to be very tactful about your questioning...' she broke off, wondering whether she was expecting too much, but he gave a grin.

'I know what to do,' he said. 'I've watched you do it again and again – just slip in an extra question. I'll do my best – I won't be as good as you at it, though.'

'You might be better, Fachtnan,' said Mara. 'Most people like you, and I'm certain that Caireen loathes and detests me. You'll do well, I'm sure.'

'What about us?' asked Moylan and Aidan, speaking in unison as usual.

161

'Well, I was thinking that you, Moylan, and Hugh worked very well as a team during the last case that we dealt with, so perhaps you two could work together again and talk to the people around Caherconnell – find out what they were doing around the time that the cows were being taken for milking. Find out whether they noticed any stranger, or any acquaintance – anyone, in fact, who was around Caherconnell at that time. Could you do that?'

Moylan gave a crisp nod and Hugh looked pleased.

'And then Aidan and Shane could investigate the farms to see who bought wolfsbane from Malachy. That's a huge task, of course, so start off looking at the farms near to Caherconnell and then spread out if you have time. Of course, you could always drop a question about whether anything is known of someone who did buy the stuff – or who definitely didn't – and that could save you quite a bit of journeying. You understand what I mean.'

'Yes, of course,' said Aidan with a lordly nod. 'And I'll explain it to Shane.'

Mara smiled her thanks, though inwardly she was quite certain that eleven-year-old Shane was far more intelligent and alert than fifteen-year-old Aidan.

'What would you like me to do, Brehon?' asked Enda respectfully.

'Well, Enda, I wondered whether you would take a note of thanks over to Blár O'Connor, the

162

wheelwright. I want to tell him how much the king admired the cradle...' She stopped because Enda was regarding her with a sceptical smile. He knew quite well that a note like this could easily be sent by one of the lads that worked under Cumhal's direction, or else by young Nessa.

Mara returned his smile. 'Yes,' she said, 'there's more than that to it, of course. You see, Blár O'Connor is in my mind as a likely suspect. Not only was he cheated by Malachy, who deliberately kept a wound in his arm from healing so that he could extract more and more silver for more and more useless jars of that salve made from comfrey, but also, because of his inhumanity in refusing to come to treat Blár's son who had been gored by a bull, Malachy was responsible for the boy's death. You yourselves told me that Blár used wolfsbane to get rid of the wolves at Binne Roe, so that would mean he had the means for the murder close to hand.'

'So you want me to nose about and to find out what he was doing on that morning at about ten o'clock,' said Enda.

'That's right,' said Mara. 'Though, in fact, I'm not sure exactly what I want you to do – probe a bit, I think, go by your instinct, see what he is willing to talk about. It might help if you had a few conversation topics in your head – questions to ask him about types of wood, that sort of thing. He and my son-in-law were deep in a

163

discussion about that yesterday evening. You see, I think that he had the strongest motive really of all of our suspects.' Her thoughts went to little Cormac. Would she kill someone who killed her son? At the moment, she thought, the answer might be 'yes'.

'I'll do my best,' said Enda.

'And your best is always worth having, Enda,' returned Mara. 'Fachtnan, would you have a word with Cumhal about the ponies. You will all definitely need to ride as you have a lot of work ahead of you. Moylan and Aidan, will you ask Brigid to put together some food and something to drink for you all to carry with you. I think Eileen is over there so she will help Brigid to do that. Hugh and Shane, would you collect the satchels from the scholars' house and bring them over to the kitchen house. You four can help with the food, then, also. I'm sure that Brigid will need all the assistance that she can get. She had a busy day yesterday with all of the excitement. She must be tired. Enda, you and I will sort out the pieces of vellum and the ink horns for everyone to carry with them. My father used to say that a note straight after an interview is worth a hundred notes made two hours later.'

They had heard it all before, even the quotation from her father, their smiles assured her, but she was not repentant. Things repeated over and over again in youth tended to stay in the memory. These boys had to retain a huge amount of information and almost every hour of her days during the terms of Michaelmas, Hilary and Trinity was devoted to ensuring that this information was fed to them in all ways possible.

'Enda,' said Mara when the other five had departed, 'I wanted to make an opportunity to talk to you. It has always been the custom at this law school to have a party to celebrate the success of a scholar, or scholars, who have passed the examination to qualify as an *aigne* (lawyer). You deserve to have this celebration. You are still only sixteen and so you are my youngest pupil ever to become a qualified lawyer. I would love to have a celebration, but I feel bad about Fachtnan. Last year was different. Fachtnan, on my advice, did not take the examination. This year, I was fairly confident that he would pass – but you know what happened. It can't be helped now, but...' She stopped and looked at him appealingly.

Enda's tanned cheeks flushed a deeper shade of rose. 'The last thing that I want is one of those parties. I remember Colman's and I thought it was a bore, and an opportunity for him to show off. I wouldn't do that, but I'd have to listen to people saying things about me...' He fidgeted for a moment and then said, 'But if you could spare me, Brehon, for an hour or so, perhaps on Saturday, I'd like to ride across to Glenslade and tell Mairéad O'Lochlainn about my good news.'

'Of course,' said Mara heartily. She busied herself sorting out some scraps of vellum from the cupboard in order to hide her smile. Enda and Mairéad O'Lochlainn, daughter of Donogh O'Lochlainn, Ardal's brother, had appeared passionately in love last winter, but Enda had taken Mara's advice and allowed the relationship to cool while he studied hard in order to pass his final examinations. Let him have a little fun, now, she thought. He deserves it. She turned around with a smile.

'I've got a good idea,' she said impulsively. 'Tomorrow is the twenty-third of June. Why don't we have a little party here to celebrate midsummer's eve and then you can all go on to the bonfire at Noughaval? This can be your celebration – but no speeches or fuss. I'll write a note to invite all of the young O'Lochlainns. Shane and Aidan can deliver it – Glenslade would be a good farm to start their enquiries about wolfsbane. Donogh O'Lochlainn always knows what's going on in the farms around his land. Who else would you like to ask, Enda?'

'Nuala, of course, for Fachtnan,' said Enda. 'And Saoirse O'Brien and her brother, young Gilla, the O'Heynes and then there are the two O'Connors.'

'What about Cuan from Newtown Castle? I don't think he gets much fun – always tied to his mother's apron strings. Would that be all right, Enda?' As she spoke Mara was rapidly penning notes to the young people from farm, castle, dun and lios in the surrounding countryside of the Burren.

'This is wonderful,' she said with satisfaction. 'Shane and Aidan can deliver these and ask their questions at the same time. Then there will be no fuss and no unease. This is the way that I like to do things.'

Enda looked at her for a moment and then said awkwardly, 'I would like to say now how much I have learned from you. I think that if I went to another law school – down to Cork, for instance, I might have learned the same laws, but I don't think I would have learned as much of how to be a good Brehon, how to keep the peace in the kingdom ... I think I will always be grateful to you and remember what you taught me.' He tailed off, his cheeks now bright red. Neatly, he gathered up the pieces of vellum, quills and ink horns on to a tray and, without looking at her, went outside with them.

How lucky that Mairéad O'Lochlainn was, thought Mara, looking after him affectionately as he crossed the yard to the kitchen house. He was tall and so handsome with his blue eyes, tanned skin, very white teeth and corn-gold hair. She would miss Enda, she thought with a sigh as she penned the last of her notes and then rapidly sorted them according to district.

Aidan and Shane were going to have to ride fast in order to be able to deliver all of these and it would mean spending very little time in each place, but that was good. If they did it tactfully, people would remember the invitation and forget the question. Enda was right. Keeping the peace in the kingdom was probably the most important facet of her position as Brehon of the Burren and she hoped that this was something that her scholars had learned from her.

Ten

Cáin Lánamna

(The Law of Marriage)

There are nine kinds of sexual union under Brehon law:
1. A union of joint property where both partners contribute transferable goods.
2. A union of woman on man's property where the woman has little to bring.
3. A union of man on woman's property where the woman is the main partner and the man has little to contribute.
4. A union of man visiting where a man visits a woman in her own home with the consent of her kin.
5. A union where the woman goes openly with a man without the consent of her kin.
6. A union where the woman has been abducted.
7. A union where secret visits take place without the consent or the knowledge of either kin group.
8. A union by rape.
9. A union between two insane persons.

'Could I just have a quick word with you, Brehon, before I go? I just want your advice about something.'

'You startled me, Fachtnan. I thought you had all gone.' But one glance at Fachtnan's worried face made her say quickly, 'Come into the schoolhouse. We can be private there.'

Once inside, Fachtnan seemed to have difficulty in beginning. Mara looked at him with surprise. He had a deeply troubled look. Perhaps he was worried over his failed examination, but somehow she did not think so. He had seemed quite happy with the offer of a teaching post; he was a humble boy. Unlike others that she had taught, this would not have been a great blow to his pride.

'Is it about your future?' she asked when the silence had grown to an uncomfortable length.

He ran his hands through his rough, dark hair and looked at her with a hint of desperation in his eyes.

'In a way, yes,' he said. 'At least I thought it might be my future, but it's all come so quickly. I wasn't expecting it.'

Mara could not resist a smile at his puzzled, worried face. 'Come on, Fachtnan,' she coaxed. 'Speak plainly. I'm too old for these riddles.'

'It's Nuala,' he said, the words shooting out of him.

'Nuala!' Mara's smile vanished. Had Fachtnan some evidence against Nuala, something that he

170

feared might reveal an involvement with Malachy's death?

Fachtnan took a deep breath, opened his eyes very widely and said in almost a whisper. 'She's asked me to marry her.'

'What!' Mara felt quite flabbergasted. This was the last thing that she had imagined. 'What do you mean? She just came up to you and asked you to marry her?'

Fachtnan nodded. 'That's right. Moylan had told her that I had failed my examination and she wanted to tell me that it didn't matter – that I could marry her and help her to manage the hospital that she wants to build at Rathborney. She said that there would be plenty of money for us both and for...' Fachtnan paused and flushed slightly, 'and for any children that we might have. I suppose it would be a union of a man on a woman's property, as the law puts it. She says that I could manage the farm and help her with her hospital, and keep an eye on the children while she was busy with her doctoring.'

'I see,' said Mara dryly, 'she seems to have thought of everything.' A thought occurred to her. 'And when did this happen?'

'Just now, just a little while ago. She came to the gate and called me. And then we walked down the road together. She said that she had something to ask me, a favour, she said.' Once again, Fachtnan blushed. 'Then she talked about the examination and then she said, "I wonder would you think of marrying me, Fachtnan?"'

171

'I see,' said Mara again. Nuala, she presumed, had her bath, washed her hair, dressed in a clean *léine*, perhaps surveyed herself in the looking glass and decided not to waste the effect.

'She's only fourteen, too young,' she said aloud, and then watching his downcast face, she asked gently, 'What do you think yourself? Would this marriage suit you? You've always been good friends, you and Nuala?'

'I did think I might marry her in a few years' time,' admitted Fachtnan. 'But this seems to have come a bit suddenly. I—' He broke off and looked at her. He looked confused and there was an appeal for help in his eyes.

'In a way this is your business, your parents' business and, of course, the business of Ardal O'Lochlainn, Nuala's uncle,' began Mara, but then she thought of her responsibilities. Fachtnan wanted help now. His parents were three days' ride away. She had to give him her opinion.

'I think if I were you,' she continued, 'I would not want, for Nuala's sake as well as for your own, to take any such important step at the moment. Nuala has just lost her father and her emotional state is not good. I think that she needs time – time to reflect, time to get over her sorrow and, above all, time for this murder to be cleared up and the guilty person found.'

'I said something like that,' confessed Fachtnan, 'but then she got very annoyed and she shouted at me that if I didn't want her, then she

172

would ask Enda, instead.'

Mara's lips twitched; she tried hard to control herself, but a laugh burst out despite herself. 'I think Enda has other fish to fry,' she said. 'If I were you, I would say no more about it, Fachtnan. When she thinks it over, she'll know that you are right. Just meet her as a friend, as usual. Don't look embarrassed, or anything. Just pretend that it never happened.'

Fachtnan looked sheepish, then relieved. 'Thank you, Brehon,' he said. 'Well, I'll be off now.'

I must go and talk to Brigid, thought Mara as the last set of horse hoofs clattered down the road. She knew a moment's temptation to tell her of Nuala's proposal – Brigid would enjoy that – but she realized reluctantly that she could not betray a confidence.

However, there were other matters to discuss with her housekeeper. She felt slightly contrite about imposing another party straight after the impromptu celebrations of last evening, but Brigid loved cooking and did enjoy an occasion to display her talents.

'Why don't you take it easy?' scolded Brigid when she heard the news. 'You're less than two weeks away from having a baby. Most women would still be lying in their beds. Why don't those lads just go down to the bonfire at the market square in Noughaval? They'll have a good time there and will leave you in peace. Why a party now? Why not wait until next week

173

when they are leaving? Fachtnan and Enda will want to celebrate, won't they?'

'I'm afraid,' said Mara, 'that poor Fachtnan has nothing to celebrate. Young MacClancy failed him in his final examination. I don't want to deny Enda of a chance to make merry, though. He did very well – not surprisingly.'

'Oh!' Brigid was silent after the exclamation. She was very fond of Fachtnan – had mothered him when he arrived as a five-year-old and had watched him grow up, always affable, always sweet-natured and never any trouble. She rubbed her fingers through her sandy hair, disturbing the neatly pinned braids. 'How is he taking it?'

'Quietly,' said Mara. 'I'm going to keep him on as a teacher – he can study in between. I'm sure that he will get through next year. In fact, I think that he would have got through this year if things had been different.' She could not mention Nuala's surprising offer to Fachtnan, but it did come into her head that it would be a good match for the boy – possibly once he had passed his final examination, and become an *aigne*, he would prefer to stay at this basic grade of lawyer rather than embarking on more long years of study in order to become a Brehon. With his wife's fortune he would have the opportunity to decide and the income to support both.

'Master MacClancy, indeed! I told you that I didn't like that young fellow,' said Brigid emphatically. 'Not a proper teacher, he wasn't.

174

Larking around and letting Aidan get above himself.'

'So I was thinking that instead of a celebration party for Enda, this year we would just have a party at midsummer, St John's Eve, but if it's too much trouble for you, Brigid...'

'Oh, don't be talking!' Brigid gave an impatient flap of her hand and Mara backed out of the schoolhouse with an appreciative smile. What would she do without Brigid?

Outside the door, she hesitated, looking down towards the Brehon's house. There was no sign of Eileen now; the baby must have woken and she had probably taken him inside for a feed. With a slight feeling of guilt she returned into the schoolhouse. Guilt, she realized, would be part of her for some time to come. Guilt that she was not with her child, and guilt that she was neglecting her work with her scholars and the affairs of the kingdom.

The schoolhouse was very quiet. Not even Bran was there. He had chosen to go with Fachtnan and she was glad of that as the big dog would love the exercise of loping along beside the pony. Mara unlocked the cupboard and looked into the top shelf. It was piled with year books dating back to before her own birth. It was a practice started by her father and she had faithfully kept it up. Now she took out the book marked MDX and opened a new page.

ANTE DIEM DUUM KALENDAS JUNIUS, she headed the page neatly in her square minuscule handwriting, detailing the death of Malachy the physician.

Everything was very quiet. And then a swallow flew in through the open door, banked and swiftly flew out again, with a shrill twittering sound, the cuckoo sounded from the nearby wood and outside the window two beautiful peacock butterflies chased each other in the sunlight and briefly flew inside, perched on the open cupboard door and returned towards the sweet-smelling outdoors. In the distance a cow bellowed with that sudden, explosive moo that meant her calf had strayed, and then the softer reply came and once again everything fell silent.

Mara wrote on, describing the events of the eleventh of June, two days before the Kalends, as the Latin calendar phrased it. She wrote fully, describing the terrible death and noting the events that may have led up to it, but stopped when she was halfway down the page. When would she be able to finish this page, she wondered? When would the affair of the secret and unlawful killing of Malachy O'Davoren, physician in the kingdom of the Burren, be solved?

The shadow at the doorway made Mara, deep in her thoughts, raise her head with a start. Her daughter, lightfooted as always, stood there.

'Aren't you looking pretty. I love that blue gown on you!' said Mara impulsively.

'I made it myself,' said Sorcha coming across the flagstoned floor and dropping a kiss on her mother's cheek.

'I'm not surprised,' said Mara. From a very young age, Sorcha had loved to create. Like her father Dualta, and Dualta's father, the stone mason, she was good at everything that involved the hands and the eyes. Brigid taught her to weave, to spin and to sew, while Cumhal patiently sieved and prepared clay for her to make small models, and even taught her a little wood carving when her hands were strong enough for the tools. She had been a happy and charming child, loved by all, flitting in and out of the schoolhouse like one of the summer butterflies, always busy, always singing and laughing.

Was she happy now? wondered Mara, reaching up and smoothing the brown hair with an affectionate hand. What was Oisín like as a husband? He always seemed so immersed in his affairs, absent mindedly patting Sorcha as though she were a well-behaved but unobtrusive dog in the household. Her thoughts ran on as her daughter took up Brigid's theme of not overworking and then she suddenly switched back as Sorcha finished triumphantly by saying, 'And Oisín thinks that you made a big mistake.'

'What big mistake?' asked Mara.

'Oh, Mother,' Sorcha sighed in an exasperated manner. 'You haven't listened to a word that I am saying. I'm talking about your work. You really should not have sent Boetius MacClancy away like that. Oisín thinks quite highly of him.'

177

'And what does Oisín know about law affairs?' queried Mara, doing her best to suppress the tart note in her voice.

'Oh, more than you think,' said Oisín's wife serenely. 'Oisín knows so much. He meets so many people and picks up things. He is very talented,' she finished proudly.

'But not actually a qualified lawyer, and certainly not a Brehon,' pointed out Mara, trying to sound amused.

Sorcha shook her head at her, endeavouring to make her blue eyes look severe. 'Oisín wants me to talk to you seriously about this, Mother. He is sure that he can get Boetius MacClancy to come back again. Oisín met him this morning. Apparently, Boetius hasn't found too much to do at the Doolin law school. Siobhan actually tried to get him to weed her garden to keep him occupied!'

'Good for Siobhan,' said Mara lightly. 'So has Oisín been over to Doolin this morning? He must have been up at the crack of dawn.'

'No, he met Boetius MacClancy over near Kilcorney. He's staying with Caireen at Caherconnell.'

'I hope she realizes that her reputation will be ruined if she keeps an unmarried young man in the house,' snapped Mara. After all her careful preparation of Fachtnan, he probably had a wasted journey if that wretched man was there sitting beside Caireen and making sure that she watched every word she said.

178

'Oh, Mother, don't be so old-fashioned,' said Sorcha with a laugh. 'After all, her son, Ronan, is there. Oisín met him, too, this morning. Apparently, Brehon MacClancy is advising them both about legal affairs. Now, come out of this gloomy place. Come back and sit in the garden and we'll both enjoy our babies. Eileen is just giving him his bath. My little Manus has had his and now he's fast asleep, God bless him, he's a great boy to sleep – much quieter than the other two.'

'I'll just finish this and then I'll be over,' said Mara. She would have a few minutes with her baby son. And she would send Eileen for a short walk so that she had him to herself.

After Sorcha's words it was no surprise to Mara to see the heavy, ungainly figure of Boetius MacClancy clumping his way across the grykes, just as the abbey's bells rang for the noonday recitation of the angelus. He was looking extremely hot, Mara was meanly glad to see. He had shed his cloak so his large stomach protruded even more under a *léine* damp with sweat. She handed little Cormac back to Eileen and rose to her feet. Boetius was not making good progress on the uneven ground so she had plenty of time to walk down the road and into the law school. Cumhal could direct him once he arrived. This was going to be an interview conducted on formal grounds, she decided.

Boetius entered the schoolhouse with heavy

step and the air of one who is doing a favour. Mara regarded him warily. Cumhal had showed him in with a cold courtesy which almost made her smile – Brigid had obviously lost no time in telling her husband the story of Fachtnan and the failed examination. However, she tightened her mouth and bade him sit down. She decided not to offer any refreshment. In any case, Cumhal, as usual reading her mind, had not waited to take an order. After all, this man was here for his own ends, not hers. He had been well paid for his work and she had no reason to treat him as a guest.

'You wanted to see me?' She came to the point quickly.

He was a little taken aback at that. She could see him turning matters over in his mind as he fingered his red beard and looked at her with his sharp eyes. Then he seemed to make up his mind and he smiled at her in a genial fashion, though his small green eyes were cold.

'I'm sorry to see you looking so unwell,' he said with false concern. 'It's not surprising really. All this is far too much for you. After all, it's only ten days since you gave birth. You can't be expected to investigate a murder and teach your boys with all that you have to do. Fergus's wife, Siobhan, was saying this to me yesterday; she scolded me thoroughly for abandoning you.' He gave her his small-boy-roguish look and leaned back on his chair, crossing one leg over the other, while eyeing her narrowly.

Mara leaned forward and adopted a confidential air. 'Do you know, I feel wonderful,' she breathed, conscious that she sounded a little like Caireen at her most effusive. 'I feel so full of energy and confident that this troublesome affair of the murder will soon be solved and the guilty person brought to trial at Poulnabrone. All seems to be so plain to me, now.'

That took him aback. 'Whaa ... Who?' he stammered.

'I'm afraid that I can't share my thoughts with anyone outside the law school,' she replied smiling sweetly. 'Well, let's talk about you; what are your plans? The last time we spoke I got the impression that you were going to settle at Corcomroe and assist Fergus.'

Boetius lifted his sandy eyebrows and endeavoured to look contemptuous as well as pitying.

'Not much there for a man of my ability,' he said loftily.

'Fergus, like myself, prefers to manage his own affairs, I suppose.' It was as near being rude as she could possibly reconcile with her conscience and her views on the high standards of personal conduct required from a Brehon, but to her surprise, Boetius did not take offence.

'It must be difficult to have a young man come in and tell you how to manage your affairs,' he conceded amiably.

'Not at all,' Mara beamed kindly at him. 'It wouldn't bother me. I would be quite confident that my way was best, and I'm sure that Fergus is the same. We have the benefit of long experience, of course.'

This silenced him for a moment. She could see from the calculating look in his eye that, like a chess player who has seen his first onslaught fail, he was now rearranging his plans. She began to feel slightly sorry for him. After all, despite his heavy, middle-aged appearance, he was still a young man. Perhaps she had been too hard on him. Still, she was interested to hear what his next move might be. If it were conciliatory, she would be amiable, perhaps give him a note to some Brehon of her acquaintance – many might be glad of a young man to help out during the hot summer months when thoughts turned to holidays by the sea or in the mountains.

'I wonder, Brehon,' he said with heavy formality, 'whether you have ever thought of the future.'

'Frequently,' said Mara briefly, watching his small eyes narrow. At least, she thought, he has given up calling me Mara or *Mamó*.

'I notice that your curriculum is singularly old-fashioned, though.' Now he sounded more confident.

'Indeed,' said Mara frostily with a lift of one black eyebrow.

'For instance there are no studies focusing on English law.'

'This is a Brehon law school.' Mara adopted

182

the kindly tone that she used when explaining something simple to a new scholar.

It annoyed him, of course. His answer came quickly and hotly.

'And yet Brehon law has been declared to be outside the law by Henry VIII, and the Pope, the Holy Father himself, has condemned the lack of punishment for thieves and murderers.'

Mara shrugged. 'The Holy Father must do as he feels right,' she said politely. 'Brehon law was the rule under which our forefathers lived and it has served the country well.'

'I know on very good authority that the new king, Henry VIII, has given very extensive powers to the Earl of Kildare. One of the matters that he particularly wants him to address is the lawlessness that is encouraged by not having the death penalty for crimes of robbery, violence and above all murder. Brehon law is to be out-lawed in all parts of Ireland.' He regarded her closely for a moment and then said softly, 'I wonder what you feel about that, Brehon? Do you regret your lack of knowledge of English law, or will you, perhaps, be content in your role of wife and mother?'

'I think that I have a fair knowledge of English law,' said Mara, trying not to show how much the young man was irritating her. 'I know about their terrible prisons, how they torture people to make them confess to crimes, how they hang beggars who steal a loaf of bread, how they put young children in prison and even hang them.'

183

'Well, well, well,' said Boetius tolerantly. 'You ladies are tenderhearted as I've said before. But,' he waggled a large finger in front of her nose, making her long to slap it out of the way, and said triumphantly, 'you can't hold back the tide, you know, Brehon. Like it or not, English troops and English laws will soon be here in Ireland.'

'Perhaps you are unaware,' said Mara sweetly, 'that the Earl of Kildare, and his English followers, have just been heavily defeated at the hands of King Turlough O'Brien and have gone back to the east of Ireland with their tails between their legs.'

Boetius waved his hand in the air. 'A temporary setback,' he said contemptuously. 'Make no mistake, Brehon, England will conquer Ireland and I see it happening quite soon.' He laughed lightly but watched her closely as he added, 'I am hopeful that if I can establish myself during the next few years, the Earl of Kildare will put the conduct of law and order in these western parts under my control. But, first of all, this affair of the murder of the husband of an unfortunate woman, and mother, will have to be solved and the culprit punished according to canon law.'

'But for now I am Brehon of the Burren and the kingdom is ruled by Brehon law, not canon law,' pointed out Mara.

'So much the worse for it!' His tone was definitely meant to be rude and she lost patience.

184

'I won't keep you,' said Mara coldly, rising to her feet and walking towards the door. 'I don't think that the matter of the murder of Malachy the physician has anything whatsoever to do with you. However, it has to do with me and therefore I have work to attend to. And I'm sure that you have some serious thinking about your future to do.'

She watched him go with a smile on her lips. If he were a dog, she thought, his tail would be between his legs! Perhaps he would go back to Caireen. Would that be another case of a union of a man on a woman's property? she wondered.

Mara felt suddenly stronger than she had for months. All her energy, which had been sapped by carrying a child and the long and difficult birth, had started to come back to her. In high good humour she hummed happily to herself as she walked back towards the Brehon's house.

If that young man, Boetius, thought he would frighten her away from doing her duty to the people of the Burren and upholding the law in which they both were trained – well, he would just have to think again.

Eleven

Bretha Comaithchesa

(The Judgements of the Neighbourhood)

The names of plants that bring evil are myriad and children and animals must be guarded from them. No path or common way across the land should have these plants growing by it.

All men are responsible for their own land and for the safety of animals and people who come on that land.

A contract to sell land is defective if the poisonous plants máelán mulchi, dithan *or* ithloinges *are found on the land within a three-year period after the sale.*

Mara and Sorcha enjoyed a quiet afternoon in the garden, each cuddling her baby and watching Domhnall climbing the apple trees, while little Aislinn happily picked the bright pink flowers of ragged robin from the edge of the small woodland that sheltered Mara's garden from the north-westerly winds. Oisín was not there. He had gone for a walk, Sorcha told her

186

mother, though Mara suspected that his walk would only take him as far as the Kilcorney woodland. He was certainly not a man to let grass grow under his feet, as the old saying had it. With his bright intelligence and his passion for whatever interested him at the moment, her son-in-law was acquiring a huge knowledge of anything to do with trees. He hung around Cumhal who distilled a lifetime of knowledge about trees and the uses of various woods, he walked over to Binne Roe to talk to Blár and to look at his tools and chat about barrel making. Everyone was interrogated if he felt they might have some information for him.

'You see, Mother,' he had said before he left, 'there will be no need to waste anything. Even the bark of an oak tree is useful – it can be used for tanning leather and Nuala tells me that it is great for treating constipation,' he stopped and referred to the small scroll that he carried in his pouch. 'No, I'm wrong! That was some other bark. Oak bark is good for treating diarrhoea and sickness. This means that I will be able to sell the bark easily. And then Blár tells me that he will purchase good-sized branches which are too small for barrel making, but will be quite right for the staves in his wheels. The smaller branches, of course, can be sold off for firewood. The great thing is to have it all organized before we start the felling. I'm making a book full of notes and adding to it all the time.'

Aidan and Shane were the first to arrive back.

They had a neat list, written by Shane, of all the farms that they could find to have used wolfsbane. Mara stared at it in dismay. Malachy must have prepared buckets of the stuff. Almost every one of the farms on the High Burren had purchased a jar. Of course, these farms were all in the valleys below the surrounding mountains on the east and west of the kingdom and of the Aillwee mountain in the centre.

'It was quite easy, really, because so many people told us three or four names where they knew that Malachy had supplied the stuff,' said Shane. 'Teige O'Brien took two jars. His shepherd put it out on Aillwee mountain before lambing and they didn't lose a single one, so he recommended it to lots of people. Apparently it worked very well and the wolves have taken hardly any young animals this season. The shepherds were all pleased and so were the cattlemen.'

So one would have suggested it to another, thought Mara sadly, her mind going to Murrough and his beloved dog, Rafferty.

Moylan and Hugh again had a neatly tabulated list of people and places. And again they were disappointed with how little to relate they had collected. There were a few vague memories – something about someone crossing the grykes with a cloak hood hiding the face, which was about the only unusual sighting – and Nuala, of course, coming along the road from Cahermacnaghten – a farmer up all night with a calving

188

cow had noticed her.

'Otherwise it was just Oisín,' said Moylan. 'Someone had seen him, not near Caherconnell, but just on the road to Glenslade – but that had been much earlier – a good hour or so beforehand.'

'That would be right,' said Mara. 'He did visit the O'Lochlainns that morning.'

Her daughter had told her that the morning of Cormac's birth – and Malachy's death – had been passed by Oisín at Glenslade chatting with Donogh O'Lochlainn.

'And someone saw Blár, the wheelwright, delivering a turf barrow to the O'Lochlainns – and at about the same time.' Hugh consulted the sheet carefully to make sure that there was nothing else and then handed it to Mara.

'No sign of Murrough?'

'No, nobody mentioned him.' Moylan shook his head vigorously.

'You've done very well, all of you – now go and have your dinner. Brigid has it all ready for you.'

'Here's Enda,' said Hugh as they went towards the pump in the yard. Brigid was always very keen on clean hands and faces before she allowed them to sit down to a meal. Mara walked over towards the stables. None of the men were around and she could probably hear Enda's account while he untacked the pony and rubbed the animal down.

'Not sure that I got too much out of Blár,

189

Brehon,' said Enda, vigorously rubbing the pony with a handful of hay. 'I think he may have guessed that I was probing. He was very polite and very helpful about answering questions, but I would say that underneath he was watching his words very carefully.'

Mara nodded her head with satisfaction. 'That's a very useful observation, Enda,' she said. 'This is the sort of thing that I wanted from you. It's occasionally valuable to ask a direct question, but generally I prefer to glean impressions and possibilities before I resort to anything like that. Did he say anything about any recent jobs that he had completed?'

'Yes, he did.' Enda regarded her with a slight smile. 'And interestingly enough he went on at great length about the turf barrow that he had just made for Donogh O'Lochlainn of Glenslade and how he had delivered it himself – on that Saturday morning.'

'And, of course, to go from Binne Roe he had to pass along the Kilcorney road, close to Caherconnell,' said Mara with a smile.

'Yes, indeed. I think I was supposed to report to you that he had a reason to be in the vicinity. He repeated the bit about the turf barrow and Glenslade twice – didn't mention Malachy's death, but it did seem as though he wanted it reported back.'

'Well, I find that very interesting. Now go and have your meal, Enda. Did you see any sign of Fachtnan?'

'No, isn't he back yet? Perhaps the sorrowing widow is proposing marriage to him – perhaps she has persuaded him to stay the night,' said Enda flippantly. Mara suspected from his grin that Enda had heard the story of Nuala's proposal. Perhaps the girl had carried out her threat and offered herself as a good proposition to Enda.

'Brigid, is Fachtnan home yet?'
'Well, I thought he did come back, Brehon.' Brigid had a worried frown on her face. 'I told the lads to tell him that I left some ale in the kitchen house for him and I thought I saw him go in there earlier – I went across to have a look at little Cormac and then I stayed for a minute to talk to Nuala – and when I went into the kitchen the ale was gone. But I must have been wrong because there's not been a sign of him. It's not like him to be late back. It's almost bedtime for Hugh and Shane. I gave them a little longer because it was such a fine evening and they wanted to finish a game of chess. I'll go down to the school now and send them off, and if Fachtnan hasn't arrived yet, I'll come back and let you know. Do you think we should send one of the men out looking for him? Or Enda? Perhaps he's had a fall or something.'
'I think that would be—' began Mara and then stopped. There was a yell from the gates of Cahermacnaghten and then the noise of two pairs of feet running frantically down the road.

'Brigid!' It was Hugh's voice.

'Brehon!' That was Shane, and Mara instantly handed the baby to the waiting Eileen and rushed to the gate. She could see them now and both faces were white.

'It's Fachtnan!' Shane screamed the words.

'He's dying!' Hugh was behind him.

'Calm down,' said Mara; her immediate instinct was to get the information as fast as possible and then to take action. She put out her hand to slow the boys down. 'Tell me, one at a time. Where is Fachtnan?'

'He's in the scholar's house.' Shane gulped. 'We thought he was dead first.'

'He's nearly dead,' said Hugh.

'He's been sick all over the place,' said Shane. 'He had a bucket. He must have used that first, but there's vomit everywhere – on the covers, on the floors.'

'Oh merciful God,' exclaimed Brigid with a terrified look. 'It's not the same thing as happened to Malachy!'

Mara stood very still. She wasn't sure that she could cope with this. Fachtnan had been under her care since he was five years old. He was one of her children. It was impossible that anything like that should happen to him.

'He's alive, though,' said Hugh. 'He groaned. We were going into our room and then we heard him groan so we opened the door and found him. He looks terrible.'

'Go immediately to Lissylisheen.' Mara began

to regain her wits. 'Take your ponies. Go as fast as you can. Find Nuala. Tell her everything, bring her straight here. Tell her to bring any medicines that she may need.'

'I pray to God that we are in time,' said Brigid as she ran down the road. Mara followed going as quickly as possible. Cumhal had appeared, alerted by the boys' yells, and without asking any questions he was helping them to saddle the ponies by the time that Mara came in through the schoolhouse gates.

Moylan and Aidan appeared at the door of the scholars' house when she crossed the cobbled yard.

'Enda's with him; he's still vomiting. It's a bit of mess in there. Do you want me to get water and buckets and things?' Aidan looked horror-stricken and hardly waited for Brigid's nod before rushing off. Moylan followed him.

The scene inside the room was appalling. Fachtnan must have been here for hours, was Mara's first thought. Of course, it was like him, if he felt ill, to say nothing and just go to his bed with a bucket beside him. Now, however, he was barely conscious, his body racked with spasms of dry retching.

'Oh, Holy Mother of God,' muttered Brigid. 'I've never seen any of the lads as sick as that. Enda, get me some water in a cup. We'll see if a few sips help.'

Fachtnan's eyes half-opened when Brigid slipped a hand under his head. He made an effort

193

to sip the water, but most ran from his mouth.

'Get some hot water from the kettle above the fire, Enda,' said Brigid. 'Pour it into that leather waterpouch hanging up above the fire. We'll put it on his stomach to ease him a little.'

Thank God for Brigid, thought Mara. She had long years of experience of boys' illness; whether it was stomach upsets from eating sour apples, or something picked up at the fairs, Brigid had all her tried and tested remedies. She stood aside watching Fachtnan's face and listening to his breathing with dread.

'Let's get him out of here.' Cumhal and one of the men from the farm were at the door. 'Come on, lad, let's be having you. Get him a clean nightshirt or something, Brigid. He'll feel better when he's not smelling the vomit. That's right, Moylan, bring that bucket here. We'll clean him up a bit and then move him out of this room.'

In a few minutes, Fachtnan was stripped, washed, wrapped in a clean linen sheet, and then Cumhal lifted him in his powerful arms. 'We'll take him into our own place, Brehon,' he said. 'He'll need a bit of nursing. That's it, lad, just get the stuff out of you. Hold that bucket there under his mouth, Aidan. Go on, Fachtnan: get rid of that poison.'

And now the word was said. Enda, returning with the leather waterpouch, stopped at the doorway, a look of dread on his face, and then, mastering himself, came in, handing Brigid the warm bundle and slipping a hand behind Facht-

194

nan's head.

It was soon over and Fachtnan slumped back exhausted.

'Let's take him now,' said Cumhal.

'Come on, lads, leave that room. We don't want you getting what he has.' Brigid's eyes met Mara's for a moment and then slipped away. She took the hot waterpouch and followed her husband from the room. Mara went too, telling the three boys to wash themselves thoroughly. For the moment they would all try to believe that this was some infection that Fachtnan had picked up. The alternative was unthinkable.

Nuala arrived just as Fachtnan was being tucked into a small truckle bed in Brigid's and Cumhal's house. She had her medical bag with her, but she took nothing from it. She just knelt on the floor, gently opened the boy's mouth and inspected the lips and tongue. Then she looked up at Mara.

'It's not wolfsbane,' she said reassuringly.

'How do you know?' It was Brigid that asked the question; Mara said nothing.

'He would have burns on his mouth and tongue, and throat also. How sick has he been?'

'Very!' said Aidan. 'Spewed up his guts.'

'How much?' Nuala was sharp and practical.

'How much?' Aidan looked horrified. 'I don't know; you don't expect me to go and measure it, do you?'

'Don't be stupid, Aidan! Go and help Shane and Hugh,' snapped Nuala. 'They're in the Brehon's garden. I told them to bring all the mint they can possibly find – every leaf of it. Go quickly – you, too, Moylan. I want it back here in two minutes. Do you hear? Go on.'

They had disappeared before the last words left her lips – glad to be doing something, thought Mara, wishing that there was something that she could do.

'The vomit was originally solid food, I'd say, Nuala,' said Enda quietly. 'By the time that I saw him though, he was just vomiting yellow liquid.'

'Bile.' Nuala nodded in a satisfied fashion. 'No black blood, nothing like that?'

'No!' Enda shook his head, appalled at the thought of vomited blood.

'How is he?' Oisín was at the door. No one answered.

'When did he first vomit?' asked Nuala.

'No one knows,' said Mara. 'No one saw him come home.'

'I did,' said Oisín. 'He came back in the middle of the afternoon. I was just sitting on the wall having a cup of wine. I spoke to him for a minute or two. Offered him some wine, but he didn't want it. He went off in through the gate leading his pony. That was the last that I saw of him.'

'We've got the mint, Nuala.' The three boys burst into the room unloading the strong-smelling green leaves from their pouches.

'Give handfuls to everyone. Now crush it and

196

put it as near to him as possible. All over the bed and as close to his face as possible. I want him to smell it. This will be safer than giving him anything to drink – that might start up the vomiting again. Here, give me some, Shane.'

Nuala took a handful and squeezed it tightly, then held it in front of Fachtnan's nose. He half-turned his face away from the strong smell, but Mara put her hand on his cheek and gently turned it back again. Everyone else was following Nuala's orders. Brigid placed the hot water-pouch on Fachtnan's stomach and added a few mint leaves on top of it for good measure. Shane was rubbing some leaves between his hands so violently that it seemed as though he would rub the skin from them. Oisín put some leaves on the floor and ground them with his boot. The room was full of the aromatic smell.

It seemed to Mara that Fachtnan's face was slightly less white. He was no longer racked by those terrible spasms and the blood beat more strongly in the wrist that she was holding. Cautiously, she drew in a breath. She tried to reckon how long it was since the last attack of retching and thought it must be almost ten minutes. Nuala was searching through her medical bag with sure hands. She looked competent, assured and somehow happier than she had seemed of late. She held up a small phial of finely ground powder and reached for the cup of water that Enda was holding.

'I think I could try some skullcap, now,' she

said. 'I think that is the right thing for him.'

With a tiny silver spoon she measured six spoonfuls into the water. Cumhal propped up Fachtnan, holding his arm behind the boy's shoulders. Nuala reached forward and suddenly seized his nose, pulling it upwards and when his mouth jerked open she poured the dose down his throat.

'Works every time,' she said nonchalantly. And then looking at the astonished faces around, she said irritably. 'More mint, quick, I'm sure there is more to get.'

'There should be,' said Mara recovering herself. 'I made a long path of it last year, leading into the wood. Take as much as you can carry, lads.'

There was a silence after they left. All the adults watched Fachtnan's face with dread. The thought of Malachy's terrible death was too near everyone's mind, thought Mara. Of course, Nuala had declared confidently that Fachtnan had not taken wolfsbane, but could she be certain?

By the time the boys were back with more pouchfuls of mint everyone had begun to breathe more easily. Fachtnan looked troubled from time to time, but each time relapsed into sleep, breathing in the mint-scented air.

'There's a sedative in that stuff I gave him,' said Nuala. 'He should sleep soundly now if the vomiting stops.'

'What made you think of the mint?' asked

198

Brigid curiously. 'I never heard of it.'

'Read it in grandfather's notes,' said Nuala in an offhand manner. 'It makes sense. Anything you give by the mouth risks being rejected by the stomach. This comes through the nose and calms everything.' She looked around at the crowd of people in the small room and said abruptly, 'I think he should be left to sleep now, so everyone should go. I'll call if I need anything.'

Everyone left obediently, except Mara who continued to sit by the bedside. Nuala looked at her and Mara shook her head.

'I have to stay, Nuala,' she said in a whisper. 'He is my responsibility. Tell me, what do you think happened to Fachtnan? Was it something that he caught from another person, something that disagreed with him?' She hesitated for a moment and then said, 'Or was it something that was given to him?'

Nuala said nothing for a moment. She looked at her medical bag, picked up a ragged piece of mint and began to knead it between her finger and thumb, and then she looked at Mara.

'I don't think that he had an infection. It would not have responded so well to the mint and the skullcap. I think it was something that he ate, or drank.'

'But what? I've known Fachtnan for fourteen years. I've never known him to be ill no matter what he ate or drank. Brigid will tell you the same. She used to say "that boy has a stomach like cast-iron".'

'Perhaps it was something poisonous?'

'But I thought you said that it wasn't wolfsbane.'

'There are more poisons than wolfsbane,
Mara,' said Nuala with a superior air. 'Many
good medicines are poisonous if you give more
than a certain carefully measured dose.'

Mara met her eyes. 'So you think someone
gave him poison – why? To kill him?'

'Probably not.'

'Why then?'

Nuala thought for a moment and then shrugged her shoulders. 'Not the right stuff. This was
probably alder buckthorn or at least the bark of
it.'

How does she know, wondered Mara? But she
said nothing.

'It's often known as purging buckthorn.'
Nuala was looking at her, perhaps puzzled by
her silence.

'Why do you think that someone did it?' Mara
looked very directly into the dark brown eyes.
The eyes were, as always, full of intelligence,
but there was a depth of unhappiness in them at
the moment that made them hurtful to look at.

'Perhaps to frighten...' said Nuala, after
another long silence.

'To frighten him? Fachtnan? Frighten him
off?' queried Mara.

Nuala shrugged again. 'Or to frighten you –
have you thought of that? There may be some-

one who would like you to stop investigating. This might have been just a warning, just someone saying "stop, or I'll do something worse, the next time". And of course that could happen. It's easy to kill someone by poison if you know enough about herbs and their uses. You could grind up the seeds of that plant "Lords and Ladies" – a plant that is in every hedgerow – and the person who drank the mixture would not survive.'

'So how can I keep the boys safe?' Mara asked, watching Nuala intently.

Nuala shrugged, the sullen look coming back to her face. 'You can't,' she said simply. 'They have to eat and drink – all except little Cormac who is being suckled by Eileen. Anything can have poison slipped into it.' She stopped and then added with her eyes fixed on the window, 'There is only one thing you can do, Mara, stop investigating the death of Malachy. It's all too dangerous. Someone does not want this questioning to continue. Why not stop? You are a woman newly risen from childbirth. No one would blame you.'

'I would blame myself,' said Mara. She put out a hand and gently turned Nuala's face so that they were eye to eye. 'A death has to be investigated and retribution demanded from the guilty person; that is the law that I live my life by and I cannot turn my back on it now.'

Twelve

Cáin Lánamna

(The Laws of Marriage)

A woman can inherit a life interest in land when her father has no sons. She is called the bancho-marbae *(female heir). If she marries a landless man or a stranger from another kingdom, she makes the decisions and pays his fines and debts. After her death, the property of a* bancho-marbae *reverts to her own kin and does not pass to her husband and sons.*

Two or three times during the night Mara woke and walked to her window, leaning out as far as she could and looking anxiously over towards the school. There were no sounds from the enclosure and no lights either. Brigid had made up a bed for Nuala in her living room, but it seemed as though all slept. Most importantly, Fachtnan must have continued to sleep. Each time Mara breathed a sigh of relief as she returned to her own bed – to rest, but not to sleep.

What had happened?

It seemed from Oisín's evidence that Fachtnan had returned at the usual time in the afternoon. Brigid had thought she saw him go to the kitchen house and she was probably right. Brigid usually was right.

But was the poisonous drug that he swallowed given to him during the day? Perhaps at Caherconnell? Could Caireen have tried to poison the boy by using one of her husband's medicines? Or did Ronan, the newly qualified physician, deliberately pick something that would make Fachtnan very ill, but not kill him – and did he do that in order to frighten Mara from continuing the investigation?

Or, more horrendous, did someone put the drug into the cup of ale left for Fachtnan on the kitchen table? Brigid's voice carried for distances of up to half a mile. If she had shouted to the other lads that Fachtnan's drink was in the kitchen, then anyone in the vicinity could have heard her.

This was the thought that robbed Mara of her sleep.

'How is he?' As soon as Mara had given little Cormac his bath and enjoyed a few private minutes with him while Eileen ate her breakfast, she went across to the law school. Brigid was flying out to the pump with a kettle in her hand. Her sandy-red hair had been neatly braided and she looked much as usual. Mara felt a rush of happiness. Fachtnan must have slept well and the night had been undisturbed.

Brigid beamed. 'You wouldn't believe it, but he says that he is hungry. Nuala is in there with him. Go in, Brehon, go in and see for yourself.'

Fachtnan was pale but looking more like himself. As soon as Mara came in Nuala rose to her feet.

'I must get back to Lissylisheen. Ardal will be wondering where I am if I don't turn up at his breakfast table. Nothing to eat for him today, Mara. Just water, and not too much of it. I've given him a dose of skullcap this morning and I'll come over again this afternoon to see how he is.'

And with that, she was out the door, and they heard her footsteps on the cobbles outside.

Fachtnan met Mara's eyes. 'That was embar-rassing,' he said frankly. 'She was there beside my bed when I woke up this morning. I thought I was dreaming.'

'Just relax. You've been very ill and gave us all a fright. You must have eaten something, did you?' Mara kept her voice light. Fachtnan look-ed in no condition to talk about his brush with death.

'No, I was so thirsty that I just drank the ale in the kitchen house. I didn't bother with any food.'

'But earlier? During the day?'

'Just a few honey cakes and a glass of wine at Caireen's – didn't like the wine much, but I thought I'd better drink it in case it seemed rude not to. And I had a bit of Oisín's – I didn't like that either.' Fachtnan's eyes were closing as he spoke. Mara got to her feet.

'Sleep now,' she said. 'I'll pop in later on. Just call if you need anything – your window is wide open.'

'This wretched murder has come at such a bad time for me,' snapped Mara. It was stupid she knew, but she was beginning to resent the way that Eileen came in and took the baby from her as though she were the mother, and that she only lent Cormac to Mara for a strictly limited time. And yet, it was true that she had no time for her own baby just now.

'Why don't you ask the king to send over Brehon MacEgan from Thomond?' suggested Brigid. 'After all, there's no hurry, is there? The man is dead. Finding out who killed him is not going to do anyone any good.'

'Except those who are innocent of his murder, but who are now under suspicion,' said Mara quietly.

'You're thinking of Nuala.' Brigid said no more about MacEgan, the Brehon of Thomond. Nuala's pale face, slumped shoulders and irritability would not have escaped Brigid's notice. 'What is it that you want to do?' she asked.

'I want to ride over to Caherconnell and interview Caireen and her son, Ronan,' said Mara fretfully. She was conscious of sounding as she must have done when she was five years old and

205

Brigid was trying to find out why she was sulking.

'Why not send for them? It's what your father would have done. Why should you go running after people like that?' Brigid had a high opinion of the dignity and status of a Brehon.

Mara moved uneasily. It was not the way that she liked to do things usually, but there was no doubt that Brigid was right.

'Very well then,' she said in a resigned manner. 'Could you ask Cumhal to send someone?' This reminded her of the man that was usually sent on errands. 'Has Seán come back yet from Thomond?' she enquired impatiently

'Not sight, nor sound of him,' said Brigid emphatically. 'But you know our brave Seán. He was probably just about to go back when he heard of the great victory, so he decided to wait and to take part in the celebrations.'

Caireen and her son Ronan arrived in the middle of the morning, when Mara was busy teaching in the schoolhouse. The five boys all lifted their heads from their book when her shrill voice sounded from the courtyard.

'No, no, we'll show ourselves in. We're quite at home here, aren't we, Ronan?' And then a minute later, still at the same high pitch. 'What a quaint place, isn't it? Everything is so old-world, here, Ronan, isn't it? Coming here from Galway, it's like going back into the past, with almost everyone living inside their own enclosures—' There was an abrupt silence.

No doubt, thought Mara, Ronan, who was no fool, had hushed his mother. She nodded to Shane to open the door to the visitors.

'Well, what busy workers!' Caireen gave Shane a sweet smile and then bestowed another on the four boys who rose politely from their seats.

'But where is my friend Fachtnan?' she demanded. 'Not ill, I hope?'

Now why did she say that? wondered Mara. After all, there were lots of reasons why Fachtnan should not have been present: he could have been sent to fetch a book from the Brehon's house, or deliver a message to Brigid, or could be out investigating the circumstances of the murder.

'How good of you to come.' Mara seated her guests and dismissed the boys for their morning break. They would normally have a game of hurling and then a drink of buttermilk or ale and a few cakes, before coming back to resume their studies.

'Yes, I'm afraid that Fachtnan is not at all well,' she said aloud, watching mother and son carefully for any reaction.

'Ate something that disagreed with him?' shrilled Caireen. 'Well, that's boys for you! Would you like Ronan to have a look at him for you?'

'No, mother, I'm sure that's not necessary,' said Ronan quickly. 'A night's sleep had probably left him feeling a lot better.'

Once again, they seemed to know a lot about the illness that Fachtnan had suffered. Was Nuala right? Had Fachtnan been given something to make him very ill, but not to injure him in any way? And, if so, would it deter Mara from carrying out her investigation into the death of a man whom, in any case, she had begun to dislike heartily?

'And your darling baby – he is well?'

'Very well, thank you. Now I would like to ask you a few questions.'

'What a coincidence!' Caireen laughed happily and then quickly tried to turn the sound into a sob. She produced a large square of linen from her pouch and held it up, delicately touching, first one eye, and then the other. 'I, also, wanted to ask you about some matters.'

'Well, you ask first,' said Mara politely.

'I just want to know what progress has been made towards finding my husband's killer?' Caireen gave a loud, and rather unconvincing sniff. 'I understand that you felt well enough to take over the investigation yourself ... a few days ago,' she added pointedly.

'Ah,' said Mara, 'as always these matters have to remain confidential to me, until I stand up at Poulnabrone and accuse the guilty person and demand a fine.'

'Poulnabrone,' Caireen informed her son, 'is one of the quaint old-fashioned customs they have here. Instead of a proper court with judges and lawyers as we have in Galway, they all go and stand around a few huge rocks that cover a hole in the middle of a field.'

'Just so,' said Mara briskly. Ronan, she noticed, looked neither embarrassed nor interested by his mother's revelations. She rather admired his composure. He was self-possessed for his age. No doubt he was used to his mother and did not allow her to disturb him. 'There is just one question that I wish to ask you before we talk about the murder,' she went on. 'I wondered whether Malachy left a will? He made none with me, but...'

Caireen looked at Mara and then looked away. 'I'm not sure...' she began but Ronan said impatiently, 'Come on, Mother, there is no secret about it!'

He turned away from his mother and addressed Mara. 'Malachy made a will leaving to his wife Caireen his house at Caherconnell, newly built by him this year, and whatever silver and possessions were in the house at the time of his death. This will was made in Galway and drawn up by a lawyer qualified in English, and native law,' he added hastily, and Mara suppressed a smile. She did not suppose that Nuala would contest the will – though as the female heir the house and land to graze seven cows should have been hers. And if she didn't, Mara would let it pass, though she was furious that Malachy had made no provision for his only child.

'I have no interest in these things at the

moment. My whole mind is on finding the murderer and seeing that she, or he, is punished,' sighed Caireen.

'Indeed,' said Mara. A useful word, she always thought. She allowed a few seconds of respectful silence to fill the room before saying briskly, 'Now let me take you back to the morning of the eleventh of June. The best thing for me would be if you could give a picture of the house as it was just before you discovered Malachy's body ... Who was in the house? Who was where? Who was doing what...? As much as you can remember.'

'Nuala was in the herb garden,' said Ronan in an authoritative manner.

Mara nodded. 'Which part?'

'I'm not sure,' said Ronan. 'Does it matter?'

'I just wondered whether you knew because you had seen her, or because someone told you that fact,' said Mara.

'I saw her from the window of my room, but I can't remember exactly which herb bed she was weeding. Yes, I remember now: it was the camomile bed.' Ronan's voice was firm and his manner casual.

'And I was in the kitchen talking to Sadhbh,' said Caireen.

'And the other servants?'

'The men were outside, seeing to the cows and the horses, and the two girls were upstairs cleaning out our bedroom.' Caireen gave a loud sniff, no doubt to commemorate spending the night

210

with her husband.

'Well, that seems very clear.' Mara beamed at them both and made a note on the piece of vellum in front of her.

'There is just one thing that puzzles me,' she said, carefully replacing the quill in the pen holder, 'and it is this: why did you, Ronan, not come to your stepfather's aid when your mother called for help? After all,' she continued, 'her cries were loud enough to be heard by Nuala out in the garden; surely they would have reached you in your bedroom?'

'I had already left the house by then,' said Ronan, looking at her steadily.

'Going where?' Mara raised an eyebrow at him.

'Nowhere in particular, Brehon. It was a fine morning and I thought I would exercise my horse.'

'Let me take you through matters again. Ronan looked out from the window, saw Nuala weeding the camomile plants, then departed to exercise his horse, while you, Caireen, were downstairs and in the kitchen.' She turned to Caireen, looking keenly at her. 'Then you decided to see how your husband, Malachy, was getting on, so you went into the stillroom, found him on the floor, tried to revive him with some water – at the same time shrieking for help – is that the way that things happened?'

'Yes, that sounds right,' said Caireen, stealing a sideways glance at her son.

'I'm just a little puzzled.' murmured Mara. 'When I spoke to Nuala a few days ago, she said that she had been weeding the patch of wound-wort and had only just moved to the camomile bed when she heard Caireen's shrieks.'

'Perhaps I was mistaken.' Ronan sounded indifferent.

'One of them looks so like the other,' suggested Caireen helpfully.

Mara waited for Ronan to speak, but when he said nothing she said quietly, 'Hardly; one has blue flowers and the other pink.'

'Of course, it would be difficult for Nuala to remember exactly how long it was that she had been weeding the camomile when she was summoned to her father's last moments,' suggested Ronan. He did not appear to be perturbed by the questioning. He rose to his feet. 'Perhaps if that is all then, Mother, we had better be getting back. There is much to arrange. We are having the wake for Malachy tonight and will be burying him tomorrow.'

'Oh!' Mara was startled. She had been so immersed in the reasons for this murder that she had almost forgotten the death itself and all the ceremonies associated with it. The wake was always a most important event where a vigil was held around the dead relative's coffin. Refreshments, sometimes even singing and storytelling, took place during the whole night and all relatives, friends and neighbours were expected to attend. 'I so regret that I cannot be present,' she said hastily. 'You will understand as I have so recently risen from childbirth...'

It was lucky that the law school party was not this evening. That would never do. As it happened, she did have a good excuse and Oisín and Sorcha could represent her. After all, Oisín was Malachy's cousin, and his heir. She, Brigid and Eileen could take care of the children between them. Ardal, of course, would accompany Nuala. Thinking of Nuala made her remember something.

'I wonder, Ronan, would you do me one favour before you go. Fachtnan has been very unwell. He was vomiting heavily yesterday evening after he came back. The vomiting was eventually stopped by a dose of skullcap, but perhaps you would check him this morning and see whether he is well enough to be allowed up.'

This would be useful, she thought, as she courteously invited Caireen to go and sit in the shade of the apple tree while waiting for her son. It would save Fachtnan the embarrassment of having Nuala in his bedroom once more, and also it would give her the opportunity of a private talk with Ronan afterwards.

'You go in; I'll wait outside,' she said politely. She went into the younger boys' room and sat on Shane's bed. Her legs were beginning to remind her that she had given birth only ten days ago.

Ronan did not spend long with Fachtnan. Mara could hear the murmur of voices, but not what was being said.

213

'He doesn't seem too bad,' said Ronan when he came out, shutting the door firmly behind him. 'He could rise from his bed if he wishes. A low diet for a few days and then he should be back to normal.'

'What do you think it was?' asked Mara in anxious motherly tones. 'Was it something that he ate?' Resolutely she did not move from her position on Shane's bed, so Ronan had to stand awkwardly, half in the hall and half in the younger boys' bedroom.

Ronan paused. 'Possibly,' he said, in such reserved tones that it had obviously occurred to him that Fachtnan had eaten cakes and accepted wine at Caherconnell yesterday afternoon.

'Nuala wondered whether someone could have deliberately tried to make him ill, not to kill him, of course...'

'Unlikely,' said Ronan briefly, and then gave a tolerant smile. 'Nuala has an instinct for dramatization,' he added scornfully.

'Yes, but if that were true, what could he have been given that would cause such violent vomiting for a few hours? Perhaps you could think of a few herbs?' persisted Mara.

'I have really no idea,' said Ronan impatiently, 'and now, if you don't mind, I'll collect my mother as we must be going.'

And so they were off, refusing a belated and somewhat insincere offer of hospitality.

'Strange,' said Mara, half to herself and half to Fachtnan, as she watched the dust cloud

214

diminish on the road to Kilcorney crossroads. 'You would have thought that a young man who has just qualified as a physician would be able to come up with the name of some herb that might have been used to make you so ill. I would wager that Nuala ran through about twenty in her mind before coming up with alder buckthorn.'

'I wouldn't think that he is stupid, though,' said Fachtnan thoughtfully. 'He gave me a very good examination and asked all sorts of questions, which showed that he understood what happened to me yesterday – the faintness and the purging and everything.'

'That's what makes it even more interesting,' said Mara with a smile. 'Now, I think that you could get up if you feel like it. Go outside and sit in the shade. Don't eat much – perhaps just a little milk.'

'Brigid, can you remember yesterday afternoon, before Fachtnan returned, did anyone come to the law school? Blár O'Connor, or anyone else.'

'Not Blár,' said Brigid, rapidly stirring one pot and then tipping some onions into another. 'I can't rightly say, Brehon. I don't remember anyone.'

'There was Nuala,' suggested Nessa, chopping some carrots vigorously.

'Oh, I don't count Nuala,' said Brigid impatiently. 'Cut these carrots a bit thinner, my girl. Big chunks like that will never cook.'

'But nobody else?'

'You could ask Cumhal,' suggested Brigid, sweeping a platterful of carrots into her pot. 'I wasn't around here too much. I went over to have a look at the baby.'

So Fachtnan could have taken in the poison – if it was poison – when he visited Caherconnell, but someone who knew the ways of the law school could also have guessed that the cupful of ale left on the kitchen table would have been for the boy who had not yet turned up for his supper. That meant that Nuala was under suspicion – but would she have done this to Fachtnan? Nuala adored Fachtnan and had done so for the last couple of years. Would she have made him as ill as that – no matter how angry she was? Mara found that it was easier to think of Nuala as angry at the rejection of her marriage proposal than to think of Nuala as fearful of discovery that she had been involved in Malachy's death. She would take her mind off these matters for the moment, she thought, and have five minutes with her baby before going back into the schoolhouse.

Little Cormac was wide awake. His slate-blue eyes were fixed on the object held in Eileen's hand. It was a cat, beautifully carved from wood and wearing a leather collar to which was stitched a tiny brass bell. Each time the cat was waved the bell chimed, and the baby's head followed the delicate clear sound.

216

'How lovely!' exclaimed Mara dropping on her knees beside Eileen and holding out her arms for the baby. 'Where did you get that?'

'Blár O'Connor brought it yesterday afternoon,' explained Eileen. 'I was walking down the road to the law school when he came along on his horse. He said that he found it on top of a shelf in his workshop and he guessed that his son had carved it for your baby. Look, it's a bigger version of the one on the cradle.'

'So it is.' Mara took the wooden toy and admired it, stroking the sleek back and smiling at the roughness of the tiny whiskers.

'He's so clever, little Cormac,' said Eileen proudly. 'He's so alert for his age.' She took the toy back from Mara and set the bell jingling again, and once more the baby's head moved.

'And to think that he is not two weeks old yet,' she exclaimed.

Mara held the baby close, touching the velvet cheek with her lips and rocking him in her arms. Cormac twisted his head towards her and began to cry.

'He's hungry, better give him back to me.' Eileen stretched out her arms and Mara reluctantly put the baby back. In any case, it was time for her to return to work.

The five boys were in their places when she came in, and as soon as she had settled herself in her chair the door opened and Fachtnan, looking a little pale, entered.

'I'm feeling much better,' he said hastily, 'so I thought I would come and join you. Are you going to discuss the murder?'

'I think we will.' Mara immediately abandoned her plans. 'Aidan, perhaps you can do the writing for us. Take a fresh stick of charcoal.' She waited until Aidan was standing beside the board, which Cumhal kept well whitewashed, before she went on. 'Now what's the first thing to do?'

'List of possible suspects.' Moylan managed to get this in before any of the others.

'What are the most usual motives for a secret and unlawful killing?' asked Mara looking around.

'Easy! A wish for gain, anger, fear and revenge.' They all chimed this in chorus. A lot of the work at the law school was memorizing these wisdom texts, many of which, optimistically, sometimes, began with the word 'easy'.

'Put in the relations first, Aidan, these will cover the "wish for gain" I would think, wouldn't you, Brehon?' Hugh looked at her for approval, and at her nod Aidan began to write on the whitened board in his large, scrawling hand.

'Does Nuala get anything, Brehon?' Aidan hesitated with charcoal in hand.

'Nothing worth having,' said Fachtnan firmly.

'What!' exclaimed Enda. 'But she is the female heir. She must get the house and enough land to graze seven cows.'

'Apparently, Malachy made a will leaving his

218

new – well, half-new – house to Caireen, and all the possessions in it,' said Mara, looking thoughtfully at Fachtnan. He flushed and looked away, and she decided not to ask him how he knew. Undoubtedly Nuala, in her honest way, had told him all the facts when she proposed marriage to him. 'I'm not sure that the will, made by somebody in Galway, is actually valid,' she continued. 'And the house is the same house, just extended, and a will made in the kingdom of the Burren should have been made by a lawyer qualified in Brehon law.'

'I'd say that Nuala would be quite happy to leave it as it is,' said Fachtnan.

Enda nodded and said, 'So next we have Oisín. How much clan land does he get, Brehon?'

'Twenty acres of mature oaks,' said Mara steadily, and forced herself to add, 'and these would be valuable to him for making casks: something that he has to buy at the moment.'

'Well, I think that Nuala should be on the list if Oisín is on – it would be about the same amount of land.' Shane was great friends with Oisín and enjoyed many a game of chess with him.

'Well, I agree with Shane,' said Aidan, and then when Fachtnan said nothing he wrote up Nuala's name.

'Now,' continued Aidan, moving to a new part of the board and writing the word ANGER with heavy emphasis, 'who do we have for here?'

219

'In this case, I think we should have "Anger" and "Revenge" together,' said Enda.

'You should have said that first.' Aidan carefully wiped the word with the damp sponge from the windowsill, patted it dry with a piece of linen from his pouch and then wrote the two words.

'I'm afraid that I would put Nuala on this list, also,' said Enda with an apologetic glance at Fachtnan.

'And Murrough, because of Rafferty,' said Moylan hurriedly.

'And Blár O'Connor because of his son,' said Shane.

'What do you mean by "dispossession" and "greed"?' Hugh looked puzzled as he read the entry for Nuala.

Aidan replied briefly, 'She was kicked out of the house and Malachy was trying to take her farm at Rathborney away from her.' He then added a few words to Nuala's entry, wrote the next two names, and stood back to allow everyone to read the board.

GREED
Daughter: Nuala – land to graze seven cows
Wife: Caireen – house
Stepson: Ronan – physician's business
Inheritor of remaining clan land: Oisín – 20 acres of oaks

ANGER & REVENGE

Nuala – dispossession, and anger at her father's greed

Murrough – poisoning of his dog

Blár O'Connor – death of his son, Bláreen

'I've just thought of something interesting,' said Enda. 'I wonder if you would think of it as being a possible motive, Brehon? If Caireen managed to get you to convict someone, say for instance, Nuala, not only would she get her house, and her son get the position of physician in the Burren, but she would also get the fine. And that would be...' he paused and made a quick calculation. 'I make it forty-two *séts* doubled for the secrecy – that's eighty-four – plus another seven for Malachy's honour price, so that's ninety-one *séts* or forty-five and a half ounces of silver. Now gentlemen,' he looked around at his fellow scholars, 'and lady,' he made a courtly bow in Mara's direction, 'is, or is not, Caireen a woman who might commit murder for the sake of a house, a position for her darling son, land for seven cows and a nice little fortune of forty-five and a half ounces of silver?'

'She'd look pretty stupid, though, if she were convicted of the murder,' said Shane bluntly. 'Then she'd be the one that would have to pay the fine.'

'She is stupid,' said Enda. His very blue eyes

221

sparkled. 'But who would the fine go to if she was convicted of the murder?'

'Who do you think?' Mara watched him with interest.

'Nuala?' asked Fachtnan hopefully.

'No,' said Enda. 'I wouldn't think so. A daughter can only inherit if the father mentions her in his will – and then only the limited ... I know,' he suddenly burst out, 'of course it goes to the nearest male relation in his clan.'

'So your son-in-law, Oisín, would be the one who would get the forty-five and a half ounces of silver.' Hugh beamed congratulations at Mara.

And he is certainly a man who would make very good use of that substantial sum of money, thought Mara. Aloud she said, 'That's right,' in as matter-of-fact a way as she could. It was important that the boys considered all aspects of the case and were not embarrassed about discussing a relative. She looked back at the board and their eyes followed hers.

'So now we have six suspects,' mused Fachtnan. 'What about "fear" without "revenge", Brehon? Have we anyone for that?'

'I don't think so, do you?' Mara looked around at her scholars.

'Usually a case of blackmail, isn't it?' reflected Moylan. 'I've certainly never picked up a hint of anything like that to do with Malachy; has anyone else?'

Heads were shaken. Nuala might be one to

talk to about this, if she weren't so prickly and bad-humoured at the moment, thought Mara, but decided not to mention her name. The scholars had enough to exercise their brains for the moment.

'There's something very interesting about this list,' she said looking at the board. 'Can you think what it might be, Fachtnan?'

'No, Brehon.' He shook his head, looking at her in a bewildered way.

'Well, that was hardly a fair question,' she said hastily, 'because I have information that you don't have. Five of the six people on that board had access to Fachtnan, yesterday afternoon – could have made him very ill, could have tried to poison him, in fact.'

'Caireen and Ronan at Caherconnell,' said Hugh.

'And Blár O'Connor passed by yesterday afternoon with a rattle for my little son, and Nuala came to talk to Eileen about herbs. Oisín, of course, lives here. The only one that could not have been guilty of trying to poison Fachtnan was Murrough.' As she spoke she was conscious of a feeling of thankfulness. She was fond of Murrough and they shared a love of the great dogs that he bred.

Aidan's jaw dropped. 'Oh, Brehon, I forgot to tell you,' he said. 'Murrough came over yesterday afternoon with a message for you to be careful not to let Bran run free in Croagh South, as the shepherd has laid bait there stuffed with

223

wolfsbane.'

'So each one of our six suspects could also have attempted to murder Fachtnan,' said Hugh with interest.

'Or at least frighten us off,' amended Shane.

Thirteen

Uraicecht Becc

(Small Primer)

The physician has an honour price of seven séts and this does not increase for any reason as a master of the profession has the same honour price as an ordinary physician.

Before a physician is allowed to practise in a kingdom, he has to have public recognition. This is bestowed by an examination of the training and proficiency by two recognized physicians.

A fine is extracted if the physician does not cure a curable illness, either through lack of knowledge or malice.

The sun was still hot by the time for the midsummer supper arrived, but it had moved from the south to the west, and Mara's garden, bright with lilies, peonies and roses, was now patched with blobs of shade.

Brigid had laid out the supper on three long linen-draped trestle tables in front of the east-facing Brehon's house – the food arranged in

225

baskets and platters down the centre. Domhnall and Aislinn were wild with excitement, shrieking to their father as each new item was laid on the tables. Mara, holding Cormac for a few precious minutes before the guests arrived, smiled at their excitement.

'It's all the colours of the rainbow! Green peas, red strawberries, blueberries!' Aislinn, like her mother, had a great eye for colour, though Domhnall, who was growing fast and eating hugely, was more excited by the long coils of sausages and the mounds of cakes of all sizes and shapes. They both wandered up and down, waiting impatiently for the guests to come back from the meadows and the rocky fields of the Burren. Eventually they appeared, looking like a flock of white birds in their snowy *léinte*. As they came nearer, Mara could see something else and she smiled as Aislinn screamed, 'Look, look *Mamó*, see what they're wearing!'

'What a sight!' murmured Mara to Eileen, as she came over and held out her arms for the baby.

Each of the boys and girls wore a garland of summer flowers: harebells, ragged robin, pincushion flowers, hawkweeds, foxgloves, orchids and hedge roses were strung together to hang around their necks. The damp meadows as well as the stony grykes had all been robbed to decorate the young revellers. Mairéad O'Lochlainn even wore a crown of tiny butterfly orchids, the snowy-white of the blooms contrasting well

226

with her head of magnificent red curls. As they came down the road, linked arm to arm, they all sang lustily the ancient midsummer bonfire-night song:

Choose the hazel of the rocks,
Choose the willow of the stream,
Choose the alder of the marshes,
Choose the birch of the waterfall,
Choose the rowan of the shade,
Choose the yew of resilience
Choose the elm of the moorland.

Almost all the girls and some of the boys bore the flowers of the yarrow plant in their hands, playfully swiping at each other with the stems. Traditionally the yarrow was supposed to protect against illness in the coming year, but it had other uses, too. Mara had no doubt that these stems would be carefully preserved until bonfire time. Elderly country people told their grandchildren that if you saw the face of a loved one as the yarrow flared up in the flames, it would mean that a marriage would take place before midsummer's day came around again. Touching a loved one beforehand with the stem was supposed to help that process.

'Look, *Mamó.*' Domhnall and Aislinn came running over. In the space of a couple of minutes Sorcha, with her clever fingers, had made each a garland and was now busy twisting some long stems of gillyflowers together to make one for

227

little Manus. On an impulse, Mara bent down and picked some soft-stemmed buttercups, piercing them with a fingernail and threading them together to make a small crown for Cormac.

'My little prince,' she murmured as she handed him over to Eileen, and, accompanied by her two grandchildren, went down the road to greet her guests. Mairéad O'Lochlainn, she noticed, had already whacked Enda three times with her yarrow stem. Young love, she thought tolerantly, and then her eyes went anxiously to Nuala.

Alone among all the young people, Nuala had not gone to the trouble of making a garland, but had stuck a few of the bright yellow flowers, known as devil's toenails, among her dark braids. Fachtnan was, rather awkwardly, holding a well-made garland of lady's bedstraw dangling from one hand, but Nuala was walking fast, well ahead of him. When he saw Nessa, Brigid's young assistant, he gave it to her with what looked like a sigh of relief. Nessa giggled and turned red, and then caught Brigid's eye and went back to frying the sausages on top of the small bonfire, safely walled off inside a circular wall of stones that Cumhal had made for outdoor cooking. Nuala glared at Nessa, scowled and then turned her gaze away from the sight of Fachtnan's garland dangling around the neck of another girl, and looked resolutely across the clints towards the distant bulk of Mullaghmore. Nuala was, obviously, not going to forgive

228

Fachtnan very easily for turning down her offer of marriage.

Was she truly in love with Fachtnan, wondered Mara, watching the girl's face with what she hoped was concealed anxiety? She greeted all of her young guests, admired their garlands, directed them to places at table, saw that there was plenty to eat and drink for everyone, but all of the time her mind dwelt on Nuala. What had prompted that sudden suggestion of marriage, she wondered? Was it something that Nuala really wanted, or did she, perhaps, just see it as a way of getting her hands quickly on her property at Rathborney? It had been obvious for a long time that Nuala adored Fachtnan, but it was more like the hero worship of a young girl for an older and very kind boy, than a truly adult love. Even when she treated him at a time when it looked as though Fachtnan's life might be in danger, there didn't seem any of the anguish that might have been expected – Nuala had been cool, competent, full of helpful suggestions – she may well have saved his life by her skill, but nothing in her manner showed even affection.

She turned to Mairéad O'Lochlainn and Enda – well they were both obviously deeply in love with each other. They could hardly have sat much closer and they continually touched, even if it was mock tussles and teasing. Enda would have to get himself a legal position as an *aigne* before he could afford to marry, but in the meantime they were going to have fun together for perhaps the last evening before Enda returned to his home.

It was the same with Saoirse O'Brien and the eldest O'Connor boy. There would be nothing to impede that marriage and the betrothal would probably be announced soon, now that Teige was back from the wars. The sooner, the better, thought Mara, as Saoirse imprinted a passionate kiss on her betrothed's lips. That would be a very suitable match between the eldest daughter and the eldest son of two neighbouring chieftains, she thought, as she carried down a plate of cakes to where Enda was sitting. She placed herself on the bench beside him and engaged him in conversation about the midsummer customs in Mayo. But her thoughts returned to Nuala; what was she thinking, watching these others? After a few minutes, Mara returned Enda to Mairéad and beckoned to Nuala, who approached slowly and reluctantly.

'Go and have a chat with Cuan,' she whispered in the girl's ear. 'He doesn't know anyone other than you very well and he looks a bit left out.' Mara had been very fond of Cuan's father, and sometimes felt slightly conscience-stricken that she was not doing more to try to free the boy from the constant supervision of his mother.

A pity that Cuan is not a bit brighter, she thought regretfully. He was a man of property and wealth, with a tower house just beside Nuala's property at Rathborney, and would make a great match for any girl, but not for

230

Nuala, unfortunately. Nuala was clever and Cuan was not. Nothing is worse than an inequality of mind, she thought, looking back at her first marriage to Dualta, the young law scholar who had attracted her when she was Nuala's age. Dualta had not been bright enough to qualify as a lawyer, but had been content to live on his wife's industry, and to allow her to finance his drinking habit at the local alehouses. She smiled slightly to herself when she thought of her divorce, conducted by herself and cleverly based on an obscure point in the Brehon law system. No man can speak of his wife's lovemaking habits between the sheets, said the law, and that was the law that Dualta had broken, drunkenly boasting of his clever wife. The law case had never been spoken of to Sorcha and Mara hoped that her daughter was unaware of it. Sorcha, gentle and sweet-natured, needed to be protected. Hopefully, Oisín would prove to be a faithful and good husband.

Nuala, a very different person to Sorcha, went across to Cuan obediently, but she did not seem to be making much effort to engage him in conversation – she just sat down and stared ahead glumly. Mara saw young Cuan make a few attempts to talk, and then flush painfully as it was obvious that Nuala was not listening.

'How are you, Cuan, and how is your mother?' Mara came to the rescue. Nuala, to her annoyance, immediately slipped away.

'She's well, Brehon, we're all well.' Cuan was

231

still flushed and embarrassed.

'Don't take any notice of Nuala,' said Mara consolingly. 'She's going through a very bad time. It's been quite a shock to her – you've heard of the death of Malachy the physician, her father, haven't you?'

'Yes.' Cuan lengthened the word, sounding rather dubious, and then added with a shrewdness which surprised Mara, 'But they weren't on good terms, were they? Wasn't there some sort of talk that Malachy was trying to take away from her the property that Toin left her in Rathborney?'

'That's right.' Mara was still bemused by the change in Cuan. She had thought him slightly simple-minded up to now. Perhaps wealth and freedom from his father had suited him. Possibly she had misjudged his mother. Maybe Cuan had begun to take up the reins of government of his lands and his silver mine. There was a note of authority in his voice now.

'He wasn't a very nice man, anyway,' continued Cuan, still with that ease of manner which had surprised her. 'There's an old man that lives up beyond my place, in Lochánn, just above the sea at Fanore. Do you know him? Padraig O'Connor. He has a fleet of fishing boats...'

'Yes, I do,' said Mara with an eye on the top table. Aidan and Moylan were getting wilder by the minute, and Enda and Mairéad had started to kiss each other in a very passionate way. As for Saoirse and the O'Connor boy, well, she wasn't

232

sure what was going on under the table ... Her presence would, she was sure, calm matters, but she did not like to abandon Cuan so soon after he had been left by Nuala.

'Well, poor old Padraig was getting a bit absentminded, nothing too much, just searching for the odd word and forgetting a few things – still pretty shrewd about giving orders to his boat captains, though – so he sent for Malachy, and Malachy came and gave him a flask of some mixture, and told him to take it every morning and every evening.'

'And it did him no good, I suppose.' Mara scanned her mind for some excuse to leave Cuan and return to her unruly scholars. Even the gentle, shy Hugh was getting overexcited and shouting remarks to Nessa.

'It was not just that,' said Cuan earnestly. 'It seemed to make him worse. I told him to stop taking it, but he said that he wouldn't like to do that – especially when the man went to so much trouble as to keep coming out and visiting him.'

'Yes, the country people are like that, aren't they, always so courteous.' Mara got to her feet, sending a long hard stare in the direction of Aidan, who had just got on top of the bench and appeared to be about to climb on to the table. 'What is that boy up to?' she asked, and then added rapidly, 'Excuse me, Cuan, I must go over there.'

Perhaps I'll send Oisín over to talk to Cuan; he'll be very interested when he hears about the

233

silver mine in the mountain above Rathborney, and also the silversmith business in Galway. He'll probably wangle an invitation to the tower house, thought Mara, a little maliciously. Let Oisín cross swords with Cuan's redoubtable mother. That would be an interesting encounter.

And then, suddenly, she stopped thinking of Cuan, and of Nuala, and of Oisín. A horse, ridden fast down the road, had pulled up at the gate. Mara recognized the rider. It was one of Turlough's men – a young relative – one of the O'Briens of Thomond.

With a murmured word of excuse, she got up and walked slowly towards the gate. Cumhal was there, he had greeted the man, and then something about Cumhal's shocked face made her stop for a moment. Was it bad news?

Her legs weakened beneath her. Cumhal, never the most religious of men, had lifted his right hand, touching forehead, breast and then both of his shoulders. He had made the sign of the cross. But why? In ordinary conversation, away from a church ceremony, there was only one reason for this. Cumhal had just been told of a death.

Instantly Mara saw it all. The triumphant journey home. And then a sudden attack. Perhaps the Great Earl had not gone back to Kildare with his tail between his legs, had lain in wait and tackled his enemy, O'Brien of Thomond, once again. This time the outcome might have been fatal...

234

Mara stayed very still, her hand on the stout trunk of an apple tree. She could not move. All her courage had ebbed away.

Cumhal's eyes met hers. Swiftly he left the new arrival and walked towards her. He had been her father's servant and then steward and farm manager since before she was born. He and Brigid had cared for and loved the small motherless daughter of their master, the Brehon of the Burren. He knew her well, could read her expressions, and he almost ran the last few steps.

'My lord is well, Brehon,' he said reassuringly. 'He sends his greetings.' And then he lowered his voice, stood very near to her and said quietly, for her ear only, 'There is some news that concerns us all here. Would you like to talk to the messenger indoors? These young people will be off to the bonfire at Noughaval soon and I'll go along to make sure that all is right with them.'

'Thank you, Cumhal,' said Mara steadily. There were only a few days to go to the end of term; the boys were excited; even Shane and Hugh were getting quite wild, daringly flicking yarrow stems at Nessa and Áine. Sorcha was sweet but lacked authority and Oisín might well decide to go off on his own affairs. It would be a comfort to her if Cumhal went, also.

What was the news? she wondered, walking steadily beside Cumhal. She greeted the young man with courtesy, inviting him to have a cup of wine with her.

He said nothing until after Cumhal had left and then sipped appreciatively at the wine.

'You have news for me, is that right?' Mara could see that he was trying to put off the moment. Her heart sank again. Was Turlough wounded?

'Well, it was my lord, the king, himself, who saw it first...'

'Saw what?' asked Mara.

'Oh, I thought that Cumhal would have told you that.' Young O'Brien had the air of wishing that someone else could tell the whole of his story, but he struggled on, 'Saw the cob, I mean.'

'The cob!'

'That's right, my lord said that it was the cob from the law school, that he would swear to that black and white face.'

'The cob,' said Mara again, but this time in a low voice. Her quick brain instantly knew the rest of the news. The cob, a handsome, heavily built riding horse, was usually reserved for Cumhal's use, but occasionally and reluctantly he lent it to Seán when his worker had a long journey ahead.

'Go on,' she said.

'Well, the poor beast was glad to see us, though there was plenty to eat where we found him – it was just next to the abbey of Emly – next to the graveyard, in fact. He had broken reins trailing – it looked as though someone tied him up – perhaps while having a meal or something.'

He stopped, but she said nothing so he continued with a grave face.

'A few of the men had a hunt around to see if they could find the rider – we thought that he might have been thrown and perhaps injured – even killed. It wasn't long before they came across him.'

Mara nodded. There would be a body; she had guessed that instantly.

'What we hadn't expected was that not only was the man dead...'

'But that he had been dead for over a week,' she interrupted.

He bowed his head with a look of surprise on his face, but he did not question her.

Of course, thought Mara. Seán was the messenger who was sent for Malachy to attend the childbirth on that morning of the eleventh of June. He had seen something – someone – doing something odd; someone in a place where they should not be; someone who roused his slow mind to suspicion; whatever it was, it had happened when he had ridden that road through Kilcorney and on to Caherconnell on the morning when she was giving birth. Seán, being Seán, would not have been able to keep his mouth shut. He had hinted, said something; perhaps asked for money. How had it been done? wondered Mara. A simple gift of food, something to eat on the journey. Sooner or later he would eat it and then the fatal poison would begin to work. He would have been discovered earlier if he had eaten it more quickly. Useless, now, to wish that he had thrown it in the ditch for the crows to find!

'He was just about recognizable,' said the young man simply. 'There was no sign of violence, but in this warm weather, it was hard to know what he had died of. But died he did! My lord got the abbot of Emly to bury him in the graveyard. He had remembered that you told him the man had no family.'

'No, he had no family.' Mara said no more. She did not wish to go into Seán's history. He had been found as a tiny child wandering along on the road near Kinvarra on the way to Galway. Her father, a compassionate man, had brought him back to Cahermacnaghten and he had been brought up by the elderly widow of one of the labourers there. Somehow he had never fitted in. He had been lazy, awkward and unreliable. Brigid and Cumhal would mourn him in a conventional manner, but they would not be deeply sorry. The people of the kingdom of the Burren would hardly notice his absence. Seán had been a misfit. Money and status was very important to him, as he knew that he lacked the status that family would give him in a Gaelic community. Was that his undoing? Did he go to the murderer and say: 'I saw you at Caherconnell – it was just at the time that Malachy the physician was murdered, wasn't it? Does the Brehon know that

238

you were there?' Poor Seán, he would not have done it subtly. He was not a man of brains, or even a man of integrity.

But she, Mara, Brehon of the Burren, had to make sure that his murderer would be brought to justice – the case needed solving just as much as the case of the secret and unlawful killing of Malachy, physician of the kingdom of the Burren.

'May we offer you a night's lodging?' she asked the young man, but was not surprised when he shook his head cheerfully.

'No, Brehon,' he said. 'I shall spend the night at Inchiquin. It's only an hour's journey from here. My brother serves the *tánaiste* there.'

Mara nodded. Conor, Turlough's eldest son and heir, had his household at Inchiquin. The young messenger would enjoy the midsummer festivities in the company of members of his own family.

'And on my way I must drop into Teige O'Brien's place at Lemeanah – the dead man had a letter in his pouch addressed to the king. It was from Teige and I bear an answer to that. And that reminds me – this satchel was lying beside him. My lord told me to give it to you.' He handed over the leather satchel. It was bleached and puckered as it had lain out in the rain, sunlight and night dews for ten days, but the straps were still buckled. He undid them neatly and showed her the contents. A change of clothing, and a linen cloth that showed the

239

remains of food – small shreds of meat and a pungent smell of horseradish. There was also a large, flat, well-padded leather pouch.

Mara took the pouch – she recognized it as one from the schoolhouse. She opened it. As she had expected, it was filled with the examination papers. She recognized Shane's neat writing on the uppermost page and put the papers aside for the moment. This was something that she could deal with afterwards. First must come the solving of the murder. She stared at the cloth in a puzzled manner. It was not the usual piece of coarse hemp that Brigid used to wrap the boys' food. This was a carefully hemmed piece of linen, the slanting stitches small and perfect – more like a fine handkerchief than anything else. Not something that Seán would have owned.

'My lord thought you would be interested to see the satchel. He thought it meant that the man had been poisoned. Anyone who struck down a man and killed him would have seized the satchel and fled, or at least opened the buckles to see what had been inside. My lord thought that Seán had died there, by himself.'

And then, with a bow, he was gone. Mara spent a while in the quiet room of her house, thinking through the implications of this latest death – murder, she told herself, and she was as sure as if she had witnessed the horrifying, degrading death of the man who had swallowed a fatal dose of wolfsbane. It would have been a terrible death, and a death unsoothed by the presence of family, friends or clergy. A death of terror, no doubt. Seán was not intelligent, but even he would recognize the fatal signs. He would have known that he was about to die just as Malachy had died.

So who could Seán have seen? There were the six suspects: Caireen and her son Ronan, Nuala – all of these were present at Caherconnell when the fatal dose had been put into Malachy's brandy glass.

And then Blár O'Connor had been on his way past the house towards Glenslade – and so had Oisín, her son-in-law and Malachy's heir. And Murrough of the Wolfhounds lived close by.

But which of those six suspects could have handed Seán the fatal food or drink that had killed him?

And what about the man who had sent Seán on that errand to Thomond? Why had he done that? Was it just the bumptiousness of a young and untried man? And yet it was strange. What was the rush? After all, she had been expected to recover and to take the reins into her own hands within days. Why had the examination papers been despatched so hurriedly to Thomond? Was it an excuse to get Seán out of the way? And if it were, what possible reason could he have for this action?

Fourteen

Heptad 3

A woman may divorce her husband on the grounds of:
1. If he repudiates her for another woman.
2. If he fails to support her.
3. If he spreads a false story about her.
4. If he circulates a satire about her.
5. If he has tricked her into marriage by sorcery.
6. If he strikes a blow which leaves a blemish.
7. If he fails to maintain a child of the marriage according to its status.

'So what we have to do now is to trace poor Seán's last movements while he was still in the kingdom of the Burren.' Mara looked around at her scholars. They were quite subdued this morning. Seán, after all, had been part of the law school for as long as any of them could remember. There was a certain tension – or was it fear? – in the air of the schoolhouse this morning when she had broken the news. They had come in exuberantly, still excited by the fun of bonfire night and now they looked at each other from the corners of their eyes – subdued by the near presence of death.

'On the other hand,' continued Mara, 'I wonder whether I should ask you to do any more investigating. The murderer is out there and still has murder in his heart. You are my responsibility and I must not allow you to run any risk.'

'So you think that Seán was murdered because he knew something?' asked Enda alertly.

'I can see no other reason,' said Mara sadly.

'But how could he?' Hugh sounded puzzled. 'How could he work it out if we can't?'

'He wasn't too bright, was Seán,' supplemented Moylan, and then flushed a bright red, looking confused and embarrassed. Hugh gave him a reproving look and moved a little to the side, as if to distance himself from this scholar who lacked discretion.

'I think that we have to treat this case as if the dead man were not someone who lived and worked in our premises. Here in this schoolhouse we can say things that we would not say outside of it.' Mara had noted the blush and the reaction of the others and knew that the boys had to be enabled to treat this murder as objectively as possible.

'Of course, the fact that he was not too bright may have led him into danger,' said Fachtnan dispassionately. 'I can just see Seán going up to someone and whispering in his ear, "I saw you put the wolfsbane into Malachy's glass" or even, perhaps, saying, "By the way, what were you

243

doing at Caherconnell on the morning when Malachy was killed?" – or some such sentence. A clever person might realize the risk of saying something like that, but Séan would not stop to think.'

'Well done, Fachtnan,' said Mara approvingly. 'You put that very well.'

'But was he near Caherconnell on that morning?' Hugh still looked puzzled.

'I don't know...' began Mara and then suddenly she thought of something. Brigid's voice, raised in anger, was clearly to be heard, telling Nessa not to empty the dirty water outside the kitchen door but to take it across the yard and pour it into the sink – that hole filled with stones that Cumhal dug every year for the disposal of waste water.

'Shane would you ask Brigid if she could spare a minute?' she said rapidly. Brigid would be delighted to be asked to help in the investigation and Nessa would be spared a prolonged scolding. The girl was willing, but, like poor Seán, not too bright.

Brigid's colour was still high, when she followed Shane into the schoolhouse, but she looked pleased when Hugh politely brought a chair for her and all the scholars turned eager faces in her direction.

'We're discussing the death of poor Seán, Brigid,' said Mara. 'This is in confidence, and it would be best not to talk about it outside this schoolhouse—'

244

'*My right hand raised to God on high; cross my heart and hope to die,*' said Brigid, rapidly crossing herself.

'It's a matter of trying to see whether there was any connection between Malachy's death and Seán's death,' explained Mara, ignoring Moylan who was doing a clever imitation of Brigid for Aidan's benefit.

Brigid turned an attentive face towards her as Mara continued, 'And I just wondered, Brigid, if you could tell us who was sent to summon Malachy when I was in childbirth? Was it Seán?'

'God bless you, Brehon, you're quite right. I never thought of that. Of course it was Seán. Was that why the poor fellow was killed? Did he see something? Well, the Lord have mercy on him, poor harmless creature! I'll tell you what, Brehon; I'd give that murderer something to remember – to kill a poor fellow like Seán that never did a bad turn to anyone.'

'Brigid, Seán may have died because he spoke to the murderer about that morning,' said Mara solemnly, wishing that she had handled this differently. Brigid was hot-tempered and impulsive. 'I am relying on you not to mention this to anyone, except to your husband, Cumhal, of course.'

'Not ... a ... word,' said Brigid emphatically. 'Now, if you've finished with me, Brehon, I'll get back to my work. Goodness knows what those girls will get up to if I don't keep an eye on them. That bonfire night seems to have addled the few wits they possess.'

'Nessa was having fun!' said Moylan mischievously. 'Hopping over the embers with—' Then he stopped and put his hand across his mouth theatrically.

'I'll give her something better to think of ... embers, indeed,' said Brigid, shooting through the door so rapidly that Hugh, who had risen to open it, was left with his mouth open.

'Now she won't think any more about murders and small matters like that,' explained Moylan with a grin at his fellow scholars, as Brigid's voice sounded from the yard.

Mara repressed a smile. Moylan was quick-witted. Hopefully, next year, he would settle down to using these wits to master the Brehon law! At the moment he was going through a silly phase, nudging Aidan to point out his joke. Aidan, to Mara's surprise, did not respond. In fact, he had been looking gloomy all of the morning. Perhaps it was Seán's death that had upset him, she thought, dismissing the boy from her mind. She had more important matters to think about.

'What I said to Brigid, I say to all of you,' she said seriously. 'Whoever murdered Malachy, and whatever was the motive, this murderer is willing to murder again to preserve their safety. I don't want anyone even hinting a suspicion. In fact, I think that though it will take a little longer, I would prefer you all to keep together in a group if I ask you to do any investigating.'

246

'Where was Seán going, Brehon?' asked Hugh.

'Boetius sent him to Thomond with our examination papers,' said Aidan. 'That's what he told me anyway.' He spoke absentmindedly, as though some unpleasant thought had come to him.

'Can anyone remember which day that was?' Mara looked from Fachtnan to Enda, but both shook their heads.

'I didn't even know that he had done that, Brehon,' said Enda, and Fachtnan nodded in agreement.

It was strange that Aidan seemed to have been more in the confidence of young MacClancy than were the two older boys. Why on earth had Boetius revealed his plans to the silliest boy in the law school?

'It was the day that we had sea trout for dinner,' said Aidan, still with a slight frown between his brows. His adolescent skin, which had improved in the last few months, seemed to have erupted badly this morning, thought Mara, feeling slightly worried about him. He had shadows beneath his eyes as if he had not slept well and he kept yawning and blinking in a nervous way.

The sea trout seemed to trigger a memory.

'I remember them – *ionach*!' exclaimed Moylan.

'The day that we built the tree house in the alders,' said Shane to Hugh.

247

'And we were playing di—' Moylan stopped abruptly as Aidan frowned at him.

'Never mind about all that,' said Enda impatiently. 'Let's go to our six suspects. Could any of them have been seen by Seán at or near the murder scene?'

'Presumably, he arrived after Malachy had been killed, is that right, Brehon, do you think?' asked Fachtnan.

Mara nodded. 'I'd say that would be right, but we can check with Nuala. My impression was that he was dead when the message arrived to say that I needed him.' Her mind went back to that morning and its horrors. She shuddered quickly and then reproached herself. Here she was alive, and almost as well as normal, and Malachy was dead. His death had to be investigated and a solution found quickly. Seán's death had shown that this murderer was easily panicked into violence.

'So Ronan, Caireen and Nuala were all at Caherconnell,' said Moylan.

Mara shook her head. 'Not Ronan. Caireen and Ronan both say that he left before Malachy's death.'

'And there would be nothing strange about seeing Caireen and Nuala there, so unless he actually saw them put the wolfsbane into the glass it doesn't seem as if it were either of them,' said Enda thoughtfully.

'So it looks as though it might have been Blár or Murrough,' said Shane knitting his black eyebrows. 'I could just imagine Seán, couldn't you, Hugh? I could just imagine him going up to someone and asking them what they were doing at Caherconnell on that morning.'

'Did he ask it that morning, when he was on his way to Thomond with Boetius MacClancy's errand, or had he asked the question before and on that day the murderer took the opportunity to poison him?' Enda put the tips of his fingers together and looked around at his fellow scholars. 'What I am thinking, Brehon,' he went on, 'is that Séan may not have been too bright, but surely if he had just accused a person of murder, he would have the sense not to eat something, however tasty, given to him by that person.'

'Yet, it would be hard to poison Seán on a normal day when he was just working around the farm – he always eats the same food as Brigid and Cumhal and the rest of them. Brigid wouldn't be cooking something special just for Seán,' said Moylan with conviction.

'So we think that he was poisoned on his journey, Brehon?' asked Fachtnan.

'There was a piece of linen in his satchel with traces of butter and a few slivers of meat, and what smells like horseradish on it,' said Mara. 'I've shown it to Brigid and she says she certainly did not give him anything wrapped in good linen like that. And she didn't give him horseradish.'

Shane whistled. 'Horseradish was clever. It's so strong that it would kill the taste of anything

249

else. I hate it. It burns my mouth.'

Mara took a deep breath. 'We must also think about Oisín,' she reminded them. 'He was one of our original suspects. Could he, if Seán had voiced any suspicion of him, have been the one who poisoned the food and disguised the taste with horseradish?' Cumhal, she knew, grew the plant in his vegetable garden. It certainly would have been possible for anyone at Cahermacnaghten to have pulled up one of them quickly and chopped up the root. While the plant was fresh, the taste was extra pungent. After a few hours this pungency died down and needed to be revived with the addition of vinegar.

'Here is the piece of linen,' she said, producing it from her pouch after she had reminded her scholars about this property of horseradish. 'I wrapped it in this oil cloth to keep it safe. Smell it; can you smell vinegar?'

One by one, they smelled and then passed it on. By the time that it reached Shane, every face was blank and every head had been shaken.

'That's what I thought, too,' said Mara. 'I could not smell vinegar, so it seems to show that the plant was fresh when its root was chopped and added to the meat – beef, I would say, from the few fibres which remain.'

'So our murderer took it from the vegetable garden at Cahermacnaghten law school,' said Fachtnan slowly.

Mara shook her head vigorously. 'Don't jump to a conclusion too quickly,' she said urgently.

250

'This is where good investigative work is important. You must check the gardens of Caherconnell, Binne Roe, and of Murrough's place at Cathair Caisleann. Every place connected with the murder must be checked; I have a feeling that horseradish may lead to the solution of these two deaths.'

'If it came from Cahermacnaghten, then Oisín could have taken a root from the garden.' Fachtnan was still logically and doggedly pursuing his line of thought.

'That's right,' said Mara calmly.

'Well, it couldn't have been him,' said Aidan. 'Oisín wasn't here. I remember he had gone over to Lemeanah the day that Seán went. I remember your daughter, Brehon, telling Seán to remind Oisín to ask to borrow a small hurley for Domhnall.'

'Unless the food was prepared earlier,' said Mara. She looked solemnly from face to face. Was she justified in using those young boys on this mission? On the other hand, it was probably not a good idea for her to ride so soon after childbirth. 'Make sure that you don't ask any direct questions,' she said emphatically. 'Ask Murrough about wolf hunts or something like that, and you can bring a message from me to Blár that we need a new turf cart for the end of the month, if possible. Cumhal plans to start cutting the turf in a couple of days' time, tell him that.'

'Is that our work for the morning?' Enda was

251

obviously dying to get going on the solving of the two murders.

'And to trace the route of Seán. Someone must have seen him. You know Seán; he would have talked with everyone. He was unlikely to have gone anywhere near Murrough's place, but he would definitely have passed Blár's place on his way to Lemeanah.' Mara looked around at her scholars and said seriously, 'I want everyone to stay together at all times and safety to be the first thought in every boy's mind.'

When the boys had left, Mara went back to the Brehon's house. She felt torn in two. One half of her wanted to solve this murder, and to wind up the year's teaching at the law school in a dignified and satisfactory manner, but the other half wanted to take her baby, to hold him close to her, to admire him, to love him, and, if she were being honest with herself, to feed him. And yet she was very lucky with Eileen. The woman was devoted to Cormac, an intelligent, unobtrusive woman who fitted well into her household. And, as luck would have it, prepared to live in same house as the baby's mother! Another woman might have wanted to keep their nursling in their own house.

'You must invite your husband over any time that you wish, Eileen,' she said, finding the woman walking up and down the parlour, rocking little Cormac in her arms and singing softly to him.

'He's busy with the sheep shearing; I would never see him normally at this time of the year,' said Eileen briefly.

'So he lives up there during June, does he?' There were several stone huts on the summit of the Aillwee mountain, Mara knew. She knew also that most shepherds took their wives and families with them. It was a fun occasion for all and the shrieks of the children often drifted down from the hilltops.

'Yes, he does. What a beautiful chess set, Brehon – made from copper and silver. I've been admiring it. Look, the queen looks a little like you and the pawns are all wolfhounds, just like your dog, Bran.'

Mara laughed, relieved that Eileen seemed happy to stay at Cahermacnaghten for the moment. 'That set was made by the young silversmith at Rathborney, and, yes, he did use Bran for a model and me, too. The set was left to me in his will by a kind old man who died last year.'

Eileen nodded and went on walking up and down. In another minute she will say that the baby needs feeding or changing or washing, thought Mara. I hardly know this woman. We should talk more. I must put aside this stupid, infantile feeling of jealousy.

'How are you getting on with your chess lessons?' she asked quickly. 'I've seen Shane teaching you.'

Eileen shook her head. 'It's a difficult game,' she said seriously. 'I keep trying to remind myself of all the rules. I go over and over them when I am rocking the baby.'

'Why do you want to learn?' asked Mara, amused by this dedication.

'I have in my mind that I would like to foster a child,' said Eileen hesitantly. She glanced at Mara and then looked away. 'If I were to foster a little boy of a high degree, I would have to teach him chess and other things, that's the law, isn't it?'

'I see,' said Mara. So that's what Eileen had in mind. She wanted to take little Cormac into her own household and foster him. Well that was not going to happen! Once the child was about six months old, he would be able to do without a wet nurse and she would feed him on goats' milk and mashed-up food. She and Brigid would care for him in the same way as they had cared for Sorcha when she was a baby. However, in the meantime, she was reliant on Eileen, so she smiled and offered to help with teaching chess when the boys had gone to their homes for the long summer holidays.

'The place will be so quiet that we won't know ourselves when they are gone!' she said, persevering with the conversation as she saw that shuttered look come back over Eileen's face. 'They'll be packing next Friday and then they'll be off on Saturday. They have all received the silver from their parents for their journey by now.'

'You have a visitor, Brehon.' Eileen stopped

her pacing and stood in front of a window. 'It looks like the *taoiseach*'s lady.'

'Go and bring her in. Give me Cormac; I'll hold him.' Mara took the baby from the woman's arms. She was glad to see Ciara. Cormac was looking so beautiful, plumper now and with a roses-and-cream complexion. She would enjoy showing him off to Ciara.

Ciara, however, was full of her own news. 'God bless him, isn't he looking wonderful,' she said, giving the baby a perfunctory glance. 'Well, Brehon, you'll never guess what happened last night at the midsummer celebrations! No, don't go, Eileen, you'll be pleased to hear about this, too.'

'What happened?' Mara turned a smiling face towards her guest, making a silent bet with herself that young O'Connor had at last put the question to Saoirse.

'We're going to have a wedding in our family,' said Ciara, roguishly prolonging the suspense.

'No!' exclaimed Mara. She was fond of Ciara and also very pleased to see her this morning. Now a question could be slid in unobtrusively and be lost in the effusive comments about the forthcoming wedding.

'Yes,' said Ciara nodding her head, her large face wreathed in smiles. 'Teige and I are delighted. Tomás O'Connor and my little Saoirse are to be wed. We thought of Lughnasa for the big day.' She turned to the other woman, 'And, Eileen,' she said warmly, 'I'm hoping that the

255

Brehon might be able to spare you for a few hours here and there to help with making the wedding gown. Would that be all right?'

'That would be fine,' said Mara heartily into the sudden silence. Eileen had not replied, just looked down at the baby in her arms. 'Eileen has had to have almost full charge of Cormac because I have been so busy at the law school and with this murder investigation,' Mara continued. 'But, of course, the boys will be off on their summer holidays at the end of the week and hopefully I will be able to take over the baby much more then. Eileen will have plenty of time on her hands then. I plan to make the most of my son and do everything possible for him.'

'Well, I'd better be giving him his bath,' said Eileen. At the door she turned and said, 'I'm very pleased about the wedding. Perhaps if there is sewing to be done, I could do it here. I wouldn't like to upset the baby.'

'Poor soul,' said Ciara compassionately as the door closed and they heard Eileen's footsteps on the stairs. 'It'll be good to keep her busy. I'm afraid that there's new trouble on the way for her. That husband of hers ... men!'

'Why? What's wrong?'

'Got himself another woman,' hissed Ciara. 'Teige's steward was full of it when he came down from Aillwee last night. Apparently the husband – what's his name...? I forget ... anyway, Eileen's husband has got himself another woman. A girl, really. No more than about seventeen years old. She's the daughter of one of the O'Lochlainn's shepherds. It's been going on since the little boy died – not her fault – no one could have guessed that a child could die from a tiny thing like that. But he blamed her, they say. That's men for you! Went straight back up and found himself another wife – probably a more fertile one this time.'

'Poor Eileen, does she know?' asked Mara.

Ciara shrugged her shoulders. 'I wouldn't know,' she said. 'I'd say no, but I suppose it was possible. You know how people love to gossip.'

'Perhaps it will all blow over,' said Mara. These things often did, she knew. She had heard that there was a lot of wild behaviour at the annual sheep shearing in the mountains. The long hot days, the short nights, the midnight dancing, the singing, the brewers of *uisce beatha* doing a good trade with their strong liquor, young men and young women working side by side during the day and enjoying themselves in the evening – there were always a few marriages that resulted from these June days, whether of the first, second or even third and fourth degree. Presumably this new marriage, if it did take place, would be one of the second degree; but this did not make it easier for Eileen. She might not want to share her husband. She might look for a divorce.

'Poor Eileen; it's lucky that she is so devoted to little Cormac,' she said aloud, hearing, to her satisfaction, how calm and dispassionate her

257

voice sounded while her mind was desperately questioning whether now, in all conscience, she could get rid of this woman at the end of six months and reclaim her baby for herself. 'It's wonderful news about Saoirse, what a pretty bride she will make!' she went on, and allowed Ciara another few minutes of motherly chat before bringing the conversation back to the evening before and the delivery of Turlough's letter to Teige.

'The messenger told you how our man, Seán, was found dead on the way to bring a message to the Brehon of Thomond?'

'May God have mercy on his soul,' muttered Ciara in a slightly perfunctory fashion.

'I just wondered whether Seán did stop at Lemeanah on his way. It would have been on the Monday the thirteenth of June...' Mara looked at her visitor in a hopeful manner.

'That's right; he did, not that I remembered, but I think the steward did. I'm not sure, but something was mentioned. Yes, of course, he did! That's how we found out that you had given birth. That was a shock! Still, all's well that ends well!' Ciara beamed at Mara happily before continuing, 'I was wondering if your daughter Sorcha was around. You see, my little Saoirse has got it into her head that the stuff for the wedding dress should come from Galway and I said to her that I would have a word with Sorcha. She'll know all about the shops there – that's what I would do, I said to Saoirse.'

'Well, let's come and find her,' said Mara rising to her feet. She was fond of Ciara, but, unlike herself, Ciara had endless hours of the day with little to fill them. There was no telling how long her visit might last. She was glad to be cutting short the interview.

Sorcha and the children were playing happily in the garden of the Brehon's house. Mara waited for a while, listening indulgently to Sorcha's expressions of excitement and joy at the thought of a wedding, and then left them together with a murmured excuse of some work to do.

'It's good that you came today because Oisín is anxious to return to Galway,' Mara heard her daughter say as she went at a rapid pace back down the road towards the law school. 'This was meant to be a short holiday and it has turned into a longer one, due to his lordship, the little prince, arriving early.'

Mara stopped for a moment and then went on. This was the first that she had heard of that, but she was not surprised. Oisín had been looking restless. He had found out all that he needed to find, arranged everything that he could arrange, so now he was anxious to get back to the city of Galway, until the day would come when he could officially take possession of the twenty acres of oaks. This would be something that she had to consider and she was glad that she had received prior warning of it. Her son-in-law's insistence that he needed to return to Galway would offer her a dilemma. She would not like, for the sake of her daughter, to say: *Oisín, you are a suspect in my murder case and as such I require you to stay in the kingdom and to be subject to the laws of that kingdom.*

But was he subject to Brehon law? After all, he had left his birthplace in Thomond over fifteen years ago. To himself he was a man of Galway – a freeman of Galway – the honour had been bestowed upon him recently. Apparently this gave him certain rights in Galway. Mara could not find that too interesting, but she knew one thing: if Oisín went back to Galway, Brehon law would have no power over him there. And was it a sign of weakness in her that she had a secret wish, for Sorcha's sake, that he might depart and not come back? And yet, such a thought went against every fibre of her training and of her love for the law. On the scales of justice, retribution always had to balance a crime.

Fifteen

Triad 175

There are three glories of a gathering:
1. A judge without perturbation.
2. A decision without reviling.
3. Terms agreed upon without fraud.

The examination papers, safe in their flat pouch of well-tanned leather, inside Seán's satchel, had not suffered by being left out of doors for nearly two weeks. The pages of neat scripts came out looking very much, probably, as they had looked when Boetius had packed them for the Brehon of Thomond to look at. There was a letter from him also. Mara glanced through it, her lip curling in distaste at the pompous, self-satisfied wording. Still, he was a very young man, she reminded herself. He might grow out of this and learn a little humility. She put it aside and rapidly scanned, with a smile on her lips, Enda's papers on the top of the pile. As she had hoped, he had acquitted himself brilliantly. His answers were models of pungency, brevity and wit, and all showed a deep understanding of the

261

law. She would have awarded him an even higher mark, but Boetius had still given him a *'cum laude'* degree so she was satisfied. Shane had done well, also; in fact it was hard to fault a boy of barely eleven who showed such knowledge of Brehon law. Moylan and Aidan had scraped a bare pass and Mara was happy with that, though she raised an eyebrow at a couple of Aidan's incorrect answers which had received a perfunctory tick of approval, but poor Hugh's paper was covered in savage underlinings and angry-looking crosses. There was no doubt that on the evidence of this paper the child could not be said to have passed. He would have to repeat the year. I'll talk to his father, myself, thought Mara, and I'll emphasize how his mother's death last year had upset Hugh and how the sudden change of teacher had been bad for a sensitive boy. She put the papers aside. She was confident of her ability to talk Cian O'Brian into an acceptance of this temporary setback in his youngest son's career; as a prosperous silversmith the fees for an extra year would not bother the man.

Fachtnan, however, was a different matter. He had already spent an extra year at the law school and this must be a great blow for him. Carefully and meticulously she went through the papers, rising from time to time to check on a fact in one of her law tomes. Boetius had marked as wrong some answers which were correct, but on the other hand he had not noticed a few mistakes.

Mara took a spare piece of vellum and began to add up the marks. If she corrected Boetius's incorrect marking, then Fachtnan would pass, by a tiny margin, but if she subtracted marks for his undetected mistakes, then he would fail.

'Excuse me for interrupting you, Brehon.' Mara had been so deep in thought that she had not noticed Cumhal come in through the open door of the schoolhouse. He was standing in front of her, looking rather troubled. She hastened to reassure him, glad of the interruption and the opportunity to postpone any decision.

'It's just that I'm a bit worried about last night at the bonfire. I told you that I would keep an eye on the lads, and that I did, but when the teacher, Master MacClancy, came up and chatted to them, and then asked Aidan and Moylan to go with him, well, Brehon, I didn't feel that I could interfere.'

'Of course. I understand, Cumhal. There was nothing that you could do. But there's probably no harm done...' Mara's voice tailed off. Cumhal was not one to worry her about nothing. He happily took the boys sailing, caving and mountain climbing, and took over responsibility for supervising them if she had to be absent from the law school. He would not be coming to report this unless he was seriously worried.

'Well, I thought the same, Brehon, but this morning when the lads were out at the pump, I could hear Aidan trying to borrow money from all of them. They refused of course, and then

263

when the others had gone in to breakfast, I heard Moylan say: "You were a fool to go on playing with him. He plays with loaded dice!"'

'What!' gasped Mara. 'Do you mean that Boetius took Moylan and Aidan from your care and then abandoned them to some gambler?'

'It's worse than that, Brehon,' said Cumhal in a shamefaced way. *He's* the gambler – and I never knew it. I'm furious with myself. I understand it now. He was always having these two silly boys up in his room in the guesthouse. Well, it was two to start with, and then Moylan got tired of it. I should have guessed something was going on.'

'But are you sure it was Boetius that Moylan was talking about?' The story seemed almost unbelievable. So much care was taken in law schools that anyone who passed the final examination was of high, moral character. And Boetius had even qualified as a teacher – he had reached the grade of *ollamh*. She knew Brehon MacEgan well. He would have the highest principles, especially in the case of awarding the status of teacher to someone – though of course the school at Duniry was a large one, and he might not have been able to get to know his scholars as well as she did with her small school.

'I'm certain, Brehon. I've just been up to the room and found this lodged inbetween the floorboards.' Cumhal held up one of a pair of dice and tossed it in the air. It fell on the desk with the number six uppermost. 'You try it for your-self, Brehon.' He held out the small cube to her.

Mara tossed it four or five times, more to satisfy him than to check on the truth of what he was saying. She had absolute confidence in Cumhal. Every time the six showed on the top.

'These crooked gamblers have two pairs of dice,' explained Cumhal. 'One lot always give a high score – usually a six – and the other pair always gives a low score – a one normally. They are quick with their hands, you see, Brehon, so they can easily swap them around. With a fool like Aidan you would only have to allow him to win once or twice, and then swap the dice and keep telling him that his luck would change. Easy enough to swap back to the high number if he looked like he was going to walk away.'

'I see,' said Mara. She tried to speak lightly to reassure Cumhal that no great harm was done. No doubt that silly Aidan had lost the silver his parents sent for his return journey. That did not matter; she would reimburse him, with a stiff lecture, of course, but the responsibility was hers and she was filled with shame. A young man of whom she had no knowledge should never have been allowed loose with her boys. 'How did Boetius come to be at the midsummer celebrations, anyway?' she asked.

'I think he is staying at Caherconnell, Bre-hon,' said Cumhal in a subdued tone, 'at least that's what Brigid told me,' he added.

Mara nodded. She would not discuss the

matter any more with Cumhal. A reserved man, he would keep to himself everything that she said to him, but her sense of loyalty to a man of her own profession forbade her to say any more. He would go now, and then she would puzzle over the matter and see how it fitted in with her thoughts about this secret and unlawful killing of Malachy the physician.

To her surprise Cumhal did not go, but stayed standing hesitantly in front of her. He had a worried frown between his eyebrows. She looked at him with surprise. He had the appearance of a man who was not sure what to say, and that was very unlike him.

'Is something else wrong?' she asked.

For answer he took a large jar from his pouch and handed it to her silently. It had been wiped very clean; the polished clay was smooth and shiny and the lid was wedged tightly into the neck. The jar had been whitewashed with a lime mixture so that any stain would immediately show on it.

All these precautions were ominous, and Mara was not surprised to see in large letters on the front of the jar the word POISON.

And on the back another legend; this time, the letters were smaller but instantly readable.

ACONITE it said. The jar contained the deadly poison, wolfsbane.

'You found this, also!' she exclaimed.

Cumhal shook his head. 'No, Brehon,' he said, 'it was Brigid who found the jar.'

266

'After Boetius left?'

There was a pause before Cumhal answered and when he did so it was with the air of a man who had resolved to tell the truth. 'No, Brehon,' he said. 'If that had been the way, Brigid would have given it to you immediately.' Mara looked at him in puzzled way and then suddenly understood. Cumhal saw this and nodded. 'That was it, Brehon. It was in Nuala's room before young Master MacClancy took it over. Nuala was busy with you – and she said that she would sleep in your room – so Brigid went to collect her things. Well, when she found that jar of poison, she put it aside and then when the news came about the physician's murder, Brigid hid the jar. When I told her about the dice she tried to pretend that Master MacClancy had the jar also, but I got the truth out of her. I told her that you had to know everything.'

Mara hesitated for a moment once she was alone again. She put the examination papers back into their flat pouch, locking it carefully into the cupboard. All the time that she was doing this, she was thinking hard. This news about Nuala was an unpleasant shock! What had persuaded the girl to put that jar of poison in her room?

Or did someone else put it there, hoping that it would be discovered?

Mara spent a long time considering the matter, but then with an effort turned her thoughts. She would see Nuala and ask her the position and

Nuala would give a straightforward reply, or else refuse to answer the question. For now, she had to consider the matter of Boetius.

Brigid, she knew, would probably know all there was to know about Boetius and his reasons for staying at Caherconnell, but, on the other hand, she would make a huge and unnecessary fuss about Mara walking across there. No, she would just go, she thought. Whatever there was to find out, she would do it herself.

'Have a lovely time,' she called out merrily to Sorcha and the children who were building a house in the garden with some lightweight hazel hurdles supplied by Cumhal. She did not pause, but kept up a brisk pace until she reached the Kilcorney crossroads. It was warm, but with a slight breeze that wafted the scent of the cream and gold flowers of the woodbine that circled around the hawthorn branches in the hedgerow. The orchids were everywhere, bee orchids, butterfly orchids, purple pyramid orchids and spotted whites, while the pale blue butterflies hovered over the delicate stitchwort flowers and the slim green bodies of the meadow pipits darted in and out of the dense clumps of road-side ivy. To her pleasure, though slightly out of breath, she felt none of the weakness that had dogged her up until fairly recently. Nothing like a bit of fury to lend strength to the legs, she thought.

Fifteen minutes later, Mara arrived at Caher-connell. The herb garden was empty, several plants were wilting from lack of water and a plentiful supply of weeds was clogging up the beds of rosemary and bugle. Nuala had not, by the looks of things, returned to tend the plants since the day of her father's death.

Mara paused by the window of the stillroom, now closed. How strange to have the window of this room closed in such hot weather, she thought. Even in cooler summer days it always stood open, making sure that air circulated and kept the precious ointments and mixtures at an even temperature. It was a shady room, facing north, and it looked quite dark when she peered in. Was Ronan working in Galway? she wondered, and then stiffened.

Most of the space on three of the walls was taken up by shelves, but against the fourth wall, the one opposite to the window, was a long broad couch with several drawings of herbs, all carefully drawn and coloured by Malachy's father, above it. It was not at them, however, that Mara looked, but at the couch – the place where Malachy used to examine his patients.

There were two people lying there, fully dressed, but with arms tightly around each other. Both faces were glued together in a long kiss and both pairs of eyes, she was glad to see, were shut in ecstasy. It was Boetius MacClancy and Caireen O'Davoren, the newly bereaved and sorrowing widow of Malachy the physician.

Shocked and embarrassed, Mara moved quickly away from the window. For a moment

269

she was appalled to think how awkward it would have been if either had seen her, but then she felt a smile tug at her lips and stopped under the shade of a large apple tree to laugh to herself. So what on earth was going on? Boetius was not that much older than Caireen's son. Was he amusing himself with a women old enough to be his mother? Or was there some other reason for this show of love? He had struck her as a young man that knew his own worth. She would have expected some pretty young girl to be his choice.

Absentmindedly, Mara reached out and with her sharp nails detached two tiny apples from the cluster of three on the twig before her, discarding them upon the soft grass beneath her feet. Of course, Caireen had something that very few pretty young girls had. She had two houses. And the one in Galway would be singularly attractive to Boetius. It was, she had heard, a fine stone house within the city walls with a large garden going back to the river. If he induced Caireen to marry him he could set up practice there in Galway. He had already told her that English law was the law for an up-and-coming young man, and with a knowledge of both law systems and a fine stone house he would probably be able to build up a flourishing practice – he might even be able to have a school.

There would have been another reason, also. Mara carefully removed a small green cater-

270

pillar from the underside of a leaf, while her mind worked busily. The walk to Caherconnell and now this quiet time under the tree had made her change her focus. She was no longer solely interested in tackling Boetius about gambling with her pupils. This matter was more serious. Many young men gambled. It was to be deplored, but mostly they grew out of it, or resorted to it with less and less frequency, as other matters took their attention.

But any man who travelled with loaded dice – and Cumhal had convinced her of that – this was a man for whom gambling was a way of life. It was easy enough to use loaded dice with a silly and rather innocent boy like Aidan, but with real gamblers Boetius would probably have been the loser. Perhaps he had built up a huge weight of debts and his eagerness to be taken on by Fergus, or better still, to take over the legal affairs of the Burren, was a measure of his desperation to pay his debts. Neither of these seemed to have worked for him. She herself had dismissed him summarily and Fergus, in his good-natured and gentle way, had probably made it clear that he was not going to retire and leave the law school work to his young cousin...

And was it possible that Brigid might have been mistaken about the ownership of the jar of aconite? Boetius had a cool impudence about him and might, once he heard that he was to occupy this room, have gone in to explore and put the jar in a hidden place. He might not have reckoned with Brigid's obsessive tidiness – it would have seemed quite likely that a room which looked clean and neat already would not have any more dusting or scrubbing done before a new occupant took it over.

Or did he openly deposit it among Nuala's belongings in order to throw suspicion on the girl?

Certainly, there were now reasons why she had to take a long, hard look at Boetius Mac-Clancy.

I think I am now cool and calm, and hopefully the pair on the couch have finished their bout of lovemaking; Mara silently addressed a gorgeously apparelled bullfinch who peered down through the branches at her and then flew away to join his more soberly coloured mate. She emerged from under the apple tree and moved quietly across the grass towards the front door of Caherconnell.

The door was opened by Sadhbh, the housekeeper. She exclaimed loudly at the sight of Mara and was full of questions about her health and about the baby's health – all of which Mara answered in loud, cheerful, carrying tones. As far as she had seen, neither Boetius nor Caireen had been undressed so it should not take them long to join her. In the meantime, she was happy to sit and sip ice cold buttermilk and chat to Sadhbh in the cool parlour.

Caireen was on her own when she came into the

272

room. Mara greeted her politely, asked after her health and then after her future plans.

'Dear Mara, always so thoughtful for everyone! How can my concerns be of any interest to you?' As usual there was a false note in her voice.

'I just wanted to check that you, and your son, Ronan, have no immediate plans to return to Galway. That, I'm afraid, cannot be permitted until the murder of your husband, Malachy, has been solved and the name of his killer announced to the people of the kingdom at their place of justice at Poulnabrone.' Mara watched with interest for a reaction.

'Whyever should we not go back to Galway?' Now her voice was shrill.

'Because Brehon law has no jurisdiction in Galway,' said Mara calmly.

'I have never come under the rule of Brehon law!' exclaimed Caireen. 'I am a native of Galway.' She tried to speak in a dignified way, but there was a definite undercurrent of alarm in her voice.

'Not any more,' Mara explained in kindly tones, 'you married a man of the kingdom and you lived within that kingdom for the last few months. You were present in the kingdom when the crime was committed – as was your son, Ronan – at least he was there on the morning that Malachy was murdered. Your other sons were absent in Galway on that day, so I have no concern with them.'

'Are you accusing me of murdering my own husband, Brehon?' Caireen's voice rose to a shriek.

Mara waited. Caireen had a voice like a corncrake – surely it must have rung through the house. She had not long to wait. A heavy footstep sounded on the stairway and in a moment he was in the room.

'Ah, Brehon, you are well, I trust? Not finding all of this too much for you? And how is your little baby? And my lord, the king?' He shot out the questions, smiling affably and smoothing his red beard, while his small green eyes darted enquiring glances at Caireen, who was mopping her eyes vigorously with an extra large linen handkerchief.

'How nice to see you, Boetius,' said Mara politely. 'I didn't realize that you were still in the kingdom. I thought that you had left and returned home.'

'You should have left while you had a chance,' said Caireen spitefully, giving her eyes another mop, accompanied by a loud sniff. 'Anyone who was present here on the day that poor Malachy was murdered is now to be kept a prisoner in this terrible, barren place until the murder is solved, and God alone knows when that will be.'

There was a silence after those words. Boetius ceased to stroke his red beard and his eyes gazed stonily ahead, looking at neither woman. Mara surveyed him from head to foot, but he did not

274

move nor glance at her.

'Do I understand that you were actually in Caherconnell, Boetius, on the day that Malachy died?' Mara spoke gently, but knew from Caireen's aghast expression that the woman had realized she had made a gaffe.

'Yes, did you not know?' He asked the question airily, placing a forefinger on Malachy's scales and rocking them gently up and down.

'On the contrary, I remember Fergus saying that you arrived at his house just half an hour before he escorted you over to Cahermacnaghten.'

Boetius laughed. 'Dear Fergus. He looks forward to my visits so much that I did not like to tell him that I had stopped off at Caherconnell on the way.'

'Let me get this straight,' said Mara gravely. 'You journeyed down from the MacEgan law school at Duniry, north of Galway, in order to visit your cousin Fergus in Corcomroe. I cannot see how Caherconnell could be said to be on your way. Naturally, you would have gone around by the coast road if you were on your way to Corcomroe.'

'You forget that I don't know the route as well as you do, Brehon,' he said lifting an eyebrow at her.

Mara allowed it to pass. Now she would probe on a different matter.

'There is something else that I must discuss with you, Boetius,' she said in stern tones. 'It's to do with the time you spent with my scholars when I was ill. Perhaps you would like Caireen to go out of the room.'

He didn't look alarmed, just laughed indulgently. 'You ladies! You are so tenderhearted! I suppose one of the boys has complained of me being a little too stern. Is that right?'

Mara waited a moment, but Caireen made no move to go and Boetius still smiled at her in the slightly mocking way, his sharp little eyes boring into hers.

'No, none of the boys have complained,' she said. 'It was Cumhal, my very trusted farm manager, who spoke to me.'

His gaze hardened, but he still made no move to ask Caireen to go, so Mara proceeded.

'Cumhal found this in your room,' she said, 'one of a pair of dice, I understand.' And she produced the small weighted cube from her pouch. Neatly, she flipped it into the air, adroitly stopping it from rolling from the table. It showed a six. Three times more she tossed it, each time allowing the six to speak for itself.

'My old friend, Giolla MacEgan, would be horrified to know that one of his graduates was playing with loaded dice and inveigling young boys into losing their money,' she remarked into the silence.

His hand went automatically to his pouch, but then he hastily dropped it when he saw her eyes on him.

'Not mine, Brehon,' he said cheerfully. 'Prob-

276

ably belonging to one of your husband's guards or some other visitor.'

'You yourself don't gamble ... Is that correct?' Mara asked the question in a matter-of-fact way.

His eyes slid from hers and looked uneasily towards Caireen, but the smile on his lips did not falter. 'Certainly not, Brehon,' he said.

'I'm very glad to hear it,' said Mara gravely. She had got what she had come for. That look at Caireen had verified her suspicions. Boetius did not want Caireen to know that he was a gambler and that probably meant that he had designs on her property. Caireen was no fool and had a proper appreciation of the comforts of life. However, she had twice been widowed and her choices for a third husband would be fairly limited. And, of course, she might enjoy Boetius's lovemaking. She had been flushed and red-lipped when she had come into the parlour.

'Now let's go back to the murder of Malachy in this house on the eleventh of June,' she said briskly. 'When actually did you arrive here at Caherconnell, Boetius?'

She saw him cast a quick sideways glance at Caireen – trying to assess whether he could get away with a lie. However, Caireen looked stonily ahead. Mara's respect for her rose. No doubt the allusion to gambling had not been lost on Caireen. She looked like a woman who was thinking hard.

'I came on the Wednesday before,' said Boetius eventually.

'And you were actually present in the house when Caireen shrieked for help, is that right?'

Again he hesitated, again he glanced at Caireen, but eventually he nodded.

'And you did not think to come to help her, is that correct?'

'I did glance in, but I could not see what I could do; it was obvious that the man was dead. In any case, his daughter Nuala was there to provide medical assistance, if any had been needed. I was on my way to Corcomroe.'

It might be true, thought Mara. He could be a fairly selfish and self-centered young man. The scene in the stillroom would have been appalling and he might well have baulked at going in there, reasoning that there were servants ready to run any errands and the wife and daughter to tend the dead man.

On the other hand, it might be that he had a hand in the murder and wished to distance himself from the house as quickly as possible. He may not have reckoned that Malachy would swallow the brandy quite so soon. Another man might have left it there for longer. The murderer would undoubtedly have hoped that he would do so.

But if he did leave the house then, where did he go? It could not have taken him more than two hours to go from Caherconnell to the law school in Corcomroe.

Perhaps he had waited to console the weeping widow – may perhaps have been the unseen

278

voice behind the vehement accusations of Nuala.

But was he the one that removed the deadly jar of aconite from the stillroom and placed it amongst Nuala's belongings?

Sixteen

Coic Conara Fugill

(The Five Paths of Justice)

*A judge must be prepared to give a pledge worth
five ounces of silver in support of his judgement.
His judgement is not valid unless he swears on
the gospel that he will utter only the truth. If he
refuses to do so, he is no longer regarded as a
judge within the* tuath *and the particular case is
referred to the king.*

*If a judge leaves a case undecided, he must
pay a fine of eight ounces of silver.*

Mara had time for a rest on her bed before the
boys returned. She heard the horses' hoofs
clatter noisily on the road and the sounds of exuberant young voices came through her opened
bedroom window. She smiled thankfully. They
were all in high spirits, buoyed up by the
thought of the approaching holiday. Nothing had
happened today, she had been right to have
allowed them out. It was a difficult task being in
charge of these young males, but nothing could

be achieved by keeping them wrapped up in linen and confining them to the law school. They had to learn to estimate danger, take chances and keep themselves safe.

She did not move. They would be hungry; Brigid would probably insist on them having a wash at the pump and changing into one of the fresh snowy-white *léinte* that were kept hanging in rows on nails in their bedroom. And then, of course, they would flock to the kitchen house. Brigid would have a good meal ready for them and they would devour it, talking, laughing, joking and teasing Brigid and the two girls, Nessa and Áine.

By the time that she had dressed and braided her black hair they were coming out of the kitchen house, wiping mouths and looking satisfied. Now would be the time to hear the story of their investigations.

'So how did it go?' she asked when they were all in their seats in the schoolhouse. She signed to Enda to shut the door. Bran lay down in front of it. This was his favourite place in hot weather and it was useful as he would stand up if anyone came to the other side of the door.

'We talked to everyone we could, Brehon. With the haymaking and everything for the last week all the fields had people in them. That made it all very easy. We traced Seán's route,' said Fachtnan. 'There were no surprises. He left here, then went down to the Kilcorney crossroads – Lorcan saw him turn and had a chat with him. Seán told him all about his errand and then rode on down the Kilcorney road.'

'Going towards Caherconnell,' interrupted Hugh. 'And he stopped there.'

'That's right,' said Fachtnan. 'Thanks for reminding me, Hugh.'

Fachtnan was being wonderfully tolerant and kind to Hugh, thought Mara. What a good teacher that boy will make if I can possibly get him through his examinations. She wished that there was a magic herb that would cure Fachtnan of his memory problems, but lacking this, nothing but relentless hard work would bring him through.

'So why did Seán stop at Caherconnell?' she said aloud.

'Master MacClancy gave him a letter for Caireen,' said Hugh triumphantly.

'That's right, Sadhbh the housekeeper told us that,' said Fachtnan. 'After that he rode down towards Lemeanah. One of the men from Donal and Maeve's place at Shesmore saw him. And then he stopped at Lemeanah. He told Sadhbh that he was the one that thought of bringing news of the baby's birth to Lemeanah – I think that was interesting, Brehon, don't you?'

'Yes, indeed, though I'm not surprised. Seán always liked to carry news; this was why he was always so long on journeys and used to get into trouble with Cumhal and Brigid, poor fellow.'

'You've left out what Seán didn't do.' Moylan broke the slightly uncomfortable silence that

282

followed her words. Seán, the murder victim, could be discussed dispassionately. Reminders of Seán, the man, made the boys feel uncomfortable.

'What was that, Moylan?'

'He *didn't* stop off at Binne Roe, so it was unlikely that Blár gave him that bread and meat – and horseradish, of course,' said Moylan.

'Nothing to stop Blár being out on the Kilcorney road inspecting some of the ash trees in hedgerows and chatting to Seán about his journey,' retorted Enda. 'And then, perhaps, giving him some food that his wife had given him. That linen cloth looked like something that a wife would wrap food in – I couldn't imagine someone like Murrough of the Wolfhounds going to the trouble of wrapping his snack in something like that.'

'True!' Moylan waved a hand. 'But Blár does not have horseradish growing in his garden.'

'But there was plenty in the big vegetable garden at Lemeanah.'

'And some at Caherconnell.'

'None at Murrough's place – he said that he used to have it but Rafferty, you know, the wolfhound that was poisoned, well he dug it up. Murrough showed us the place where it used to be – it was beginning to sprout again.'

'Anyway, Murrough didn't meet Seán that day, he said, and no one mentioned seeing him talking to him. I think Murrough would be remembered because he always has a wolfhound or two with him.'

'I think, myself, that Murrough could be cross-ed off the list. He wouldn't do that – wouldn't murder a man.'

The voices chattered on and Mara sifted and re-sifted the evidence.

'How long did Seán stay at Lemeanah?' she asked.

'It's difficult to get times from people, Bre-hon,' said Fachtnan. 'The steward remembered him coming. He remembered that he was talking to one of the shepherds about supplies and to one of the field workers about making room for the hay, and Seán said that he could wait, that he had all the time in the world.'

Mara sighed. That sounded like Seán. He was always a man who liked to lend an ear to every conversation. News was his coinage.

'Then, when Seán had told his news the steward sent a messenger to the *ban tighernae* to see whether she would like to talk to Seán, about your baby, you know.'

'And,' Enda took up the tale. 'No one could find her for a while – she wasn't in the hall or anywhere that they expected her to be and then eventually someone remembered that she had gone down into the cellars.'

'Into the cellars!' Mara was startled. What on earth was Ciara doing wandering around the cellars on a fine day?

'She had gone down there with Oisín, your son-in-law,' explained Enda. 'They were talking about wine and storage of wine and things like that. That's what the steward said.'

'And then she would have to make all sorts of enquiries about the baby and things like that; women usually do,' said Moylan with an air of a man who understood these matters.

'So, all in all, Brehon, he might have spent about an hour there,' summed up Enda.

'And, of course, once he left Lemeanah, he would be in the kingdom of Corcomroe so we thought you would not like us to be making any enquiries there,' said Fachtnan.

'No, you were quite right.' Mara spoke absent-mindedly. So Oisín was at Lemeanah that day. Thoughtfully, she took from her drawer the superfine piece of linen with the tiny slanting stitches. Perhaps it was time that she had a talk with her son-in-law.

'You did very well, all of you,' she said turning to her scholars. 'Now you can take the rest of the day off. I think Cumhal would be glad of some help with the hay. They are hoping to carry it home tonight, I think.'

'Haymaking supper,' said Hugh enthusiastically. 'I love June, don't you, Shane? First there's bonfire night and then haymaking. And then holidays of course.'

Hugh sounded very cheerful, Mara was glad to hear. He seemed to have got over his disappointment, and had been reassured by her promise to break the news herself to his father and to explain the reasons for his failure.

Sorcha was sitting sewing under the shade of an apple tree when Mara reached the garden of the Brehon's house. She was alone except for little Manus, stretched out, fast asleep, on the grass. His chubby legs, with slightly muddy knees, were as brown as the hedge skipper butterfly that fed from the pink clover beside him, and he looked the picture of rosy, sturdy babyhood.

'He crawled today!' Sorcha said as her mother sat on the bench beside her. 'Crawled! And he's barely six months old. Eileen was waving Cormac's toy – you know the one that Bláreen made for him – and the little bell was pealing, and what would my brave Manus do, but start wriggling across the grass on his tummy, and then he managed to get up on his hands and knees and the next was ... well, he was crawling! And Domhnall and Aislinn were clapping him and cheering him, and he kept on crawling around the grass and collapsing on to his tummy, but every time he managed to get back up on to his knees again. He's got all his father's determination.' Sorcha gave a fond look at her small son and rapidly put in another few stitches.

'He's worn out now, I suppose.' Life was less complicated when she was just a grandmother, thought Mara. She adored her three grand-children, but now her first thought was not to rejoice in Manus's achievement, but to wonder whether Cormac would crawl at six months. He still looked so incredibly fragile beside Sorcha's three sturdy youngsters. 'Where are the other two?' she continued.

'Oisín took them off to show them *Poll an Cheoil*.'

'I hope he's careful,' said Mara anxiously. *Poll an Cheoil* (hole of the music) was the name of a cave near to the law school. It was reputed to run for miles under the limestone of the Burren and to reach the sea eventually. Aislinn would probably cling to her father's hand, but Domhnall was bold and adventurous.

'Oh, he will,' said Sorcha placidly. 'Look at this. Brigid gave me some linen and I'm making a short smock for Cormac. Now that he's started crawling, he'll need a new set of clothes.' She held up her sewing.

'It's beautiful.' Mara took the small garment in her hands and held it up. Already the seams under the arms and along the sides had been stitched, and now Sorcha was gathering in the fullness across the chest with a series of ornamental cross stitches. Mara turned it inside out, gazing at the tiny neat stitches in an abstracted fashion.

'I shall make him five or six of these. He's bound to get them dirty within five minutes of wearing.' Sorcha's voice had broken a silence and Mara was aware that her daughter sounded slightly puzzled. She handed back the little smock quickly.

'I was just thinking how strange it is that you

can sew so beautifully and that I am so absolutely hopeless at it. Brigid taught you, I know, but then Brigid was my nurse before she was yours. Why didn't I learn?'

'You were too busy studying.' Sorcha smiled at her mother. 'Don't look so troubled!' she exclaimed. 'Why should you sew? You can do other things that are so much more important! Sewing would be just a waste of your valuable time.' She dropped a kiss, as light as butterfly, on her mother's cheek. Her blue eyes were anxious.

Mara laughed gently. 'I'm beginning to feel that you are the mother and I am the child,' she said, rising to her feet. 'You look after me as if I were one of your own brood. Now I'd better go and see if I can borrow my son for a few minutes from Eileen.' She kissed the top of Sorcha's head – it saved having to look into her daughter's eyes – and then went off across the grass.

I'm not taking pleasure in my garden this year, she thought, as she breathed in the intense perfume of the lilies in their baskets woven from the purple shoots of willow. Every other June, she had revelled in those lilies that always lined the path from the gate to the front door. Her eyes swept over her garden. The pink roses near the holly hedge were just as exuberant as ever, the gillyflowers frothed over their small fence of stone and the peonies stood tall and rosy against the pale grey limestone of the house wall. None of it gave her pleasure. Somehow I am uneasy and unsure, she thought. I've always been so organized. Everything had its place and its time. I'm not like that now. I've lost confidence, somehow. Nothing is being done right. I'm neglecting my baby, neglecting poor Nuala, wrestling with my conscience, worrying continuously but not effectively. This murder has to be solved. The scales have to be balanced.

Cormac was crying when she pushed open the door of the house, but by the time she put one foot on the stairs the small weak cry had ceased, and when she entered Eileen's room the baby was contentedly feeding. Mara sat on the bed and watched.

And ached to hold him in her arms.

The haymaking was progressing well when Mara wandered over to the farm after swallowing her small supper. During the last week the meadows had been dotted with small cone-shaped haycocks, but yesterday these had been put together, three or four of them, to make larger haycocks, the grass still showing pale, bleached circles where their smaller cousins had once stood.

'Great summers these days, Brehon,' said Cumhal enthusiastically as she joined him. 'I remember all those years when your father was here, God have mercy on him, and we had summer after summer of rain. We'd be driven demented! All the haycocks would have to be pulled apart and remade again time after time in the hopes that they would dry. And in the end the hay was hardly worth the carrying!'

'You have plenty of helpers, I'm glad to see.' Mara glanced around. Almost all the neighbours had come to join in the fun and to share the workload – the men and women, with their *léinte* kilted at the waist in order to raise them to knee height, were busily loading the carts or raking up the stray wisps of hay from the ground. Children ran around being useful or playing games, and by the hedgerows a few young women fed their babies. Tomorrow and the next day, the men and women from Cahermacnaghten would go to help in other farms. She knew from her law texts that this custom of *comhar* had gone on from time immemorial, and it added to the sense of family and tradition which was so much in her thoughts this evening.

'And here's the best little helper of the lot,' said Cumhal as Domhnall ran up carrying his small, wooden rake, made for him by Cumhal, sloped across his shoulder. 'Tell the Brehon the poem I taught you about hay in June, Domhnall.'

While Domhnall was fluently reciting the multiple verses, Cumhal regarded him with a proud smile. 'God bless him,' he said after Domhnall had run back to his companions, 'he's got a great memory. He's the image of the Brehon, your father. Please God, we'll see him here at the law school soon. He'll be the brightest and best of the lot of them.'

It was true, thought Mara, Domhnall was like his grandfather, the highly respected Brehon of the Burren. Sorcha liked to point out the resemblance between her son and her husband, but, to Mara's mind, Domhnall was a deep thinker, much more of an academic than Oisín, despite his sharp cleverness, could ever have been. Domhnall, of course, adored his father and tried to be like him in every way. Would, or could, the child's hero worship of his father last?

'Is that Cliona O'Connor over there?' she asked, looking at one of the young women feeding their babies, and Cumhal nodded.

'That's right, Brehon. I took a couple of men over and cut her meadow for her a few days ago, and she came along to help today. She needn't have bothered. It was no trouble to us to do a five acre meadow. She's worked well, though; the little fellow just sleeps in the shade most of the time with some of the other babies.'

'I didn't know that she had land.' Mara was conscious that she should not be delaying Cumhal. This was a very busy time for him, but she was curious about Cliona. It seemed ages since that morning at Poulnabrone, the morning when Cormac was born, but yet it wasn't much more than two weeks.

'She took the land instead of the silver that Ryan owed her for the divorce settlement,' explained Cumhal. 'You see, every piece of silver that he had got for the sale of the sheepskins and the cloaks he had put back into buying more

291

sheep, so he wasn't able to give her what she was supposed to have.' He waited for a moment and then, when she did not reply, said courteously, 'Well, if it's all right by you, Brehon, I'd better be getting back to work.'

'Yes, of course, Cumhal,' said Mara hastily. She waited until he returned to the cart, averting her eyes from the sight of Enda standing precariously high on top of the loaded hay and bouncing up and down to compact it. He was bronzed like a young god and had pulled his kilted *léine* from his shoulders and wore it hanging around his waist, exposing his bare chest, arms and legs to the admiration of the young girls. Shane and Hugh were racing around dragging rakes at high speed through the scarified grass and the two fifteen-year-olds were wielding dangerous-looking pitchforks to transfer one of the last few haycocks on to another cart. Fachtnan was leading a third cart back to the barn, holding the bridle and stroking the horse's nose. Mara looked around for Nuala; up to the last few weeks Nuala was always near to Fachtnan, but now there was no sign of her.

'You're well, Cliona?' Mara seated herself beside the young woman, murmuring the usual enquiry in a low voice. The fat little baby on Cliona's lap had dropped off to sleep.

'I'm very well, Brehon,' said Cliona. She looked tired, but that was not surprising. It was not easy for a young woman with a baby to manage even the smallest of farms. 'At least I have my self-respect now,' she said in decisive tones.

'I hear that you are setting up as a farmer,' said Mara.

'I thought I would,' said Cliona. 'Be a pity to waste all that I have learned. I'm looking to buy more land, but I won't rush. Let this fellow grow up a bit. I'll just increase the flock bit by bit and graze them on Sliabh Elva as much as possible.'

Mara nodded. The land on that mountain was held in common by all members of the O'Connor clan. Cliona was an O'Connor by birth as well as by marriage. She would be able to graze as many sheep as she could afford free of charge and keep her five acre meadow for the young lambs and for summer hay.

'And the neighbours are helpful to you?' she enquired.

Cliona nodded. 'Very helpful,' she said. 'Blár and his wife can't do enough for me. Blár calls around most days, and Áine loves to look after the baby for me. Look, she made this little smock for him.'

The baby was wearing a short smock, very like in shape and size to what Sorcha had been sewing for little Manus. Mara bent over to admire it, taking the tiny hem in her hand and turning it over to look at the stitching. It lacked the exquisite embroidery that Sorcha could do, and the stitches, though neat, were far bigger and less uniform than the stitches on the piece of linen that had enveloped poor Seán's last meal.

293

It looked as though the deadly dose of wolfsbane had not been given by Blár O'Connor.

Enda, from his high perch on top of the hay, was the first to see the new arrivals.

'Brehon, the king is coming!' he yelled. 'They are coming down the Kilcorney road.'

'The king!' All pitchforks and wooden hayrakes were immediately abandoned, and there was a rush of all the workers towards the gate leading to the road. Even the women by the hedgerow gathered up their babies and walked across the field. Turlough will have a magnificent guard of honour and won't he love it, thought Mara affectionately. She stayed where she was for a second and then, suddenly changing her mind, she got to her feet and ran towards the house.

I don't care, she muttered rebelliously to herself. I don't care if he's asleep, being fed, being changed, or having a bath, he's my baby and he's coming to see his father.

'He's asleep,' said Eileen defensively, as Mara pushed open the door.

'He can sleep all night,' returned Mara firmly, scooping up Cormac in her arms and holding him against her face for a moment. She loved the warm baby smell of him. 'Come on, my little prince,' she said gaily, 'come and meet my lord, the king.'

Everyone stood back as she came out of the gate and allowed her to go forward. The horses were coming at a rapid trot and then slowed down. The bodyguards reined in and Turlough advanced alone.

'You're wearing my favourite gown; I love you in green,' he said enthusiastically, as he swung himself from his stallion like a man of half his age and threw his arms around her, abandoning his horse for his bodyguard to catch. 'And there's my boy. You've grown, little fellow! Soon have you a warrior!'

Mara smiled. This was the second homecoming, but somehow it was the best. Her confidence had suddenly flowed back. She would solve this crime, ensure that the murderer paid the fine and then they would all get on with their lives and have an idyllic summer. She stood back by the gate and allowed him to greet the crowd. What a king he was! He remembered so many faces, admired the babies, asked the mothers eagerly whether they had seen his tiny son, had a knowledgeable discussion with Cumhal about the virtues of hay cut in June, slapped the backs of the scholars and told them to behave themselves over the summer holiday and to spend at least twelve hours every day studying.

'That's what I did when I was your age,' he declared to the enormous amusement of the crowd. The baby woke up, stared at the eyes, so like his own, and then began to cry.

'Perhaps he needs feeding,' said Mara.

'He's just bored. Wants to go out fighting,'

295

said Turlough with a grin. Expertly supporting the floppy head he swung him vigorously to and fro in his arms. Cormac stared and then after a few minutes of this violent exercise, he just closed his eyes and slept.

'There you are,' said Turlough complacently. 'I'm a good man with babies.'

Ardal and Nuala arrived quite soon after Mara's invitation had been delivered. Ardal was riding his new strawberry mare and Nuala was seated on a handsome bay. There was no doubt that Ardal looked after his niece well and gave her the best of everything. The girl looked very unhappy, though. Her tanned skin had a sickly, yellowish tinge to it and her brown eyes were full of misery.

'How do you think that Cormac is looking, Nuala?' Mara held out the baby for the girl's inspection. Despite everything, she still had a high opinion of Nuala's professional judgement and skill.

'He's doing well,' said Nuala after a few moments. She weighed the baby in her arms, held out a finger to be gripped by the tiny hand, unwrapped the linen swathes, inspected the little limbs, raising the arms and legs in turn, before continuing, 'You've been lucky with Eileen, Mara. He's put on weight and he is beautifully looked after. Look at his skin – no trace of a rash, or soreness.'

'Please God we'll see you with your own little

296

baby soon, Nuala,' said Turlough. He was a sentimental man and the sight of Nuala with the baby in her arms moved him.

'You'll have to find me a husband then.' Nuala tried to smile, but her eyes were bleak.

'Find you one!' roared Turlough. 'I bet there is a long tail of them from here to Thomond, isn't that right, Ardal?'

Ardal smiled gently. Like Turlough, he seemed moved by the sight of the motherless and fatherless girl with the baby in her arms. Perhaps marriage would have been the best thing for Nuala, thought Mara, but then looked at the angry frustration in the brown eyes and knew that the girl had to be left to try to achieve her dreams of being a physician before anything else.

'Shall we eat out here?' she asked lightly. 'Sorcha and Oisín will be coming across in a few minutes. I'll send one of the men to fetch the cradle and little Cormac can stay with us.'

Brigid was a miracle worker. Although busy with the haymakers' supper she promised steaks, some roasted parsnips and a tasty wine sauce in honour of the king. She and Eileen would manage easily while Áine and Nessa continued to feed the haymakers. Sorcha, more domesticated than her mother, handed over the baby Manus to his father and went to help them with the food.

'I'll get the wine, Mother,' said Oisín after his wife had gone. He dumped his small son on the grass with an order to Domhnall not to let his brother eat anything he shouldn't or crawl too far away.

'It's very difficult looking after Manus,' said Domhnall seriously to Mara. 'I don't mind looking after Aislinn, because I can tell her if she does something wrong then I won't play with her, or I won't give her something, but Manus can't talk so you can't give him any punishment if he misbehaves.'

'That boy's a lawyer already,' said Ardal with quiet amusement. 'Retribution must follow crime; a good principle.'

'It is indeed,' said Mara thoughtfully. The principle was a good one and one that she had to act on without any more delay. There had been two crimes, she thought sadly. Retribution had to follow. Tomorrow, she told herself. Tomorrow, when the scholars have returned home; tomorrow I must deal with this.

'Mara, I've been thinking about your young Enda,' said Turlough, coming and joining them on the bench in front of the holly hedge. 'He's a clever boy, isn't he? I was wondering if he would like to work for me. You see, Tomás Mac-Egan is getting old and he doesn't like stirring too far from his fireside – none better so far as the brain is concerned, but the legs are getting stiff. He's been talking of retiring, but I don't want to lose him. An energetic young assistant would be just the thing for him.'

'I think that would be a wonderful idea,' said

Mara warmly. 'Enda would do well, I'm sure. Do you want to ask him now? I know that he would like to start work as soon as possible. His family have had sad losses with their cattle and he would like to contribute. Perhaps let him have a month's holiday – he's worked very hard this year – would that suit you?'

'Yes, let the lad have his holiday – no rush,' said Turlough. 'Anyway, I'm hoping to have a bit of a holiday myself here in the Burren with you and the little fellow. Conor is very well at the moment; he can look after things in Thomond for me.'

'That's good.' Mara glowed at the thought of a month together. It was good news about Conor, Turlough's eldest son and the *tánaiste* (heir). His life had been despaired of; everyone had been sure that he was about to die of the wasting sickness, but thanks to the medicines from a monk at the abbey he had made a good recovery.

'Will you tell Enda the news now?' she asked. 'They will all be off tomorrow morning. Domhnall,' she called, 'I'll keep an eye on Manus if you will run over and tell Enda that we would like to see him for a minute.'

Enda had put on a clean *léine* and was looking very handsome and very adult as he strolled over with little Domhnall. It was hard to believe that he was still a month short of his seventeenth birthday – he had none of the usual awkwardness of an adolescent. He listened to the king's proposal, his tanned face flushing a becoming pink and thanked him with a mixture of politeness and warmth.

Mara smiled wistfully. How they did grow up! For a moment she missed the old exuberant Enda. Her eyes followed him as he sedately moved away down the path, greeting Oisín in a dignified manner, bestowing a bow on Sorcha, and then she laughed, as suddenly, instead of going out of the gate, he scaled the wall with a single leap and began to run wildly down the road, the noise of a barely muted whoop sounding above the voices and laughter from the haymakers' supper. She looked at Turlough and saw the grin on his face.

'He'll liven up Tomás MacEgan,' he said.

'He's a bright boy; he'll learn from Tomás; I see a great future in front of him.' said Mara. 'Give him a few years to earn money and then perhaps he will go on with his studies and become a Brehon – that's if he does not weigh himself down with a wife and family too quickly.'

'Now my lord, here's a wine that you will enjoy,' said Oisín, appearing at their side, holding two glasses. He had decanted the wine from the barrel into a flagon and then carefully poured it out. Mara held hers to the light, admiring the rich red. She sipped, rolled it around her mouth and sighed with satisfaction. It was rich and smooth and tasted of blackcurrants. It would go wonderfully with the promised steaks.

'Thank you, Oisín, that was well chosen,' she

said. 'Nothing like the first glass from a new barrel.'

'Have you told my lord about my idea for the small barrels?' he asked eagerly.

He was so knowledgeable, so clever, Mara thought, as she sipped her wine and half-listened. Quite a showman, too. He didn't sit down, though there was a convenient seat. He stood in front of the king and of the O'Lochlainn *taoiseach* and expanded on his ideas, explaining how air tainted the wine and displaying all of his knowledge of trees and the various woods. There was no doubt that he was talented – not just a good businessman, but a showman also. Both Turlough and Ardal became fired with enthusiasm for these new barrels and converted to the wisdom of using oak to hold the wine. Oisín manipulated that enthusiasm so cleverly. After a few minutes Turlough was almost convinced that the original idea was his own and was full of plans to get orders from all of the chieftains of his acquaintance, and Ardal, in his quieter way, was caught up by the excitement, suggested various good ideas and promised some of his men to help with the tree cutting during the winter months. When Mara got to her feet and wandered over to check on Cormac, she could have sworn that not one of the three men even noticed her departure.

The haymakers' supper was going well, she thought. In fact, everyone seemed happy except for one person. She sighed and went to sit beside

301

Nuala.

'Enoying yourself?' she asked.

Nuala nodded in a perfunctory manner, but did not reply.

'Nuala,' said Mara gently, 'there was a jar of aconite in your room in the guesthouse – the room that you vacated for Boetius. Did you put it there?'

Nuala stared at her and then laughed without humour. 'I'm not a very efficient murderer, am I?' she said in a harsh voice. 'Imagine just sticking it under the bed and then leaving it there!'

'Did you put it there?' persisted Mara.

'Can't you guess?' said Nuala impatiently. She rose to her feet and went off to join Ardal. Mara allowed her to go. She sat very still and gazed across at the distant heights of Mullaghmore. The mountain was even more beautiful than usual – pale blue with the swirling terraces plainly marked in the clarity of the evening air. She did not follow Nuala, nor call her back. There was no point in wondering about the jar of aconite. It wasn't important. The truth was plain to her now. Tomorrow, when the scholars had departed, would be the time to reveal it.

'Tell me all of your news from Thomond,' said Mara as they sat together after their meal was finished. The haymakers had gone home, Ardal and Nuala, in response to a whispered request from the girl, had ridden away and only Mara, Turlough, Sorcha and Oisín were left sitting in the quiet garden. The table was still covered with a linen cloth but most of the dishes and plates had been taken away. On the table was a flagon and four of Mara's precious crystal glasses, brought by her father from the holy city of Rome, and these were filled with the deep crimson wine that glowed against the snowy whiteness of the cloth. A pale cream-coloured platter of applewood lay in the middle of the table with a small, rounded cheese and some slices of Brigid's delicious, heavily buttered soda bread arranged around the cheese. The light was beginning to go in the subtle way of a June night; the reds and blues of the vividly coloured flowers began to fade and the white lilies took on a special intensity. The swallows still darted in and out of the barns in the law school enclosure, but in the distance the nightjar called and over towards the east a sliver of new moon showed above the horizon.

'No news – no news being good news,' responded Turlough. 'The Earl of Kildare has gone back to his stronghold with his tail between his legs. No one will call him "The Great Earl" again if I have anything to do with it.' He smiled the smile of a victorious man and, tilting his wine glass, swallowed the last drop.

'The king of England will not let him be defeated again,' said Oisín quietly.

Turlough looked at him in an annoyed fashion. 'You taking to soldiering, Oisín? You seem to know a lot about it.'

Oisín shrugged. 'I've got better things to do,' he said. 'I'm a busy man, but I hear news. I talk to the people who come in on the ships. England is a powerful country. If Henry VIII wants to conquer Ireland, he will do it and he will give the Earl of Kildare more support. It might be better to keep quiet and hope to be forgotten.'

'Let's not talk about war and things like that tonight,' begged Sorcha with a quick glance at Mara. 'Tell me, my lord, what do you think of your little son?'

'I think that he is as beautiful as his mother.' Turlough, no more than Sorcha, did not want to carry on with this conversation with Oisín. This victory over the Earl of Kildare had been the highlight of his ten years as king and he didn't want anything to tarnish the bright sheen of exhilaration. He bent over the cradle and tucked the woven wool blanket more closely around his little son.

'And how's this wretched business of the murder of Malachy going?' he enquired.

'Going well,' said Mara, and saw Oisín look at her sharply, struck, no doubt, by the quiet confidence in her tone.

'Have another glass of wine,' she said sweetly, taking little Cormac from his cradle and rising to her feet. 'I shall just take Cormac up for his last feed and then I'll bring him back down again. I'll leave you to look after the two men, Sorcha,' she added. 'Do have some more, Oisín. It was well chosen by you, and I'm sure that you will enjoy it.'

Brehon law is so merciful, she mused as she climbed the stairs to Eileen's room. The penalty is straightforward; if the guilty person cannot pay, his or her family or clan can step in and help. She thought briefly of English law. Could she possibly be able to work under that system where a terrible death from the headsman's axe would be the only possible outcome from a successful investigation? She thought not. Yes, retribution had to follow crime, but it need not destroy the guilty person.

Seventeen

Di Chetharslicht Athgabala

(On the Four Divisions of Distraint)

A Brehon, or those in training for that office, should be of unblemished character. His word will be taken by the court so he must guard against the slightest untruth.
   A lawyer who falsifies a record or who swears a lie may be removed from the kingdom.

Today is the day and now is the time, said Mara to herself. The boys had packed all their goods into the satchels, hung by the side of the ponies. Hugh's father, who lived in the kingdom of the Burren, had already come to fetch his son. He had listened patiently to Mara's explanation as to why his son had failed the examination and had proved to be sympathetic to Hugh's vulnerability, and they had ridden away, apparently on the best of terms. He was the only parent to come to collect a son. Shane, the youngest scholar, lived in northern Ireland, but he would travel with Fachtnan and his father would come

306

to pick him up at Fachtnan's home in Oriel.

Only Aidan lacked exuberance. Mara tightened her lips to conceal a smile as she looked at his glum face. He must be wondering how he could make his way home without a penny left for the journey. His pony would need rest and food at wayside inns and so would he. She felt cruel as she watched him; perhaps she should have put him out of his misery yesterday. But on the other hand, he was an easily led boy and she didn't want him to start this gambling habit. That was why she had said nothing until this last minute. However, he had been punished enough by now, she decided, so she beckoned him over and put some silver into his hand.

'This is a loan,' she warned him, 'but it will turn into a gift if you can promise me to keep away from dice playing for the next two years. What do you say?'

Aidan, of course, immediately swore that he would never look at dice again. 'Anyway, Brehon, I have no luck,' he said, turning his hands palms-uppermost to the sky and smiling at her appealingly.

'Very well, then,' said Mara, trying to keep a stern face. There was something so engagingly puppy-like about Aidan that it was hard to be angry with him. He would grow up, she told herself. Basically he was a sweet-natured boy, just cursed at the moment with a silliness and a lack of common sense. Perhaps he would mature in the holidays and return as a reformed character.

307

He was a nice boy, really, she thought, as he bent down and patted Bran, and then touched the tiny hand of the baby in her arms. He looked at the silver appreciatively and thanked her awkwardly, and ran to join the others.

The boys were all mounted, now, all shouting farewells as Cumhal, Brigid, the two girls, Nessa and Áine, joined Mara and Bran. Fachtnan, Enda and Shane turned to the north. The three of them would ride together until Galway, and then Enda would go north to Mayo while the other two struck the north-east route to Oriel. Moylan and Aidan went south; they lived near to each other and so would have each other's company on the route home.

'Now you can have a rest,' said Brigid. 'That's a relief to be rid of all of them.'

'I suppose so,' said Mara. It should have been a relief. And yet, somehow, she was conscious of a feeling of being deserted – a left-over sensation from her childhood, when the end of June spelled the end of companionship and fun, intellectual stimulation and competition. The fate of an only child, she thought, remembering how she would wander around the empty schoolhouse and the deserted yard desolately, and then go down to Lissylisheen and find Mór O'Lochlainn...

This reminded her of Mór's unhappy daughter, Nuala, the long-awaited, much-loved daughter of her friend.

'Brigid,' she said, 'could you send one of the

308

girls down to Lissylisheen to carry a message from me to Nuala – just to say that I would like to see her.'

'I'll send Áine,' said Brigid. 'Nessa can rock the cradle for his little lordship here. He looks sleepy. Eileen has gone off to Lemeanah Castle this morning. She said that you knew all about it ... something about sewing. I said that we'd manage fine – now that all the lads have gone.'

Áine had no sooner departed when there was a sound of a horse's hoofs on the road. Not a visitor! thought Mara, feeling exasperated.

'It's the young MacClancy,' said Brigid, and then corrected herself. 'Master MacClancy,' she said in reserved tones that carried a wealth of meaning.

'I'd better see him,' said Mara. 'I'll go into the schoolhouse. Here, take Cormac, Brigid.' Boetius was not looking his usual confident self. He had the bearing of a man who has faced a hard decision and is still not sure what to do. He took his seat in the schoolhouse, smoothed his red beard and looked at her without the annoying twinkle in his eye. In fact, he had a rather hang-dog expression on his face.

'Brehon, I've been thinking over our last interview and trying to understand your manner at that,' he said, with the air of one who has been exposed to unreasonable suspicion.

'Oh, yes,' said Mara, looking back at him with what she knew was a blank expression.

'I felt that I ... I, a fellow lawyer, was under

suspicion.' He tried to force a note of complaint into his voice, but could not help his uncertainty pervading it.

Mara left a pause before saying firmly, 'Yes, that is true.'

'I thought then that I should throw myself on your mercy.' His confidence had begun to return. The twinkle was just about perceptible in his green eyes, and he smoothed the beard with the air of one who knows that he is irresistible when he adopts the small-boy air.

'Go on,' said Mara gravely.

'You see, I was not in the house when Malachy died...' he hesitated, seemed about to add something and then stopped, looking at her appealingly.

'You lied then, when we spoke last.'

'It was Caireen,' he complained. 'I don't know why she said that I was at the house. Perhaps she really thought that I was still there – perhaps she didn't know of my errand, but I wasn't ... you see...' Once again he stopped, but when she said nothing he went on in a tone of forced lightness. 'You see, I was there the night before, but then Malachy asked me to do a task for him, a legal matter ... it was something that Malachy wished to keep secret, so he told me to leave the house early – not long after dawn so that I would not be seen – and to tell no one. I thought it best not to betray his trust and to go along with Caireen's statement that I was still in the house.'

Why secret? thought Mara, but aloud she said

310

merely, 'Where did you go?'

'To the pass near Rathborney – to Lochánn, just above the sea at Fanore.'

'Why...?' began Mara and then she stopped. Suddenly her conversation with Cuan at the midsummer feast flowed back into her mind. And she understood! It all fitted. According to Cuan, Malachy had given this old man at Lochlánn a potion. What was his name? Yes, Padraig O'Connor, a man with a fleet of fishing boats – a well-off man, then; a man who had accumulated riches by his own industry and who, therefore, was entitled to leave those riches to whomsoever he chose. Malachy had been feeding this poor old man with some sort of syrup that addled his remaining wits. There was only one reason to do this...

'He sent you to make Padraig's will!' she exclaimed, and Boetius looked at her in a slightly alarmed fashion.

'How do you know?' he said suspiciously. 'Malachy swore that this would be just a matter between us both.'

She ignored that. 'Go on,' she said.

'Well, you're right, though I don't know how you guessed. I left Caherconnell at dawn, or soon afterwards. I walked my horse on the grass past any houses so that no one could hear me pass. Malachy had warned me that it was to be a secret that I came from him. I was supposed to stay with Fergus and then when the old man died, to pretend that the will was made a week

311

later – and at the request of Padraig.'

'Go on,' she said, though she guessed the end of the tale.

'Well, I got there eventually – you wouldn't believe the amount of times that I had to hide and wait for a load of cows to be driven past or something. And I went into the place and found the old man.'

'Out of his wits, no doubt,' said Mara dryly.

'Well, yes, he wasn't too bright,' admitted Boetius, 'but eventually I managed to get him to sign his name to the will and then I went on down to Fanore – had a drink or two at the inn there – and eventually made my way down the coast and popped in on Fergus and his wife.'

'Why are you telling me this?' asked Mara after a long silence.

'Just to show that I couldn't have murdered Malachy,' said Boetius eagerly. 'Look!' he delved in his satchel and produced a scroll of vellum and handed it to her.

'Dated the first of July, 1510,' observed Mara.

'That's because Malachy told me to put that date on,' said Boetius impatiently. 'He thought that the old fellow would live a month or two, and when he died Malachy would be called and then he would discover the will.'

Which he would have in his own satchel all the time, thought Mara. Aloud she read the will – a simple one.

'"I bequeath all of my possessions to Malachy O'Davoren in consideration of the care and devotion he has shown in nursing me and helping me with the illness. All goods within the house, all of my fishing boats, all monies owed to me are for Malachy."'

At the bottom of the will was a wavering signature, and below that in a firm and assured hand the words: Boetius MacClancy.

'Your name could and should be erased from the list of lawyers for this,' said Mara icily. She held the piece of vellum between her finger and thumb, eyeing the man with disgust.

'I told you this in good faith; I wouldn't have thought you would be a woman to betray that,' said Boetius smugly.

'What good faith?' said Mara stormily. 'You told me this to save yourself from an accusation of murder – an accusation that you could not otherwise disprove. You have achieved your end; I no longer believe that you killed Malachy, but I now know you to be guilty of the crime of the fraudulent extortion of a signature from a man who was not *compos mentis*, whose wits were addled by potions from a man who, like yourself, betrayed his profession and his teaching.'

'I know I shouldn't have done it, but...' began Boetius.

'Of course, you shouldn't have done it,' retorted Mara. 'I suppose you are going to tell me that he offered you a bribe and that you needed the money to pay your gambling debts. Get out of here, go on, you disgust me, I don't want your

313

presence in my schoolhouse even for one more minute.'

Boetius got to his feet, looking alarmed. 'What are you going to do?'

She was glad to hear a slight tremor in his voice and to see a shamed flush on his freckled skin. How long it would last she didn't know. Let him suffer and perhaps he might be careful never to do such a thing again. For the sake of Fergus, Brehon of Corcomroe, this young man's cousin, she probably would not shame him publicly, but it would do no harm to have him looking over his shoulder for the next year or so and dreading the revelation of his disgrace.

'I don't know,' she replied unhelpfully. 'Now get out before I call Cumhal and have you thrown out.'

When he had gone she spent some time gazing at the vellum. Eventually she sighed, took a sharp knife from the drawer of her desk and began to scrape the skin, removing the lying words of the forged will and leaving a smooth new surface for some more worthy document to take its place. Her hand did the work skilfully, but automatically, and her mind was free to be busy.

The old man from Lochánn became the target of Malachy's greed because his possessions, and his fortune, were the product of his own industry and were his to leave as he wished. Everyone, thought Mara, should make a will while their wits were sharp and while they were capable of judging how their goods could be distributed after their death. And then she laughed at herself.

As Brehon of the Burren and *ollamh* of a law school, she, Mara O'Davoren, had accumulated a large amount of silver. In addition to that, she was the sole owner of the farmlands of Cahermacnaghten with its cows, sheep and poultry; with its rich grazing meadows and fertile fields. She had made no will!

Until the birth of little Cormac, her fortune would have passed in its entirety to her daughter Sorcha, which, of course, meant into the hands of the ambitious Oisín. On that morning of the eleventh of June, if Mara had died and the child had died with her – and without Nuala's skill that may well have happened – then Oisín would have become a very rich man, indeed.

She got to her feet. She would have to do something about Nuala before she did anything else.

The girl was sitting on the wall outside the Brehon's house staring moodily at a butterfly-covered clump of red valerian that grew out from a pocket of soil between the stones. She sat so still that the butterflies sucked from the flowers without alarm, but they rose in an agitated cluster of warm reds, browns and purples when Mara came towards her.

'This stuff is very good for relieving depression,' said Nuala indicating the plant. 'I was thinking that I should try it.'

315

Mara sat down beside her, looking gently at the sad face and the intelligent brown eyes, now so full of misery. *For I the LORD thy God am a jealous God, visiting the iniquity of the fathers upon the children unto the third and fourth generation of them that hate me*, she thought. Malachy, in his last few months of life, had done much evil, and this evil now seemed to live on and be visited on the head of his unfortunate daughter. Something had to be done quickly before this girl, with all of her wonderful promise, was destroyed.

'Nuala,' Mara said rapidly, 'last night I talked with my lord, the king, and we agreed that you should go to Thomond. There is a great physician there, famous throughout Ireland. You have heard of Donncadh O'Hickey – he will take you on as his pupil and if he finds you as advanced as we think you are, you could be qualified as a physician within a year. Are you willing to do that? You won't be too lonely in a strange place?'

'Of course, I'm willing!' Nuala's tanned face suddenly blazed with excitement, the flush of colour turning the yellowish tinge that she had worn since the death of her father back to its normal, healthy summer hue. The light came back into her brown eyes and they glowed.

'And you won't be too lonely there because Enda is also going to Thomond – he will be working as assistant to Brehon MacEgan.'

'Not Fachtnan?' enquired Nuala, and then she

316

laughed. 'Not that he wants anything to do with me now. I asked him to marry me and it gave him a fright. Did he tell you?'

'Yes, he told me.' Mara decided that honesty was the only course with this intelligent, perceptive girl. 'I think that you and Fachtnan have a very good relationship,' she said gently, 'but I don't think that either of you are ready for marriage yet. You both have your professions to think about and it's not a good idea to tie yourself down too early.'

'I don't care as long as I get qualified. When can I go?'

'Turlough is going to talk to your uncle Ardal this morning,' said Mara smiling. 'I should say that you can go as soon as he is able to take you over there. He will want to see you well settled. Allow him to present you with some new gowns before you go. It would be good to look grown-up, wouldn't it?'

'Yes,' said Nuala fervently. 'Yes, I don't mind wearing gowns if there is some reason for it – no silly veils or headdresses, though. I couldn't stand that. I don't mind pinning my plaits to the top of my head, though.' She stopped and the joy on her face became muted. 'Do you mind me leaving? Am I allowed to go? Am I still a suspect in the murder case?

'No,' said Mara. 'No, Nuala, you are not a suspect, though you didn't answer my question about the jar of aconite in your room. How did that get there?'

'I took it straight after my father died. I saw it on the shelf and put it into my bag. I was pretty sure that was what killed him. And then the news about you came and I rushed over to Cahermacnaghten and just left it under my bed.' Nuala hesitated and then said in a rush of words, 'I'm sorry I didn't tell you before. I ... I suppose I was just in a bad mood.'

'I understand.' Mara rose to her feet and said lightly, 'Now, I must go and find my son. You go back to Lissylisheen and wait to hear about this from Ardal, before you mention it to anyone. The king will be over later on.'

There was no sign of Turlough, however, in the house and no sign either of his two bodyguards. Mara crossed the road and scanned the fields, but she could not see him. He had still been dressing when she had gone to see the boys off, but, of course, Boetius had taken quite a long time to tell his story. And then she had sat thinking for some time in the schoolhouse – perhaps putting off the moment when she would have to confront the murderer. And then she had spent time with Nuala. To her alarm she realized that it was some time since she had seen her baby son.

'Brigid,' she called as she saw her hard-working housekeeper spreading a line of well-scrubbed *léinte* out on the low hedge. 'Brigid, have you seen the king?'

'He's gone over to Lissylisheen, Brehon.'

318

Brigid's high-pitched voice carried well across the field. She finished laying out the last of the *léinte* – now the hedge looked like a bank where twelve boys reclined in the sun – and came across to Mara.

'Yes, he said that he had some business with the O'Lochlainn so off he went,' she said in more normal tones.

'Of course.' I should have guessed, thought Mara. Turlough was never a man to let an idea simmer. He had been very enthusiastic about having Nuala come to be an apprentice to his own physician and as soon as he had breakfasted he had ridden over there.

'Where's everyone else?' There was a strange empty feel to the place. No one was visible but Brigid herself. Of course, work had begun on the bog where the turf for the winter fires would be dug out in neat rectangular shapes and stacked to dry, before being brought back and stored in the large, open-sided barn. Most of the men would be there this morning.

'Cumhal has taken Sorcha and her three little ones to Fanore,' said Brigid. 'Don't you remember? It was all fixed up. I gave them a basket of food and some fruit – they can drink from the stream there. They were so excited, Domhnall and Aislinn, God bless them. They'll love it there. And baby Manus, too.'

'But where's my baby?' Mara asked looking around. The oak cradle was there, under the shade of an apple tree, but it was empty. No

319

baby was to be seen. Nessa appeared from the storeroom carrying out cabbages.

'Oh, Eileen came back; she decided not to go to Lemeanah after all. She has just taken little Cormac for a walk, down towards Kilcorney crossroads,' said Brigid nonchalantly, turning to go back across the field.

'A walk!' exclaimed Mara, and then quickly and sharply, 'Where's Oisín? He didn't go with the rest of the family to Fanore, did he?'

'No, Brehon,' said Brigid. 'The last I saw of him, he was crossing over towards Kilcorney.'

Eighteen

Do Brethaib Gaire

(On Judgements of Maintenance)

The law must not only protect society against the insane; it must also protect the insane against society.

No fine can be demanded from an insane person and no punishment can be given for an offence committed while the mind was not in balance.

Exploitation of the insane is against the law. A contract with a person of unsound mind is invalid and anyone who incites an insane person to commit a crime must, himself, pay the fine of compensation.

It was a warm day, full of sunlight, birdsong and the heavy perfume of flowers, but Mara felt as if she had suddenly been dropped into the depths of a dark, cold cave. Every fibre of her body felt frozen, almost paralysed. Her hands shook and her tongue became suddenly dry. She could not move; she could not speak. Her eyes followed

Brigid on her way back to her basket of washing, but both her tongue and her limbs had lost all of their power. She needed help, but there was no one there to give it.

And then suddenly the spell was broken. A large warm body beside her, a hot tongue licking her hand.

And then she knew what to do. Only she could accomplish the rescue. Only she and her faithful dog, Bran. Anything else was too dangerous. She would have to rely on her wits and her instincts. Without a word, she crossed the road and went across the stone-paved field.

Bran trotted at her heels. Normally he would be running, hunting for a stick that she could throw for him, chasing around in circles, looking for hares, racing up and down, but now he sensed her terrors and he just went with her. A powerful and comforting presence. She could have gone down to the Kilcorney crossroads, walked the road, called for help at Lissylisheen, but instinctively she knew that this could be perilous.

In any case, she guessed where the murderer had gone. And across the clints was the quickest way.

The wind had died down and the day was hot, dangerously hot. This heavy, thundery weather could drive the unquiet spirit to desperation. What was planned, she wondered, trying desperately to drive herself to go faster? To run was impossible for her just now. She was a woman who had given birth recently and the deep grykes between the clints could twist an ankle or break a leg.

Frantically her mind ranged over the possibilities as her legs moved as fast as she dared to go. Did the murderer plan to use little Cormac as a bargaining tool? *Do not accuse me of the murder of Malachy and of Seán and I will let you have your baby back.* That was the most likely, she told herself, but deep in her mind she feared something worse.

There was no sign of anyone in the fields. The stony ground of the High Burren was used only for winter and spring grazing; now, at midsummer, the cows would be fattening contentedly on the rich grass of the valleys or wandering on the mountain common land. There was no sign even of anyone replacing a stone on a wall, or looking for a missing animal. The hay had mainly been cut so most of the farmers would be at the bog today. It would have been comforting to see someone, someone in whom she could confide, who would come with her, but she thought it might have been unwise. This was a matter that she had to solve for herself. She looked down at Bran and felt reassured. Bran would obey her smallest gesture.

It seemed an eternity before a few trees were to be seen in the distance. Malachy's oaks were down there, down near to the church and the small graveyard. She turned to the right, going south; the way was rough but she trod it almost without seeing any of the hazards. Not long now, she told herself. Every nerve in her body was alive and tingling. Her breath came short and her heart seemed to bang against her ribs. The dog beside her uttered a long, low growl. She did not know whether he saw something or whether he had picked up on her mood.

Or whether, perhaps, he had sensed some evil in the air.

'Heel,' she said to him sharply and he obeyed instantly. This murderer, she knew, would be brittle – anything could break the tension and if that happened the baby would die and probably she would also. For her own life she cared little if she lost her child, she thought, and for a moment despair almost overwhelmed her. She bit her lips and dug her nails into her palm. How could she have been so stupid as to abandon her baby and leave him without a guard while she spoke to that absurd Boetius. She could not blame either Turlough or Brigid. She should have given orders that the baby was not to be taken off the premises, should have kept him under her eye. The fault was hers. She had mis-judged this murderer. The relationship had led her astray.

She could not fail now. She had to be equal to the situation. This murderer was frightened, almost certainly mad, but not truly evil. She felt Bran's nose against her hand and somehow con-fidence began to come back. When the moment came, she would find the right thing to say. The

324

dog was her only hope if all else failed, but Mara had been trained from a very early age to rely on words, and words would be her first weapon.

She dare not allow herself to think that there might be two dead bodies at the end of her quest, but that thought kept rising up from the back of her mind.

Now they had left the High Burren and were going down the steep hill. Luckily, there was a well-trodden path here and she knew that it would lead to where she wanted to go. Malachy's woodland reared up high to the left of her and to the right was the old iron gate leading into the churchyard. It stood open and she slipped through it, the silent dog at her heels.

Just by the gate was a large yew tree, studded with the poisonous tiny red fruits. Mara stopped beneath its branches.

Waiting, watching, wondering.

On the other side of the graveyard appeared a man. He also was almost concealed under a yew, the twin to the one where she stood. A handsome, florid man, a dark man, dark hair, dark eyes, brown skin – from the race of Dubh Daibhrean. It was Oisín and, though he made no move, she knew that he had seen Eileen arrive and had followed her. Of course, he would have seen her from the oak woodland; she would have been conspicuous as she crossed the stony ground of the High Burren.

The graves were mainly on the south side of

the small ancient church, small grassy mounds, sometimes with a block of limestone to mark where the head lay and sometimes a small wooden cross. At the far side there was a small mound – a very little mound; it had not subsided; the soil still had the look of being freshly dug, but the small body beneath hardly raised it.

Kneeling beside the mound was a woman. And the mid-morning sun struck a ray of light from the knife in her hand.

And lying on the grass beside her was little Cormac – not crying, not moving, as still as if he were dead.

Mara went forward and knew that this time, of all times in her life, her tongue could be her saviour. She sat down on the grass beside her tiny son and fixed her eyes on Eileen. Bran lay down beside her, his nose touching the little body. There was no sound of distress from the dog and she knew that her son was safe. She had known it already. Something within her had sensed that the connection between them, as strong as the umbilical cord, was still unbroken. Still, she had to check, so she reached out and placed a hand on him. He lay immobile, too immobile, but his soft, round face was warm. She could hope. She could afford pity.

'You have suffered greatly,' she said compassionately to Eileen. It took every inch of self-control that she possessed not to scream at the woman, not to snatch up her son and hold him to her breast. She breathed deeply, willing her face not to show emotion, and fixed her eyes on the woman who had stolen her son. Yes, the eyes were certainly insane.

'My baby was murdered by that man Malachy, the physician.' Eileen's pupils were huge and dark and her voice was sleepy.

'So you killed Malachy,' said Mara gently.

Eileen nodded. 'I killed him,' she agreed. 'He had to suffer! He died like a dog and he deserved it.'

'What happened?' asked Mara.

'You've guessed it already, I'd say.' Eileen's voice was dreamy and indifferent. 'My husband came back from the hills and when he saw the salve that I was using he shouted at me. He told me that you should never put comfrey on a wound that has gone bad. He knows about these things, but I didn't. And I had put pot after pot of that stuff on the baby's arm! It was such a tiny thing in the beginning, just a bite from a cat. And every time I put the salve on I was making it worse.'

'Was your husband angry with Malachy?' Mara kept her voice low and gentle. Keep Eileen talking at all costs. The knife was still in her hand, but surely Mara's own strength and the dog's strength balanced that deadly weapon.

But why did little Cormac sleep as though it was his final sleep? Why had the voices not woken him?

'No, he was just angry with me.' Eileen's voice was dull and sluggish now. 'He didn't go

327

near Malachy. He didn't dare in case he offended someone – that's the type that he is. I was the one that he blamed. He told me that I was stupid to go on using the salve when I could see that it was doing no good. He showed me the red streaks on the baby's arm. And then he went back up to the mountain – he had just come down for some more wolfsbane to poison the wolves. The sheep were more to him than his own child! And that night my baby went into a high fever. I could do nothing. I tried everything I knew, but at dawn, my baby died. And he was so beautiful. No boy in the world was ever as beautiful as he.'

Mara felt a sob rising in her throat. She could not speak for a minute, and in that minute Eileen acted. From behind where she was sitting, she took a flask, tilted it to her mouth and then put it down. After a moment, she gasped and then she sat very still. The pupils in her eyes grew even darker. Sweat oozed from her forehead and her hair was damp. Continually she licked her lips and swallowed noisily.

Suddenly she lunged forward, knife in hand, not towards the baby, but towards Mara herself, aiming straight at the heart. There was a rustle from the yew tree as Oisín started forward, but Bran was quicker. Instantly he seized the woman's wrist in his strong white teeth, holding her firmly. Her hand trembled uncontrollably and the knife dropped to the ground. Mara took her hand from the baby's face, picked up the knife and placed it in her pouch. Oisín, she noticed, had drawn back into the shadowy depths of the yew branches. She was grateful for his instinctive understanding of the situation. The essential thing now was to find from Eileen whether a drug had been given to the baby, and if so, what drug.

'Let go, Bran,' she said in a low voice.

'I wanted to kill you; I wanted to keep your baby. If you were dead he would be left with me until he grew up.' The voice was slurred and the eyes quite insane. 'It would have been a quick death for you. Malachy had a slow death. I took some of the wolfsbane that my husband had in his store and I brought it to him – he thought I had come to pay him. I gave him the piece of silver, and then when he went to put it in his box I dropped the powder into his glass.'

'Why did you kill Seán?' asked Mara gently. Her hand was back on the baby again. Surely there was something wrong with him. She felt his neck. To her alarm she realized that her fingers were wet with the hot stickiness of sweat. She lifted him up into her arms. His little body felt limp.

'What have you given to my baby?' she asked urgently, her earlier question put aside, unimportant, now. 'Why have you done this?'

'Because you have everything and I have nothing,' said Eileen.

Once again, she put the flask to her lips, turning it upside down against her mouth so as to

329

drain the last drop. Then she took it away and flung it wildly, aiming high so that it soared through the trees that surrounded the little graveyard.

'But soon you will have nothing,' she gasped. 'Your baby will die soon and then you will know how I felt.'

'Eileen, tell me what have you given him?' Mara tried to keep her voice cool, tried to make it sound like a casual enquiry. As Brehon, she had often to deal with a case of madness and she knew that it was important to keep calm. Soon Eileen would be beyond speaking. The woman's eyes stared blankly ahead, her mouth had rigid lines to each side of it and saliva poured out uncontrollably down her chin.

'What was it, Eileen? What did you give him?' Mara held her baby close; already a slight drool had appeared in the corner of the tiny mouth. She looked an anguished appeal, but Eileen was beyond words. She had slumped over on her side and now her eyes were closed.

In a moment Oisín was by her side. 'Let me take him; let's get him back home. I waited because I thought you might get information from her, but it's no good. Leave her. She will soon be dead.'

For a moment Mara half-held out the baby to him, but then she shook her head. 'No,' she said. 'No, I'll hold him quietly here. It can't be good to disturb him. You go. Go as quickly as you can. Fetch Nuala from Lissylisheen. Tell her

330

everything. Tell her about the sweating and the saliva...'

Oisín knelt at Eileen's side, his quick eyes darting over her, feeling her hands, pulling up an eyelid and peering into the eye, noting all symptoms. Then he put his own hand on the woman's heart.

'Racing!' he said with a grimace. 'She won't last long at this rate.'

With a feeling of dread, Mara put her own hand on her baby's tiny chest. The little heart beat, but there was no difference as far as she could tell. Oisín quickly moved her hand, lifting it off and replacing it with one brown finger.

'Seems normal,' he said shortly, and then he was gone, running vigorously out of the gate. Mara could hear the noise of his sandals banging against the stone of the road, going at full speed towards Lissylisheen.

The woman on the ground beside her opened her eyes and gazed at the baby in Mara's arms.

'I'm dying,' she whispered. 'Get me a priest.'

For a moment Mara wavered. It was a sacred duty on all to fetch a priest to a dying person. But what about her baby? The sweat continued to flow from his neck and now even from his forehead, and the few scraps of fluffy hair on his head were damp, but his tiny feet and hands were stone-cold. She held him close to her breast and almost felt as though the beat of her own heart was keeping his heart working. Perhaps it was a mortal sin not to fetch the priest;

331

she didn't know and she didn't care. This woman had used poison to kill Malachy – that might be forgivable, but she also killed poor innocent Seán who was guilty of nothing but a love of gossip, she had made Fachtnan seriously ill and worst of all she had given poison to a baby. She did not wish her harm, decided Mara, but she would not risk her baby's slender hold on life in order to go and fetch a priest.

'Don't trouble yourself,' she said softly. 'Just lie quietly.'

Eileen groaned, but said no more.

I should know what to do, thought Mara. She had assisted at many a deathbed; the lawyer, as well as the priest and physician, was a frequent companion for the dying.

'Do you repent of your sins?' she asked.

Did she nod, or not? It was difficult to be sure as paralysis seemed to be setting in. Mara decided that it was a nod and went on with the ritual.

'*Deus meus*,' she said solemnly, hoping that the God she evoked was a merciful God, '*ex toto corde poenitet me omnium meorum peccatorum, eaque detestor, quia peccando, non solum poenas a Te iuste statutas promeritus sum, sed praesertim quia offendi Te, summum bonum, ac dignum qui super omnia diligaris.*' In Eileen's name, she expressed sorrow for her sins, and her belief in the goodness of God, and went on to promise to sin no more. '*Ideo firmiter propono, adiuvante gratia Tua, de cetero me non*

332

peccaturum peccandique occasiones proximas fugiturum. Amen.'

Everything was very still. Even the pigeons in the nearby wood had ceased their cooing. The sun had moved and the stone church cast a dark shadow over the two women and the baby. Eileen suddenly groaned. It was a strange sound, very deep, as if it came from the depths of her being. She gasped. Her back arched as if from some unbearable pain. Her eyes opened widely. Her hands went to her breast and then fell away. Suddenly the light went from her eyes with that awful finality – as if the lamp of the soul had been quenched.

She was dead.

And then, a minute later, there was a sound, the sound of horses being ridden down the narrow road at full gallop. The noise of voices, shouts, Turlough's voice above all.

And then he was through the gate and kneeling at her side, the man of arms, the king of war, and he was sobbing like a child.

'Hush,' she said, and then automatically, 'don't wake the baby.'

And then Oisín was there, carrying a bag and Nuala following him. The girl didn't say a word to Mara, just knelt down, lifted the eyelid, peered into the blue-grey eye, placed her ear to the tiny chest.

'Have you got whatever she gave him?' she asked.

'She flung the potion over there somewhere.'

Mara whispered the words, still keeping up in her own mind the fiction that her baby was in a normal, healthy sleep. And then she noticed that Oisín was already rooting around in the undergrowth.

'Would there have been any left?' Nuala's eyes went towards Oisín and then back to the baby. Her questioning was sharp and unemotional. Turlough still sobbed, on his knees beside his little son and even the bodyguards had tears in their eyes, but Nuala was completely focused on her task.

'No, I don't think so.' Mara answered the question in the same tone as it was put. 'She swallowed it, drained it, I saw it upside down, and then she threw it.'

'How did she seem – before she collapsed?'

'Sleepy,' said Mara. Neither of them used Eileen's name.

'That fits,' said Nuala with satisfaction. 'I've read about this in my grandfather's notes. She poisoned herself with hemlock, I would say. Very easy to get hold of that. It grows in lots of the hedgerows around here. She knew a lot about herbs and she was always anxious to know more. I seem to remember that hemlock was one of the things that she asked me about.'

'What can you do?' Mara could barely whisper the words. She forced them out, though, because the words in the back of her mind were: *can you do anything?*

'Most poisons have some sort of antidote,'

said Nuala. She had a cheerful, authoritative note in her voice. Turlough stopped sobbing, wiped his eyes with his handkerchief and looked at Nuala with some hope on his face.

'How bad is he?' he asked, his voice still broken.

'Not very bad,' said Nuala reassuringly. 'I would think that he has had quite a small dose. When we were coming along, Oisín told me about the woman's heart beating so fast and I was worried that I would find the same with Cormac, but his heart is normal. And the pupils of his eyes don't look very enlarged, either.'

'Got the flask,' shouted Oisín. He leaped the wall, rushed forward, unthinkingly striding through a large patch of stinging nettles, carrying it carefully upright.

'Let me smell,' said Nuala, and then gave a nod of satisfaction as he put it under her nose. 'I think I'm right,' she said. 'It does smell of hemlock. It has a smell of mice. I know it. Like some other poisons, you can use it in a medicine. In fact, a small dose can help against other kinds of poisoning.'

'What are you going to do, Nuala?' Mara was glad that Turlough asked the question this time, because relief had made her own heart thud so fast that she could hardly draw a breath.

'I'll have to wait until Ardal gets here. I sent him on to Caherconnell. He's bringing me some stuff from the stillroom, there. He has instructions to trample down Caireen if she gets in the way.' Nuala gave a cheerful grin and Mara began to feel better.

'I might have to make him sick – I don't like doing it with such a tiny baby, but it may be the best thing to do.' As she was speaking, Nuala slipped her finger inside the baby's mouth and was peering down the little pink throat.

'Nothing like wolfsbane,' she said. 'That would have burned the mouth. I didn't think so, but I wanted to make sure.' She sniffed the baby's mouth and smiled. 'I think she gave him a little hemlock in a lot of honey; he smells of honey, don't you think?'

Mara bent over and inhaled her son's breath. 'Yes,' she said, 'yes,' and then with great relief, 'oh yes, you're right.' Surely no woman who had fed a baby at her breast would have tried to kill him.

'Here comes Ardal.' Oisín was at the gate before Ardal had time to dismount. He grabbed the bag from the chieftain and flew back down the path, holding it open so that Nuala could pick out what she wanted.

'There we are, this is what I wanted.' Nuala was calm and decisive, pointing into the bag. 'Tannic acid. Do you remember I was telling you about that, Oisín?'

'Comes from oak trees, well, well, well.' Oisín took out the little flask and unstoppered it, sniffing its contents. 'Smells of bark!' he said happily. 'I can let you have lots of oak bark when you are a famous physician, Nuala.'

Nuala didn't smile. All her attention was concentrated on her tiny patient. She took him from Mara's arms and raised him up and down gently as if to remind herself of his size. Then she handed him back to Mara and found a tiny spoon from her bag and gave it to Oisín.

'Fill the spoon,' she said to him. 'When I give you the word, just pour it straight down his throat.' Quickly she put her finger under the tiny chin, tipped the baby's head back, slipped a finger in through the toothless gums, pressing down the tongue, and said urgently, 'Now!'

And Oisín, as if he had been born to the profession, slid the spoon into the pink mouth and poured the dose down the throat.

Cormac shuddered in Mara's arms, opened his eyes indignantly, gave an enormous hiccup and then began to cry.

'Good,' said Nuala with satisfaction. 'I was wondering how to rouse him. With an older child or an adult you would just make them walk up and down for about ten minutes, but crying is just as good. Don't rock him, Mara, that will send him to sleep.'

'Give him to me,' said Oisín. He took the baby from her arms, handling him expertly and touched his finger to the small soft cheek. Cormac's head twitched. Then Oisín touched the other cheek and Cormac reacted again. Next Oisín slapped him vigorously on the back and this time the large hiccup was followed by a spurt of watery vomit.

'Good,' said Nuala again. 'Well done, Oisín. I must remember that. Of course babies get sick easily. Probably there isn't much need to give them potions to make them vomit.'

'Let's keep him awake. Go on, make a noise, bang something.' Directing his words at the two bodyguards, Oisín jigged the indignant, howling baby up and down a few times, rubbed his stomach and then once again tapped him neatly on the shoulder blades. This time, little Cormac heaved and vomited vigorously.

'That'll be it, I'd say,' said Oisín, looking at him with satisfaction. 'Here you are, Mother, you have him back.'

Mara took the baby and held him close. Oisín had been clever, quick-thinking and adroit. His silent presence under the yew tree had been of great comfort to her. He had given her every chance to find out what drug had been given to the baby by Eileen and had only intervened when Eileen brandished the knife. He had summoned Nuala and the others without the waste of a second. He had immediately gone to search for the flask, knowing that it would be needed. He had handled the baby expertly. She owed him much. Somehow they had always had a slightly tense relationship – perhaps her own adoration of her lovely daughter and her reluctance to let her go had been at the root of that tension. That should, and could, end now, here in this tragic graveyard. Now was the moment to set things right between them. She looked at him and smiled.

'Oisín,' she said warmly, 'if you call me "Mother" again, I'll strangle you.'

Nineteen

Audacht Morainn

(The Testament of Morann)

No sin is greater than that of kin-slaying and suicide is regarded as a form of kin-slaying as a person who kills themselves, kills that which is nearest and dearest to him. It is a deed that fills all men with horror and it can only be condoned in the case of one who is temporarily or permanently deranged.

'So tell us all about it. How did you decide that it was Eileen?'

Mara sighed inwardly. She wished that she didn't have to answer this question. She had just returned from a difficult interview with the priest at Kilcorney. Of course, it did look suspicious, the woman dying out there in the graveyard, her body slumped over the grave of her dead child, but she did not believe it to be any of her business to point the finger of suspicion and have Eileen declared a suicide, her body to be buried in unhallowed land, dug into some crossroads.

'She had seemed very ill and then she died. I recited the act of contrition and she appeared to acknowledge it.' Mara kept her tone neutral and cut short the interview by rising to her feet and excusing herself on the grounds of her legal duties. The priest would be even more suspicious when he heard of the judgement at Poulnabrone that Eileen was responsible for the murder of both Malachy and Seán, but that was a week away and by that stage the woman would be safely buried beside her baby son.

'I should have guessed before,' she said now in response to Turlough's query. 'It was stupid of me; but of course, I was feeling stupid on the day that Ciara came over and when she first spoke of Eileen.'

'Just the after-effects of childbirth,' said Nuala in a slightly superior manner.

'But I can't think what she said of such significance,' said Sorcha. 'And I wasn't just after childbirth,' she added to Nuala with a smile.

'She spoke of the child dying of a fever — Eileen's son, a very well-cared-for child – I should have enquired about that – should have found out that Malachy had been treating the child for a small wound and that he had been giving her comfrey to put on it – the same case as Blár, really, except that the child was very young, ran a fever and died of it. I perhaps didn't want to upset her – didn't want to bring up the subject until she did, herself – or perhaps,

341

if I'm being honest, I didn't want to think of a baby dying, not when Cormac and I had just gone through so much. But I just told myself that I should respect her privacy.' It was sad, thought Mara, that if Eileen had not cared for her child so carefully she probably would not have brought him to Malachy. Very few of the farming community used the physician except in the case of an accident. Most had a knowledge of herbs handed down from mother to daughter, or from father to son. Most would have doctored a child's infection themselves. No doubt, Malachy realized that Eileen, unlike most wives of shepherds, had her own silver gained from the sale of her embroidery at the markets. He probably gave her the same salve made from comfrey as he gave Blár, and it had the same effect of closing up the wound too quickly and allowing the yellow pus to fester inside the arm. The child, not being much more than a baby, sickened and died quickly.

Mara rose to her feet and picked the baby from his cradle. She could not bear to have him out of her sight now, though he seemed to show no ill-effects from whatever dose that Eileen had given him.

'Let's go and have our supper, now,' she said. She was not going to allow any more discussion of the murder, she decided. She would make her report to Turlough as king of the Burren, then she would tell the people of the kingdom when they assembled at Poulnabrone at the end of

342

June. After that the whole affair would be finished. She led the way down the path between the baskets of sweet-smelling lilies. 'We'll have supper indoors,' she said over her shoulder. 'The sun seems to have deserted us tonight and those wretched midges might start biting.'

The air was very heavy, she thought as she lit a few candles in her room. She hoped that the fine, sunny weather was not at an end. The air was still and the sky stayed overcast during their meal. She was not surprised when a clap of thunder came, just after Ardal and Nuala had left and Oisín and Sorcha had gone across to the guesthouse. Sorcha would come back later to feed little Cormac.

'That will clear the air now,' said Turlough, pushing open the casement window and leaning out. 'A few hours of heavy rain is just what the countryside needs to get the grass growing again. What are you thinking about? You look very thoughtful.'

'I was thinking about a wet nurse for Cormac,' said Mara.

'Hmm,' said Turlough. He seemed to be about to say something else, but then checked himself. She understood his feelings, but Sorcha could not be asked to look after two babies for much longer. In any case, Oisín was restless and anxious to get back to Galway.

'There's a girl with a baby a little older than Cormac – Cliona is her name. I conducted her divorce case just the day before Cormac arrived. She's struggling to look after a small farm and a herd of sheep at the moment, but it can't be easy with a tiny baby to care for. I was thinking that if she agreed to live with me, either here or at Ballinalacken Castle, for six months, I would engage a man to look after her farm. Cumhal would help me to choose someone and he could keep an eye on it as well. What do you think?'

'I think that's great, if you are happy with her, are you?' Turlough gave her a keen glance. 'You never seemed too happy with Eileen, did you?'

'No,' said Mara. 'I thought it was just me; I thought I was jealous of her. I should have relied on my own instincts. There was something strange about her. She said so little. I didn't feel that I ever got to know her. Of course, I should have found out more. I blame myself so much. I could not have prevented Seán's death – that happened while I was still ill and before Eileen ever came into this house. But she gave Fachtnan something to make him very ill and then...'

'There must have been more than that, more than the fact that her own child had died; what else led you to her? Was she your only suspect? You said something about Blár O'Connor and Murrough of the Wolfhounds.' Turlough's question after a minute roused her from her thoughts. He looked at her keenly and she hoped that he had not guessed her vague suspicions of her own son-in-law.

'The real clue of course was the linen cloth

that obviously wrapped the fatal bread and meat, spread with horseradish and poisoned with wolfsbane,' said Mara. 'I could not imagine Murrough of the Wolfhounds even possessing a cloth like that. Everything is very rough and ready in his household. I did consider Blár, but I saw some stitching done by his wife and it didn't look the same at all. The stitches on that cloth were beautifully done, small and even – just like Sorcha's in fact, except that there was something slightly strange about them, just a slight slant to the left, and again, I should have listened to Ciara, because she – you know how she chatters on and everything just pours out – well, she mentioned something about Eileen being left-handed. It all just came together in my mind yesterday – that's why I insisted on Cormac sleeping in our bedroom last night...' She stopped, shuddering at the terrible risk to her baby. She should have taken Brigid into her confidence a little – made up some reason why Eileen should not be allowed to look after the baby. Had the woman really intended to go to Lemeanah – a good half hour's walk away? She suspected not. The poison had been prepared and was to be used at the first sign of danger – perhaps taking the baby from her care the night before had alerted her.

'So it was all a matter of sewing,' remarked Turlough, taking out his own handkerchief and examining the stitching on the hems. 'I wonder who made this for me. Do you know, I don't think I have ever seen you with a piece of needlework in your hand.'

'I'm too busy,' retorted Mara. But to herself, she thought she must try to make something for Cormac – a little smock perhaps when he began to crawl – a smock of pale harebell-blue to match his eyes. She would ask Sorcha to teach her. Brigid would be too shocked at the very idea and would immediately offer to make six smocks.

'And, of course,' she said aloud, 'Eileen was probably seen by Seán coming away from Caherconnell on the morning that Malachy died. You know what a gossip Seán was. He probably mentioned it to her idly when he stopped off at Lemeanah Castle on his way to Thomond with the examination papers. She panicked. She was already – this is just surmise, but she was an intelligent woman – she was probably already aware that her husband had lost interest in her and that the knowledge of her crime would certainly have made him divorce her – so when Seán said that he had seen her on that morning of the eleventh of June, I'd say that she went indoors, took some of the new supply of wolfsbane that her husband had just obtained to poison the wolves on the mountain, picked some horseradish from the vegetable garden at Lemeanah and made him a meal. Seán, poor innocent, would have accepted it. Apparently he was hanging around for quite a while because he wanted to tell the news of my baby personally to

346

Ciara and she was nowhere to be found. Eventually she was discovered in the cellars with Oisín – he was selling her wine – so there was plenty of time for Eileen to get the horse-radish – there's plenty of that in the vegetable garden at Lemeanah and their cottage is just beside that garden. She spread it on the bread, sprinkled it with wolfsbane, added a few slices of beef and knew that he would be guaranteed to eat it.'

'And Fachtnan?' enquired Turlough. 'How did she poison him?'

'That was easy for her to do. By that stage she was living here and in and out of the kitchen – she may even have helped Brigid to make the food for the scholars on that day. I'm not sure why she did it – to frighten me off, I suppose. She may have decided that Fachtnan was a special favourite of mine, or she may just have chosen a cup of ale at random – from her point of view it probably didn't matter – an attack on any of the boys would scare me. Nuala thought that dose was not meant to kill...' And then Mara stopped. There was something that she wanted to say and Nuala's name had just come up in the conversation.

'Anyway, that's enough of that,' she said decisively. 'Let's think about Cormac's christening.'

'I was thinking about that too,' said Turlough, his face brightening. 'I suppose we'll have to wait until my cousin, the Bishop of Kilfenora, gets back from Rome, but in the meantime we

347

can do some planning.' He looked at her hesitantly. 'We'll have to choose godparents for him,' he said, and then, rather tentatively, 'I was wondering about Ulick Burke for his godfather.'

Mara just managed to stop herself making a face. She disliked Ulick Burke, but on the other hand he was a good friend of Turlough's, had willingly and happily come to his aid and fought by his side in the recent battle against the Earl of Kildare. In any case, he was guaranteed to brighten up the solemn event, heavily weighted with all the O'Brien nobility, with his scandalous anecdotes.

'After all, this little fellow has a king for a father, he needs someone of importance to be his sponsor,' pleaded Turlough.

'Yes, Ulick is just right,' said Mara graciously. 'I'm happy for him to be Cormac's godfather and then Nuala can be his godmother.'

Never would she be able to pay the debt that she owed to Nuala, but to make the girl godmother to the king's son would be some small token of Mara's love and gratitude.

And Cormac, she thought, might benefit from the nobility of one side of his godparents, but she hoped that he would also benefit from the brilliant intelligence on the other side. A prince he might be, but he would never be king. Turlough had his grown-up sons to inherit his kingdom. No, Cormac, like his mother, would be a Brehon and balance the scales of justice in the kingdom of the Burren.

348